KU-794-709

Vanessa Hannam was brought up in the Quaker village of Jordans. She left school at sixteen and became a couture model for the House of Worth. She then became personal assistant to the Director of The Contemporary Art Society at the Tate Gallery. She married and had four children, during which time she studied singing with Walter Gruner at the Guildhall, performing in concerts, oratorios and amateur operatic productions.

In 1983 Vanessa Hannam married a Member of Parliament. She has worked as a journalist and was for many years a fund-raiser for Cruse Bereavement Care. In 1992 she became a magistrate.

CHANGE OF KEY

David Lovegrove's marriage to Joelle was a sham even before her frequent trips abroad highlighted their growing estrangement, and her neglect of their young daughter, Polly, has hardened his heart. Meanwhile, he has been offered a Government position, which would enmesh him deeper in politics. David has some tough decisions to make. Then, beautiful opera diva Anna Frazer comes into his life. When Joelle, faced with divorce, threatens to take Polly abroad, David is devastated. But this nightmare is soon eclipsed by tragedy. While David endeavours to do the right thing, others are making their claims on Anna . . .

VANESSA HANNAM

$\blacklozenge$

CHANGE OF KEY

Complete and Unabridged

ULVERSCROFT
Leicester

First published in Great Britain in 1998 by
Headline Book Publishing
London

First Large Print Edition
published 1999
by arrangement with
Headline Book Publishing
a division of Hodder Headline Plc
London

British Library CIP Data

Hannam, Vanessa
    Change of key.—Large print ed.—
    Ulverscroft large print series: romance
    1. Great Britain—Politics and government
    —Fiction
    2. Political fiction
    3. Large type books
    I. Title
    823.9′14 [F]

ISBN 0–7089–4101–X

Published by
F. A. Thorpe (Publishing) Ltd.
Anstey, Leicestershire
Set by Words & Graphics Ltd.
Anstey, Leicestershire
Printed and bound in Great Britain by
T. J. International Ltd., Padstow, Cornwall

This book is printed on acid-free paper

To the memory of Elizabeth Harwood,
a sublime singer and a precious friend.

With thanks to all my family and friends for their patience, to Richard Van Allen for his help and Georgina Perry, my brilliant amanuensis. And to Daisy Lettuce and Josie for taking me on such restoring walks during the writing of this book.

The fountains mingle with the river, and
  the river with the ocean;
The wings of heaven mix forever with a
  sweet emotion.
Nothing in the world is single;
All things, by a love divine, in one
  another's being mingle.
Why not I with thine.

Percy Bysshe Shelly.
Set to music by Roger Quilter.

Prologue

Earth clattered on to the bunch of violets. Anna took her eyes from the hole in the ground where her mother's coffin lay and looked at her father's face; it betrayed no emotion. He wiped his hands together as if to remove the traces of soil he had thrown and rid himself of an inconvenient episode. Anna tightened her grip on the hand of her young brother Shamus. She could feel his sobs gathering momentum. His whole body shook. Anna wanted to cry with him, call her mother back from wherever she had gone, hear her gentle voice with its quiet, healing wisdom, the only voice that could silence Anna's father, Angus Frazer.

They had bought the violets the day before, she and her sixteen-year-old brother. Her father had forbidden flowers for Violet's funeral; 'donations to cancer research' the friends and relations had been told.

Anna looked down again. A thin scattering of rain began to fall. The flowers struggled bravely as Violet herself had done during the last few months when Anna had come from London to be with her. Spring was going

1

out like a lion and a chill wind funnelled round the bleak Glasgow churchyard. She pulled her brother closer as the grim figure of her father turned and strode purposefully away from the huddled group of mourners.

'Did you see that, Anna? He threw the earth on to our violets deliberately,' Shamus said quietly.

Anna knew her brother was right. She had thought the same herself, but today of all days she was going to try to pour oil on troubled waters. Before she could reply, she felt a gentle touch on her shoulder.

'Come away now, children. Yer father will be needing you back at the house.' It was Aunt Jeannie, Violet's sister.

Anna turned. The three of them stood together and Jeannie embraced them. She put a firm hand on the back of Shamus's head. His hair stood out stiffly, accentuating the thinness of his face. It had been cut short, the regulation for the boarding school he now attended. Anna watched as Jeannie pressed her hand firmly about his shoulder. He looked frail, neither man nor boy; it was as if his neck might snap in the wind. His tie was stained with tears.

The wind was biting as the mourners moved slowly towards the gravel path which led to the road, a few of them talking quietly.

Anna felt an urge to be alone, to say a last goodbye to her mother, the best friend she would ever have. She wanted to tell her not to worry, send her peacefully on her long journey.

'You go on and wait for me in the car, out of the cold. I'll only be a minute,' she said. Jeannie's eyes, so like her sister Violet's, met those of her niece for a moment. She gave an understanding smile as she walked away. Anna could see Shamus's shoulders begin to shake again.

She walked back to her mother's grave. The churchyard was now empty. A pool of rainwater had collected about the brass plate on which Violet's name was written. It caught the light as a slant of watery sun appeared between the clouds.

Anna lifted her head and looked towards the sky and sang, in the rich contralto voice she had inherited from her mother, the first song Violet had taught her: 'Blow the wind southerly . . . ' The sound did not falter, the words rang clearly as Violet would have liked. The little group walking towards the cars stopped and stood very still; they listened and hurriedly sought their handkerchiefs.

As the last words of the song floated away on the air, there was silence.

Aunt Jeannie wiped away a tear. 'That lass has the most beautiful voice I've ever heard. It could raise the dead, it could. If my dear sister heard that, it will have sent her on her way a happy woman.'

1

'Do I have to stay with Granny Lavender? She smells of fish.'

David Lovegrove glanced towards his eight-year-old daughter Polly with a mixture of irritation and amusement. She sat in the passenger seat of his BMW clutching her pink fluffy toy from which she had never, in his recent memory, been separated.

'You mustn't talk like that, Polly. Your grandmother is very fond of you and, anyway, what do you mean fish? Perhaps you mean smoke, she's always trying to give it up, you know.'

'Truly, Daddy, she does. It's because she's always boiling horrible bits for the cats, fishes' heads and things, even the eyes. Mrs Duvver threatens to leave if she goes on doing it. She says the cats should eat tinned food like other people's do.'

Polly prattled on, and after a bit David stopped listening. He swung the car off the M25 and on to the A217 on the outskirts of London. Driving back into the city always made him feel just a little depressed, but he reminded himself that on this occasion

5

he was not returning to do battle in the chamber of the House of Commons. No, tonight, he thought with pleasure, he was looking forward to his favourite opera, *The Marriage of Figaro*, at the Coliseum. And just for once, all the arrangements had been made by someone else — his sister. It was her birthday present to him.

He brought his attention back to Polly. She was still elaborating on the smells in his parents' house.

'It's not cigarettes. Mummy smokes and she doesn't stink. Why is Mummy always away?' Polly's voice assumed a whining tone and she started to suck her thumb.

'Don't suck your thumb, Polly, it will make your teeth stick out.'

David patted his daughter's knee. He felt a pang of guilt. Polly needed her mother. When he and Joelle had planned a baby, he had not thought through the question of Joelle's career. At that point she had been a freelance news reporter, doing bit part hack work for regional television. But now she was a top news presenter with a satellite TV company and her trip to Egypt was the most challenging assignment yet.

'I had a horrible dream last night,' said Polly.

'Oh dear, what was it?' he asked. Polly

6

often had dreams. Sometimes they were oddly prophetic, as if the child had some sort of second sight.

'Well, Mummy, you and I were in this big boat, or maybe it was a car, and then it fell into a big bit of water and I tried to rescue Mummy because I couldn't see you anywhere and she was stuck . . . ' Polly's voice trailed off and she buried her face in her toy. Her words became muffled and David glanced at her. Her face looked troubled but then she suddenly broke into a laugh. 'Daddy, look at that dog. It's wearing a funny paper thing round its head. Perhaps it's a circus dog.'

The dog, a smooth-haired mixture of labrador and some sort of terrier, stood mournfully by its owner, waiting at a pedestrian crossing. It looked embarrassed and sad and David had a mad thought that dogs, like children, are born in love with the first thing they see, and easily transfer that devotion to a human friend . . . He wondered if the dog understood that the old man who owned it had probably spent the major part of his weekly pension on taking it to the vet and fitting the collar to stop it worrying the large sore patch that David could now see on its back leg as he slowed down to let dog and master cross the road.

Thankful that Polly had forgotten about the dream, David embarked on a conversation about dogs in general and particularly Ross, their golden retriever, to whom Polly attributed human intelligence. In the back seat, Ross slept on, oblivious.

As the car pulled into the elegant square where his parents, Charles and Lavender Lovegrove, had lived for thirty years, Polly sat up very straight. She was about to say something important.

'When I have a dog of my own when I'm grown up, I won't leave it because I want it to be a happy dog . . . and I still don't want to stay here for the night but as it's your birthday, Daddy, I promise I won't cry.'

David stopped the car and gently pulled his daughter towards him. He nuzzled the top of her head; it smelled of shampoo and grass.

'Darling Polly. You are the most precious thing in the whole world, and you mustn't be sad. Mummy doesn't want to leave you, but she has to because of her work which is very important and we must both be proud of her.'

The door of the large house in Vincent Square opened to reveal the tall, thin figure of his mother, Lady Lavender Lovegrove.

Lord Lovegrove heard his wife's voice in

the street below his study window. He rose clumsily from his desk chair, upsetting the dregs of his cup of afternoon tea on to the report on his desk. Gloomily he watched it form a dark stain on the bottom of the page and thought wryly that it was a suitable comment on the subject of condoms for conjugal visits in prisons.

He quickly took a large silk handkerchief from his breast pocket and dabbed the stain. The large paisley square, together with his customary bow tie, was part of his distinctive mode of dress. He had been looking forward to the visit of his only grandchild Polly, and his heart sank as he heard his wife's imperious voice floating clearly as a clarion call up to his fourth-floor hideaway.

'You're rather late. Charles will have to give the child her tea and put her to bed. Mrs Duvver has left something in the larder. I have a meeting of the Licensing Committee.'

Charles thought how much that greeting said about his wife of thirty-five years. Her granddaughter did not have a name, and never, but never, was he referred to as Grandpa. It was all connected with Lavender's obsession with her pedigree. An earl's daughter, albeit an impoverished one, she always called herself Lady Lavender, but she looked down her nose at Charles's hard-won spurs, a working Labour peer in the House of Lords. She had been a good-looking woman and he was fond of her in his way, but time had not mellowed her.

He glanced out of the window at the group on the pavement. David was his mother's son, he had her height and the same sandy fair hair, but they were as disparate in character as they were alike in looks.

'Oh, I'm sorry, Mother,' David said patiently. He put his arm round Polly's shoulder as he spoke and she nudged into the curve of his body, looking up at the top window of the tall house.

'Where's Grandpa?' she asked. 'I've brought my new video for us to watch together.'

Charles came down and took delivery of his grandchild. He was glad Lavender was going out, he and Polly could play backgammon. Lavender would not approve of a child of eight playing racy games, it was not in her perceived idea of suitable activities.

As David drove to his house in Battersea to change, he suddenly felt tired and fed up with his life. Nothing was quite right and yet it should be. He and Joelle were, to all intents and purposes, the perfect high-achieving couple of the nineties. But it was no fun being lumbered with the fallout of an absent wife. He dreaded getting back to the stuffy house where Friday's breakfast dishes would be mouldering in the sink. The house, so beautifully decorated by Joelle, had begun to show signs of neglect. It had been a relief to be at the cottage where his sister had made sure everything was perfect. Meg was terribly domesticated. He couldn't think where she got it from; certainly not their mother, that was for sure. He couldn't understand why his domestic life was so ghastly; other people managed perfectly well when both parents worked, but then perhaps there was a little give and take. Recently he had begun to realise that with Joelle there was only take and no give.

As he neared the house there was a flurry of movement on the back seat as Ross leapt up. The nice thing about Ross was his enthusiasm for arrivals, a triumph of hope over experience — David remembered there was no dog food.

In the kitchen he rummaged for something to give Ross to eat and found only a poppadom and a stale green pepper. The au pair, Karen, was nowhere to be seen but there was a saucer of stale cigarette ends on the kitchen table. He had suggested more than once that she should be replaced with a more full-time housekeeper or nanny, and he would gladly have paid the wages. He had even gone so far as to interview one potential nanny, but Joelle had insisted that they couldn't afford it. But David had more or less made up his mind that the days of making do with the grudging piece-meal arrangement with girls like Karen were at an end. He got back in the car and drove to the all-night deli to get Ross some mince.

2

Anna Frazer looked at the brown plastic pill box, opened it, and took out the beta-blocker. She sat alone for a moment in number four dressing room. She was sharing it with two of the other principals in *The Marriage of Figaro*, Barbarina and Marcellina. It was four o'clock and the others had not arrived. They had no need to get here early, but Anna had had to arrive in plenty of time to get to the wardrobe so that Cherubino's costume could be altered to fit her. It had been quite a task as she was so much slimmer than the scheduled singer, and then there was the business of the wig. Anna's mane of auburn hair was in no way suited to the part of a teenage pageboy embarking on an affair with his mature mistress, a beautiful Italian countess. She was to have light-brown hair tied back with a wide blue satin bow which set off the gold and silver of her pageboy suit. During the fitting the wig lady had remarked on how well the blue enhanced the colour of her eyes.

Anna stared at her reflection in the mirror. She savoured this quiet, private moment.

Soon the place would be humming with excitement.

The cover for Cherubino had not been able to perform because she had a heavy cold and there was no way that Rachel Perry, the original, could get back in time. There was a strike at Heathrow Airport, timed to coincide with Easter, and flights from Basel, where Rachel had been singing, were cancelled. It gave Anna a chance every young singer prays for. Her only regret was the absence of her mother. If she had still been alive she would have dropped everything and come to London for this moment. Anna resisted a tear; at this point she could not afford to be emotional. She took the beta-blocker knowing that within minutes she would feel confident and in control.

Her mind turned to food. She must eat now in order to give her stomach time to digest. As she left the dressing room, she flicked off the lights. The room became dark except for the grey light from the thick glass in the ceiling under the busy pavement above. She thought with a ripple of excitement of the next time she would see it. Too late now to worry about the hastily learned libretto. She hummed some of it as she walked to the canteen along the womb-like dark green backstage corridor lit only by dim yellow wall lights. The theatre was only just back to normal after the chorus had come out on strike for more pay and improvements to the lavatories, but nothing much had come of it and even now there was the faint smell of sewerage wafting along the corridor. The single ladies' lavatory shared by all the principals had flooded yet again.

Since Anna had become a permanent member of the English National Opera Company, her life had changed completely. She was only just getting over the terrible year during which her mother had died. It had seemed as if everything conspired against her, although after her mother's death her teacher had remarked that her voice had found a new dimension. Her personal life, however, was still a mess, but she wasn't going to think about that now.

The canteen was busy; some of the chorus, as usual in a gang, were indulging in their customary good-natured badinage. Anna remembered the days when she could afford to lark about before going on stage. Now she hardly dared talk in more than a whisper on the day of a performance, and there were certainly no parties the night before; in fact, her social life was nonexistent. But this was a small price to pay for the satisfaction of fulfilling her ambition.

Anna heated a meat pie and chips in the canteen microwave and, giving her friends in the chorus a wave, sat by herself, setting the *Figaro* score upright against the ketchup bottle. She was still having trouble with the dialogue between the arias; the translation was so very different from the one she was accustomed to. She had sung a small part in the previous season's production after being noticed by the chorus master and Cherubino was her next step up the ladder. A metal chair clattered against the floor and Anna looked up.

'May I join you?' It was Celeste Robertson, the young Welsh soprano who was singing Susanna. 'I thought I might find you here. How are you feeling?'

'Better since this afternoon's rehearsal,' replied Anna, dipping one of her chips into the ketchup on her plate. 'That dressing-up scene should be the easiest thing in the world, but it always gets me in a state, and as for the escape scene, did we ever get it together?'

'Don't worry about it. No one will notice and, don't forget, if you lose it sing anything on one note — the conductor will hold up his hand and bring you in at the next bar.'

'Well, thanks for being alongside me. You were rock solid. As long as I don't lapse into

16

the other translation, the one I'm used to, I'll be OK.'

'I can never understand why a work like *Figaro* needs so many different translations. You would have thought that in the course of two hundred years there could be a definitive version.' Celeste picked up her cup of tea and cradled it in her hands. She looked at Anna through a faint wisp of steam and thought what a lovely face she had. She was impressed with Anna's professionalism. She knew that Anna had been through some sort of family or personal crisis; she had had to pull out of the chorus very suddenly and all sorts of rumours had circulated. Celeste liked her, and had spotted Anna's star quality from the start but, hand on heart, she had been doubtful about her ability to survive the tough world of opera with all its cutthroat undercurrents. Today, however, she had seen a different Anna, one which suggested those beatific looks were perhaps deceptive.

Celeste took a swig of tea, put down her cup and gave Anna's hand an encouraging squeeze. 'You're going to do brilliantly,' she said warmly, 'and I'm very pleased that you're back in the company. I thought when you bunked out last year that it was your lot, as it were, sort of 'had your chance missed it' syndrome, especially after you had done so well with Countess Ceprano.'

Anna returned Celeste's friendly gaze, but decided not to elaborate on the events of the last turbulent year. There was only one person in the entire world who knew it all, whom she could trust completely, and that was her flatmate, Meg Lovegrove. No, she decided, she must not make the mistake of letting her personal life spill over into her professional one.

Anna made her excuses and went back to the dressing room. She wanted plenty of time to get ready. She had elected to do her own make-up and she was due for a final fitting for the wig. When the first call 'Beginners on stage' came through the Tannoy at seven o'clock, Anna had nearly finished doing her face. She felt good in the light-brown tieback wig, and the flattener she wore to disguise her ample bosom fitted her comfortably. She carefully put on her thick, dark, false eyelashes and surveyed the handsome young boy in the mirror. She knew she was going to be more than all right. 'Fifteen minutes, beginners' came the call and Anna's adrenalin started to run. When the five-minute call came, the bug really got to her, that heady mixture of icy-calm determination mixed with pure joy and terror.

Anna thought about the several hundred members of the audience draining the last of their drinks twenty minutes later, as she made her way down the dimly lit corridor, keeping her eyes on the white painted line on the floor. *Figaro* demanded a big set and it took up most of the room backstage. She approached the thick black curtains behind the set. The stage manager, complete with earphones and microphone, raised his eyes from his console of switches and gave her an encouraging wink.

The deputy stage manager, only recently out of music college, was 'on the book'. She stood in the prompt corner. Seeing Anna, she stretched out a steadying arm. 'Mind, you're the second person who has nearly kicked the bucket.' Two inches from Anna's blue satin shoe stood a bucket of broken glass ready to be tipped into another for the sound of Cherubino's fall through the greenhouse roof under the countess's bedroom window. Avoiding the bucket, Anna nearly fell into the jumble of safety harnesses, spare cables, fire extinguishers and Hoovers that cluttered the prompt corner. And then she was on.

3

As she stood waiting for David in the foyer of the Coliseum, Meg shivered and pulled her shawl tight about her shoulders. She had come out without a jacket. The beauty of the April day had fooled most people into a premature celebration of spring.

Meg's day had been marred by a confirmation of most things she had come to expect where her mother was concerned. She felt angry with herself. She was thirty-one years of age and as her mother had pointed out, 'It's surely time for you to take care of yourself.' The remark had been delivered in the dispassionate and commanding tone from which Lavender seldom strayed, except perhaps when she spoke to or about Jamie, Meg and David's older brother.

Meg had not been able to control the resentment in her voice as she replied, 'When have I ever had to do anything else, with a mother like you?' Her mother's face had displayed no emotion.

Lavender's features, beautiful in her youth but now strangely compressed in a complex network of tiny wrinkles, caught the bright afternoon sun outside the house in Fulham. For a brief moment Meg thought she saw the glint of a tear at the corner of one of her eyes, but then Lavender turned and got into her car. As she did so she offered a dry cheek for Meg to deliver the traditional peck.

Meg had turned and walked away. She should have known getting her mother to come and see the flat was a waste of time; Lavender was merely doing what she had always done, raising her hopes and then taking a fiendish pleasure, or so it seemed to Meg, in exploding her dreams. It had been the same with everything. The worst had been the puppy; even Jamie had spoken out about it. 'Surely, Mother, you could let her have it. I can keep it in Scotland when you want to go away, not that you ever do go away except to come here.' But her mother had been adamant and her father had taken it back to the shop. That was when Meg should have learned that she and David would have to fight their own corner, but then David had given in to Lavender and gone into politics — and he was definitely regretting it.

There was something about David that made Meg feel safe. The sight of his face looking around the throng of people in the foyer to find her instantly dispelled her feelings of disappointment and anxiety.

21

Several women had seen him arrive. His wholesome good looks always attracted attention. He was a tall, slightly shambolic figure, dressed in a bottle-green corduroy suit and his usual bow tie. His thick sandy-coloured hair touched his collar. He certainly did not fit the perceived appearance of a Member of Parliament of any party — rather more an academic or perhaps an art dealer. It was the bow tie. He had got that from his father. David adored Charles, and Lavender's deficiencies as a caring wife and mother acted for them as a bond. They used to laugh indulgently about her, even to her face, whereas Meg went quietly to her room and wrote in her diary.

'Megs darling,' greeted David in his gravelly voice. He had a way of attaching a slight chuckle to the end of his sentences. He did this now as he said, 'So how did it go? I can tell by your face she rained on your parade as usual.' He pressed her arm and guided her through the crowd towards the bar. 'Let me get you a huge drink.'

'She won't budge,' Meg told him over a large gin and tonic. 'When I actually got her to see the flat I thought she might be softening, but I was wrong.' Meg looked up at David. She bit her lip and gave a slight gasp. 'David darling, I forgot to say happy birthday. I am a selfish cow, talking about myself. I have your present in the car. I'm going to give it to you at dinner. Did I tell you my flatmate, Anna Frazer, is taking the role of Cherubino tonight? The principal is stuck in Basel. Anna is a marvellous singer. She seems to have jumped out of the chorus from nowhere — it all started when the chorus master heard her in a concert at St John's Smith Square. He knew she was good, but not quite how good. She is joining us for dinner. I hope you don't mind.'

David's face clouded a little. He wanted to have a cosy evening with his sister and, besides, they had a lot to talk about. He had known all along that his mother, who was trustee of her father's estate, would never release money for Meg to use as a down payment on a small flat. The money had been left in trust and provided a small income for each child. Neither David nor his brother had any objection to a small amount of capital being advanced to Meg to help her buy a flat, but Lavender held the decisive vote. It was typical of Lavender to raise Meg's hopes even to the extent of going to see the flat, and typical of Meg to think things would ever be different, but then that was part of Meg's charm — all her geese were swans.

23

They made their way to Meg's usual seats, stage box left. The curtain lifted. David was tired after the weekend in Sussex, looking after Polly and a pile of constituency work — surgery cases and work for his minister — and then on top of it all, a confrontation with his mother. Lavender always managed to make a normal situation seem full of hassle. He knew his father enjoyed his role with his first grandchild, but Lavender was a different story. She was as grudging about Polly as she had been about her own children — except, that is, for Jamie, but then as she constantly repeated, Jamie was born an adult. David could not avoid drifting into sleep. He felt his head slumping.

Cherubino stood holding his wide-brimmed hat to his chest but nothing could disguise the tall female beauty, bearer of the richest of mezzo voices. David's desire for sleep quickly evaporated, and he was enchanted. This young woman was clearly destined for great things. He watched Cherubino's every move, the slight edge of nerves making the performance all the more robust and vigorous. He noticed an interplay between her and the conductor, Justin Stein, another bright young star on the horizon; it was redolent with sensuality. From his lofty vantage point in the stage box David could see the conductor clearly for Cherubino's first aria, 'Is it pain? Is it pleasure I feel and with feverish ecstasy fills me?' Was it his imagination or was there a sub-plot going on here? The conductor mouthed all Cherubino's words but his attention to the other singers was markedly less obvious.

After the final curtain call, David and Meg went to wait for Anna in the corridor outside the principals' dressing room. 'Anna isn't back yet,' said the dresser. Evidently a great discussion was taking place on stage, with Anna coming in for some well-deserved congratulations. The applause for the understudy had been tumultuous. David had felt the adrenalin. Even looking down on to the stage from the box, Anna's popularity was obvious. 'She's gorgeous,' he had found himself saying to Meg, but he was not prepared for the surprise which now approached in a great flurry of excited approval. He saw her over the shoulder of Celeste Robertson, the bouncy Susanna, and could hardly believe his eyes. The brown-haired beauty whom he had watched with such delight had a mass of Titian curls. In one hand she held Cherubino's hat and wig. 'She looks like a Pre-Raphaelite painting,' he muttered. Meg looked at her brother. He was smiling with pleasure. Anna caught sight of Meg and before she could say anything, Meg was upon her.

'You did it! You did it!' cried Meg. 'The best Cherubino I've seen for years. Darling Anna, there's no stopping you now. Oh, by the way, this is my brother David. He's joining us for supper in my theatre club around the corner.'

The long-lashed eyes gazed at him from a flawless face. Anna Frazer radiated health and vigour. She was beautiful and, above all, vivacious. She took David's proffered hand enthusiastically and accepted his hastily offered congratulations. Their eyes met and held, each acknowledging the other's approval.

The tiny dressing room was crammed with people, including Anna's singing teacher, a couple of old school friends from Scotland with whom she had completely lost touch, and, of course, Justin. There were even a few people she couldn't place but they all got a special greeting. Anna knew enough to know that a star on stage has to continue the performance off stage.

Eventually the dressing room emptied of visitors. Anna and the other two soloists divested themselves of their costumes which were swiftly removed by the dresser before any harm could befall them. Then Anna was alone. The other two soloists had gone off as fast as possible. They were old stagers and were used to the fuss after a performance but Anna needed a moment alone to savour her success. She stood in front of her mirror in a sleek black dress, her hair swept up on top of her head. She just needed to touch up her mascara and add a hint of lipstick, and she would be ready to join Meg and David just across the alley from the stage door. Meg had understood. Justin, of course, had made his usual thin excuses and escaped.

As with most things, Anna had come to realise that when something went well, there was a price to pay. She had achieved her ambition, but she had no family to share it with. She knew if her brother Shamus had been able to make it he would have been over the moon, but he couldn't afford the fare down from Scotland and anyway the school would never have let him out. He was entering the last term of his A levels and he had to get good grades if he was to get into one of the London music colleges. As she stood and looked at her reflection, she remembered the last words her father had spoken to her: 'If you go back to that life of yours, I don't want any part of it.' And then he had taken another drink, his face flushed with anger, and bawled at her, 'Yer turning into a whore, Anna! Yer mother would have gone the same way if I hadn't saved her.' And that's when Shamus hit him.

She never knew how her father found out about the abortion, but he certainly used the knowledge to maximum effect. The only redeeming feature of his behaviour was that she was sure he never told her mother. Justin had met Anna off the train and taken her straight to the nursing home. After the abortion, Meg had been wonderful, but the flat was freezing. It had no central heating and seldom got the sun. It was the worst time Anna could remember. And then she had gone to Scotland to nurse her mother. She had thought Violet was rallying.

'Promise me, Anna,' her mother said, 'you will follow your star, not like me. If it wasn't for you and Shamus I wouldn't know why I had lived all this life of mine, not doing the thing I should have done, using the gift God gave me. Use your gift, Anna. It will be your passport to happiness, and look after Shamus. If you leave him here with your father, he will be like Orpheus in the underworld.' Her mother had sighed, gently sunk back on the pillow and died.

Anna wondered what Shamus was doing now. She would tell Meg during dinner the news she had just received — probate on her mother's small estate had been wrapped up and she had been left enough money to buy a small flat. She planned to have Shamus living with her when he got into music college. She would miss Meg, she was the best friend Anna had ever had. But whether or not they shared a flat, they would always be friends. There was shorthand between them. Meg had understood how she was feeling tonight. She knew she needed a silent communion with her mother, but one thing she had never discussed with Meg was her father.

Anna touched up her make-up, then turned on her high-heeled shoes and made for the stage door. Two or three admirers were waiting for her outside in the cold. They eagerly pressed programmes into her hands for signing. She was on her way. Nothing would ever be the same again.

4

Anna sipped her red wine gratefully. The three of them sat at a round table in front of a log fire. The fact that it was gas and the Georgian panelling had been installed in the last few years did not detract from the cosy authenticity of the room. Meg had been a member of the exclusive dining club for some time. Most of the clientele were actors, singers or writers but with so many friends in the opera world Meg had not found it difficult to get someone to put her up for membership.

The menu came and Anna stole a glance at the other diners' plates. She liked the look of the venison sausage and onion mash. David chose fish — lightly poached halibut in a parsley sauce. Meg was a vegetarian and went for vegetable bake in filo pastry. With the food ordered, Anna relaxed and took a closer look at Meg's brother. She had heard a lot about him, but his being an MP had been an instant turn-off for her. Her father's bigoted rantings had long ago made her decide that the two subjects she should avoid at all costs were politics and religion, particularly the latter, which had been the Pandora's box from which her father extracted the many small miseries of their family life. But David Lovegrove belied her preconceived ideas of what a politician was like. He had an easy manner, and Anna particularly noticed his instinctive good manners. He had a way of setting the tone without seeming to do so, and it was not long before Anna realised he did not talk about himself except with an endearing self-deprecation. She found herself being gently coaxed into talking about herself and yet never once did he ask a leading question.

He did not have Justin's way of making you feel as if he thought he should be somewhere else, and never once did his manner have that faint ring of patronisation she had experienced from men when they knew she was a singer. She still remembered the priest at her mother's funeral. 'Still doing a little singing, Anna?' he had asked her. Her tart reply, 'Yes, and are you still doing a little praying?' had led to her father's order to 'Go and wash your mouth out with soap, and while yer at it, wash that paint off yer face. Yer look like a Jezebel.' She never talked to Justin about these things. His concentration span relating to anything other than himself was limited, to say the least.

The three of them fell into an intimate conversation as if they had always been a close trio. Prior to Anna's arrival, David had not had time to hear the full details of Meg's afternoon with their mother. He asked her now and Anna listened carefully.

'Well, I can kiss goodbye to the idea of buying a flat,' said Meg. 'I simply can't afford it. I've managed to save a couple of thousand or so but it's not enough to put down a deposit.' David gently put his hand on her arm.

Anna saw Meg's face flush a little as she talked about her mother. Meg had an obsession about being left on the shelf with no home of her own and no security for her future. Meg's thirtieth birthday had been a traumatic affair. 'I will be an old maid,' she had wept over the coffee and toast Anna had brought her in bed as a birthday treat.

Strangely, Anna felt no embarrassment at being part of this very personal dialogue between brother and sister; in fact it paved the way for her to confide her own news.

'Well, on the subject of properties,' she began, 'my mother's estate has finally been settled and Shamus — that's my brother, David — and I have been left just enough to buy a small flat or house in London.'

'But that's marvellous!' Meg exclaimed,

genuinely pleased for Anna. They had often talked about how much each of them would like to be able to buy somewhere of their own and be done with paying for unheated rented accommodation.

While the two women discussed where Anna should look for a property, David listened and looked.

David had never slept with another woman since he had been married to Joelle. He had never wanted to. He didn't notice the body language of the women who found him attractive and would gladly have dallied with him, be it for five minutes or five days, and such women were legion in the carpeted corridors of the House of Commons. But just recently the state of his marriage had begun to open a small window through which he could see the sun on a girl's hair as she swung down the street or the shape of his secretary's waist as she leant over the filing cabinet. Joelle's independence had emasculated him, but watching Anna now, he felt the stirrings of long-forgotten passions. It was not just the sound of her mellifluous voice, as pleasing when speaking as in song, it was the earthy quality of her body, her well-formed breasts which now brimmed from the cleavage of her black dress as she leant forward to talk to Meg. He would like to have laid his face on them and smelt the fragrance of her skin. He loved the way her eyes flashed as she spoke. Everything she said was laced with a fiery animation. Her singer's training had given her a way of delivering her words with great precision, using her lips a lot, and when she smiled she revealed perfect teeth. David found himself wondering what she would look like without any clothes on.

'David and I will be your first dinner guests,' he heard Meg say. He came out of his reverie with some embarrassment, half thinking Meg was aware of his private thoughts about Anna. 'You were miles away,' she said. 'Worrying about Polly, I bet. Our mother is not keen on children, to put it mildly,' Meg explained to Anna.

'I won't tell you what I was thinking, but I will certainly be thinking about it again,' he replied.

David spent hours listening to other people's problems in his surgery, and he had chosen the disabled as his particular interest in parliament; he was chairman of the backbench all-party group. His experience in the field had taught him a lot about human nature and he could define qualities of endurance in a flash. Anna Frazer was a fighter. It was clear from the few things she had said about her family that her home life had been traumatic, and the death of her mother last year had obviously affected her profoundly. She would not be drawn on the subject of her father, and when David asked about him he received a sharp kick under the table from Meg, but not before Anna had revealed that he had forced her into nursing and she had commenced her training at the Glasgow hospital where her father was a leading ENT specialist.

David then changed tack and established some facts about Anna's singing career, a topic on which all three felt comfortable. David's other chosen speciality in parliament was the arts, which he felt had suffered under years of Tory rule. This was one area where he saw eye to eye with his mother, who divided her time between raising money for obscure arts charities and sitting as a magistrate. If her particular causes had not been so esoteric, he might well have taken more of an interest, but Lavender's prejudices and obsessions seemed curiously out of touch with people's needs. David saw many flaws in an imperfect system. He did not see an emergence of a triumphal underclass, he saw the reality of a mindless opportunity gap.

'My mother always sang,' Anna told David.

'She taught me and my brother to play the piano from a very early age.' Her face darkened. 'Her career in music ended when she married my father. The only types of music he allows in his home are church music or oratorio and never on Sunday.'

David found out that Anna had had singing lessons with a friend her mother knew from her own college days, who had encouraged Anna to sing in local competitions and concerts. Soon she acquired enough confidence to think of taking up music professionally. She auditioned and was accepted by the Scottish Academy of Music in Glasgow. She got a local authority grant and with the help of a music prize she made her decision and gave up nursing. As she put it to David, 'There was a bit of family opposition, but I have never for one moment regretted it.'

'I should think she didn't,' Meg chipped in. 'She won the most valuable prize in Glasgow which helped her to get to the Guildhall in London and then to the Opera Studio.' Here she had studied the mezzo repertoire. She had performed in several open festivals in and around London, and her first solo opportunity had been Dorabella in Mozart's *Cosi Fan Tutte*.

David wondered how she had managed

financially. He asked her, admiring the way she used her hands as she spoke. Her long fingers were those of an artist. He loved women's hands. Joelle's were strangely hard and inflexible. He looked at Anna. He could hardly keep the electric approval he felt from his face as she told him how she had worked as an usherette at the ENO in the evenings. While she was at the Opera Studio she had met Meg, who had been PA to the administrator for three years and had just taken on a new position as an events co-ordinator and corporate fundraiser.

'What is your next ambition?' David asked.

'I can answer that in two seconds,' replied Anna. 'I have an obsession with Octavian in *Der Rosenkavalier*. It's one of the all-time greats, Strauss's love affair with the female voice at its most sensual. The moment when the high-born page Octavian delivers the silver rose, the official love token from the elderly suitor, to the beautiful young Sophie and their eyes meet and their voices soar in recognition of what must follow — I get goose pimples just talking about it. I heard Sally Burgess do it when I first started to work at the Coliseum. I have almost every recording ever made.'

'And I should know,' interjected Meg. 'I

have to listen to them from morning to night.'

Recently David had been reading a lot of Jung and particularly his theories on coincidence. He had just purchased a new CD of *Der Rosenkavalier* and had tickets for the forthcoming performance at Glyndebourne. He was about to ask Anna to come with him but something stopped him. He would ask her, but not yet. He must think carefully; this was no ordinary casual meeting. Anna had had a profound effect on him.

* * *

As David let himself into his house in Battersea, he heard the phone ringing. The au pair was out, as usual, and he hurried to turn off the burglar alarm, stumbling over a suitcase in the hall, and got to the receiver just as it stopped ringing. The answer machine clicked into action and he heard Joelle's voice. She was ringing from Luxor. For an instant David felt like leaving her to deliver her message. He had been feeling unfamiliar urges as he had driven home, all of them with Anna in mind. Hearing Joelle's voice was almost like being caught in the act of making love to Anna.

He listened in the dark.

'Darling, it's me,' Joelle's bright voice announced. 'Everything is going very well. The conference is attracting a lot of attention. I have some news. I'll have to stay on for an extra two weeks —'

David snatched the phone off its hook.

'Joelle, I've just got in. What do you mean, another two weeks? Who the hell is supposed to look after your daughter? I have to go back to parliament. I've had as much as I can take. Do you hear me?' David realised he was beginning to shout.

It was a bad line with a lot of crackling. Joelle's voice became conciliatory. 'It's very important, darling. Exciting things are happening here and I'll get a huge fee. Tell Polly I've ordered her the most beautiful kaftan and that I love her. If you get stuck, I left the number of the domestic agency on my desk.' David could tell she was about to ring off.

'Listen, Joelle. Something is going to have to change. I can't live like this any more.'

Before David could say any more, there was more crackling on the line. He just heard Joelle saying they could talk when she got back, then a click and the line went dead.

David sat slumped in an armchair. He didn't turn the light on. He saw the room in the dim light from the street lamp outside. Everywhere was quiet, and then he heard a whining from somewhere at the back of the house. He remembered with a start that Ross was shut in the kitchen.

Ross could hardly contain himself when David opened the kitchen door. He was up on his hind legs washing David's face. There was a definite smell of dog in the room. It was probably the warmth. David had insisted on a gas Aga when they bought the house. Ross and the Aga were just two of the things Joelle disliked about their domestic life — Ross, because he left a trail of hairs and muddy paws wherever he went. Joelle was a clean freak. Their Colombian cleaner, Beatrice, spoke very little English and Joelle used pictures to communicate with her. Her latest attempt to persuade Beatrice to clean up Ross's hairs by showing her a picture of Ross and the Hoover had been a failure. Beatrice had complained to David in pidgin English, 'Like dog but no want Hoover him.' There had been quite a sulk and David had been worried that Beatrice would leave. He knew she only stayed because she was devoted to Polly. They had found some mysterious way of communicating. Beatrice did everything for Polly. She had even taken her to Peter Jones to get her school uniform.

David had given up worrying about the lack of vocabulary. Beatrice got what she wanted without words but he did wonder if her lack of English was in fact a ruse. She clearly understood a great deal more than she let on.

David made himself a cup of camomile tea, took a handful of dog biscuits from Ross's special tin, and went back to the sitting room. He put on his favourite recording of *Figaro*, sat down in the semi-dark and listened to Mozart. Ross laid his head on David's knee, grunting appreciatively as David fondled his ears and fed him biscuits.

In the stillness of the empty house, David allowed himself a rare luxury, time to think, and it occurred to him with a frightening clarity that he wanted more than anything in the world to make love to Anna. He wanted to hold her, whisper into her hair, hear her practising in some distant corner of his house, go shopping with her, walk high on the Downs with her with Polly between them, know that when he looked up from his chair on a winter's evening there she would be. He felt in his heart a terrible ache for all the things he had never had in his marriage to Joelle. It wasn't that he was unhappy, but being with Anna tonight had made him realise the gulf between happiness and compromise. He didn't want things just to jog along any more.

Later, as he removed the bedcover from the valanced bed, he took great pleasure in letting it fall on the floor. Joelle always insisted he fold it and lay it on the banisters outside their bedroom. He left his clothes in disorder on the chintz chair. And he left the snowy-white monogrammed towels which Joelle had extravagantly bought from the White House on the marble floor of the bathroom. He felt a pang of resentment when he thought about all the money Joelle had spent doing up the house. Thousands of pounds on things like clothes closets, extraordinary built-in cupboards with a place for everything. David would have preferred his old-fashioned wardrobe which had belonged to his grandfather, but one day he had come home to find it had gone to auction. Looking back on it, David wondered how he had been so very easygoing about all the assaults Joelle had carried out on his life. It was as if she had been determined to sweep away all the things that were part of his background. He decided he had spent long enough being told what he should be; from now on he would have a go at just being.

5

'Shall I put some oil on your back?' Joelle heard the rich male voice as if in a dream. She had been asleep by the pool for some time. She turned over, carefully gathering her swimsuit about her. It was Felix Khamul who stood there, blocking the light afternoon sun. Joelle was taken aback by the intimacy of the offer. Before she could say anything, Felix continued, 'The sun is hotter than you think. Even now, early spring, you can get very burned.' He admired Joelle's slim, tanned body as he spoke. An expensive body, he thought. European women did not usually have that softly tanned look at this time of year. They usually peeled off their clothes and then much of their skin as they lay exposed in a way he still found offensive. But not so the waiters and pool attendants who never saw their own women except veiled or in the dim corner of the marital bedroom. The European female crotch was endlessly compelling to them, especially now near the end of Ramadan when abstinence left them frustrated. The ribald jokes made in the bars would certainly have sent these women running for cover.

'How kind,' Joelle replied. He couldn't see her eyes through her Ray Bans, but she was smiling invitingly. She slowly removed the sunglasses. 'I was just about to go inside. I have some work to do. I have to modem my latest report and await a call from my programme editor.'

Joelle reached for her silk wrap and skilfully tied it about her. She began to gather her things into a Cartier beach bag. Felix noted the trappings — trophies from extramarital relationships, he assumed. He had been watching Joelle for the last week. She was a smart girl. Something about her singled her out from the usual camp followers of the diplomatic world — media trash, easy on the eye and easy to bed. But Joelle was a challenge. He had played backgammon with her the previous day; he had almost let her win, close enough to make her think she had nearly got the better of him. It took great skill to calculate the moves in this game, whose winning depended to a large extent on luck. But he had been impressed. She had a coolness about her. It was obvious she was used to a sophisticated life. Felix had been surprised when he had been handed the dossier on Joelle Lovegrove to learn she was married to an English politician. Her

44

parentage, however, was no surprise — born in Cairo to an English diplomat married to a Frenchwoman. The dossier reported a longstanding affair with one of the network's cameramen, albeit very discreet. The husband probably hadn't known. The husband was clean, a well-thought-of MP specialising in altruistic fields such as disablement and the arts, not ambitious, but the husband's family sounded interesting. His father had been a powerful force in the judiciary, and the mother was the daughter of a left-wing English aristocrat. Felix couldn't quite see how the glamorous and cosmopolitan Joelle fitted into all this. Felix had no particular fondness for the British. His father had sent him to an English public school which had cured him of that. He suspected Joelle's husband would have been one of the breed who taunted him with endless refined cruelties. It was in fact the school that had forced him to change his name from Abdullah to Felix, and even this had not silenced the sniggerings and jokes about dagoes and wogs. He had developed a silent brooding hatred for these people.

But one thing he had realised; if he could survive those years at an English public school, he could survive anything. He had to admit one other thing: the

English experience had taught him how to dress. Today he wore strictly Savile Row. His frequent visits to London kept him well stocked with replacements. He would fax in advance, sometimes sending his own bales of Egyptian cotton to the shirtmakers in Jermyn Street.

Felix seated himself on the edge of the chair next to Joelle. 'May I?' he asked, getting out a gold cigarette case. Joelle nodded. As he lit a small, dark, Egyptian cigarette, she admired his perfectly manicured hands. He wore an ornate gold ring on his wedding finger. She had known he would come and find her. She had announced loudly her intention to go to the pool when the conference closed and the delegates dispersed for their free time. She knew he was staying at the Sheraton with the official party; most of the media were booked into the hotel on Crocodile Island. She knew he would find out easily enough. She had let a few things slip when she had played him at backgammon last night. There were always games on the go. It was as natural to the Egyptians as breathing. Joelle was aware that he had given her points, and their eye contact during the game had been sufficient to leave the ball firmly in his court, with a predictably favourable response from her should he wish to see her again in more intimate surroundings.

'I should be honoured if you would have dinner with me tonight,' he said now. 'I would ask your husband's permission, but he is so far away that I fear that is not possible.'

He was, of course, subtly letting her know that he had run a check on her. She was not surprised.

'Well, I should be delighted,' she answered graciously. 'I shall look forward to it.' She hoped she didn't betray the eagerness in her assent. Felix Khamul was the man of the moment. It was not only his film star good looks — unusually tall for an Egyptian, olive skin, perfect teeth and dark brown eyes with healthy whites, no doubt because, as she had already noticed, he never drank alcohol. Being a Muslim, this was strictly forbidden. He could have passed for an aristocratic Italian. Joelle had been wondering exactly how old he was. His thick black hair had begun to grey elegantly about the edges, adding a touch of gravitas to his appearance. He came from a very old and distinguished family in the Lebanon and spoke perfect French. His family had moved to Egypt and become immensely rich from cotton and sugar. They had large estates near

Alexandria, and Felix owned properties in London, the south of France, Washington and Palm Springs. He had two wives. One was a devout Muslim, herself from an old family, who lived in seclusion in the family villa in Alexandria. The other was a young American; she lived in Palm Springs.

Felix enjoyed a life of unparalleled luxury. He had a private jet and a yacht in the south of France, he belonged to the Gezira Sporting Club in Cairo where he excelled at tennis, the Eagle Club in Gstaad where he skied with his children, and the Union Club in New York where he played backgammon with the jet set. This had led him to Monaco where he won the backgammon tournament and began to mix with the world's lotus eaters and high fliers. But it was not his lifestyle that had first attracted Joelle to him, although she knew enough about herself to acknowledge that money was indeed a powerful aphrodisiac. It was his power in the political arena. When he spoke at meetings, his quiet, grave voice silenced the hall to an almost hushed reverence. He was known to be ruthlessly opposed to fundamentalism in any form, and he had been the driving force behind seeking out the terrorist group that had made an attempt on the president's life. The terrorists had been dealt with swiftly, in a way that only the Arab world would understand.

Joelle was not quite sure what his remit in the regime actually was. He seemed to have the president's complete confidence. She had bravely asked him about his position yesterday when she interviewed him for the network. 'Think of me as the Arab world's Talleyrand' had been the enigmatic reply. This had only increased Joelle's interest. She had always admired Talleyrand as one of the greatest figures in French history, surviving at least four different regimes as a trusted adviser and keeping his head when others lost theirs.

Felix arranged to have his car pick Joelle up at eight o'clock. They would dine at the Old Winter Palace Hotel in the centre of Luxor. He told her to bring something warm as he planned an expedition after dinner. She should let her companions know she might be back late. He gave her his mobile telephone number where he could be reached at any time.

Joelle did a couple of hours' work in her room. The hotel provided hacienda-type chalets, surrounded by a rose garden and looking out on to the Nile. She bathed and changed into a cream silk trouser suit. For warmth she chose a pale ivory cashmere shawl. She surveyed her handbags, and decided on a brown crocodile clutch bag. It had just enough room for a toothbrush, compact, lipstick and credit card, and a crisp white handkerchief for good measure. She gave one final look at herself in the mirror before she switched on the air conditioning. She was glad she had had her thick dark hair cut short and feathery before she left London. The effect was both elegant and feminine as it petalled round her fine sculptured features. She wore very little make-up; her eyes, a bright blue, shone to their best effect when left to nature since her lashes were naturally thick and dark. But she had taken trouble with her lips tonight. The effect was dramatic, the bright red matching the huge costume rubies she had clipped in her ears. She knew heads would turn.

She was about to leave the room when the phone rang. Fearing it might be David, she thought of ignoring it. She didn't want her evening spoilt by feelings of guilt. But it rang on so she answered it. It was the concierge, his voice sounding unusually respectful. 'Madame,' he crooned, 'Monsieur Khamul's car and security guard are awaiting you.'

6

The black limousine had tinted windows and smelt of leather and men's aftershave. Joelle slid back into the capacious seat and felt a wave of pleasure. It was dark outside the car, very dark. The Egyptian night comes with the same dramatic abruptness as does so much in the East. Joelle loved these extremes, she found them exciting, they made her feel alive. They filled her with a sense of destiny, which she found strangely comforting.

The previous evening she had sat on a grass bank with the other hotel guests, and to the strains of Mozart watched the golden orb of the sun drop behind the violet-hued mountains on the west bank. The music had made her think of David and Polly, and the growing restlessness she felt about her life with David. She knew he was a good man, and she had loved him passionately once. He had represented security. She had been ambitious for him. She had visions of him becoming important in the government, of herself being a powerful hostess, but the years of being the unseen, unacknowledged wife had been frustrating and disillusioning.

There was simply no role for someone like her in the British parliamentary system.

It hadn't taken her long to forge an impressive career of her own. She had become respected in her work, an authority on Middle Eastern affairs. She was trilingual in French, Italian and English, she had contacts, and she was becoming quite a pundit. She had even been asked to write a profile on the powerful figures in the Arab world by the *Economist*. This was why the evening with Felix would be a delicious mixture of work and pleasure. But she felt a pang of alarm in the back of her mind. She found Felix much too attractive for comfort. She suspected he would try to take her to bed and wondered whether she would be able to resist, but then she looked at the two figures in front of her in the car and with a slight shudder reminded herself of just what getting involved with someone like Felix actually meant.

They were driving over the bridge which linked Crocodile Island, on which the hotel was built, to Luxor. A family lived under the trees by the bridge, their only shelter a bamboo shack. Earlier she had noticed their brightly coloured clothes hanging out to dry. She was struck now by the stark contrasts in these people's lives and the lack of social conscience born of the fatalistic nature of their beliefs. 'Have that family lived there long?' she asked the bodyguard, observing that his eye had been caught like hers by the swaying lanterns of the family, which hung over a table where they seemed to be eating an evening meal.

'Yes, madame, they have lived under that tree for ever. They used to have to migrate to higher ground in the rainy season, but since the Aswan Dam was built this area no longer floods.' Picking his teeth with an ivory stick, he continued, 'That's why the hotel could be built. Before, the place was only fit for crocodiles. Now we have reptiles of a different kind,' he joked, catching her eye in the mirror. Joelle felt a mild twinge of alarm and reverted to the subject of the family.

'I noticed them last night when I went with my girlfriend shopping to the souk,' she said.

'Forgive me, madame, but you did not go alone to the town in the evening, did you?' the guard asked, removing his tinted glasses to look at Joelle more closely.

Joelle had indeed been to the bazaar in the evening and both she and the journalist had regretted it. They had been hassled and followed and neither had liked to admit how scared they had been.

'Madame was lucky not to have come to any harm. May I advise you not to do this again?' The bodyguard fixed Joelle with a look which meant 'listen'.

The Old Winter Palace Hotel, reminiscent of the British Raj, stands much as it has done for a hundred years. Its clientele remain the smartest and most selective of travellers. The first indication of its old-world charm is the red carpet which welcomes the guest's arrival, stretching opulently down the sweeping steps to the road. Joelle had been there many times as a child. Her father used to take the family at the end of Ramadan, exactly this time of year, Joelle reminded herself, as she noticed the crescent moon hanging over the Nile. Felix awaited her at the top of the steps, alerted to her arrival by a call from the security guard. They had spoken excitedly for several minutes. Joelle still could not get the hang of Arabic, but she caught a few words and her name had been mentioned at least twice.

Felix took her arm proprietorially as they walked through the marbled hall to dinner. There was a flurry of excitement from the staff as they entered the dining room, and several diners showed irritation at the commotion Felix caused by his entrance. A middle-aged English couple near by were particularly put out. Assuming as most English people do that the best way to make yourself understood in a foreign country is to shout, the man summoned the head waiter and loudly complained of the slow service, demanding to know why Felix had been served before him. Hearing this, Felix summoned the wine waiter, asked what the couple had ordered, and sent them a suitable bottle of wine with his compliments. Joelle was not at all sure about this. She thought the wine would be returned, but instead it was received with much appreciation. 'I've seen the man before. That Colonel Blimp act is a scam; in fact he speaks perfect Arabic,' Felix explained softly, as Joelle tried to avoid looking at them. 'He was a British Secret Service agent. He is what is known as a sleeper. I expect he is sending information about this trip. People like that never retire,' Felix added in a conspiratorial voice.

Joelle raised her glass to her lips and sipped some of the excellent claret which had arrived with the first course. 'Oh, so you never know, he might be useful to you one day. Do I fall into the same category?' She laughed, leaning forward a little as she spoke, noticing that Felix drank only water.

'No, my dear. You are a beautiful woman, but it is still a man's world and, on the contrary, it is I who can be useful to you.' He touched the inside of her wrist as he spoke and the effect was electric. Suddenly her appetite disappeared and all thought of resisting his appeal evaporated; she wanted to be alone with him to hasten the inevitable.

He saw the look in her eyes. He could read women like an open book, but Felix was a man of refinement. He liked to stalk his women, like a panther, enjoy the foreplay. He would relish the indulgence of the long Arab night. This was no ordinary woman; he wanted to savour each little bit of her, including the ritual of finding out more about her, so that the mantle of lovemaking would fit her better, would permeate her body and mind. He planned to take her to the Valley of the Kings in the darkness. He wanted to get inside not only this woman's body but also her mind. This was the sweetness of the challenge, to have this emancipated European woman throw her independence to the desert dust and bask in his shadow. She knew the power of her beauty but she did not know its dangers. A Muslim woman hoards her beauty like a jewel, she uses it sparingly and wisely.

'I hear from Mohammed, my guard, that you went alone with another woman to the souk,' Felix said quietly. 'You are lucky no

56

harm came to you. I am surprised that with your knowledge of the Arab world you did something so foolish. It is the end of Ramadan, the men are mad with lust and, as you know, European women are highly prized.' He spoke gravely, he wanted to seem avuncular.

'We were silly, I see that now,' she replied, defensively, 'and you are right, I should have known better, but one forgets. With so much tourism, one assumes that Western women will be able to behave as they would in their own countries. You have a woman president, but the political scene has not opened to hear the Islamic voice and allow it to participate in democracy. Surely this is the only way forward? In the West everyone is allowed to express themselves. If you continue to exclude the extreme groups, they will become much more dangerous, especially given their views on women. Why don't you begin a dialogue with the more moderate members?'

For a moment a dark shadow passed over Felix's face and his eyes hardened. 'My dear, as you may know, my family originally comes from the Lebanon where there has always been a conflict of cultures, and now as all voices gather round the table, things are much better. But here, in Egypt, it is more complex. The population will have reached eighty-six million by the year two thousand and twenty. This will bring burgeoning social problems. They are already apparent. Tourism is an economic necessity. These people you speak of are radical, violent, fundamentalist extremists, and they have to be stamped on ruthlessly. You've seen what they can do to the economy. Believe me, it is the only way. Madame President knows this. She is a remarkable woman. I have great respect for her, but she is dealing with pockets of unimaginable ignorance. Have you forgotten that most of the women in upper Egypt are still circumcised? And it's not men who do it to them. It is the grandmother, and she performs the circumcision on the mud floor of the family home. Western women are an obsession with these men. They cannot touch their own women outside wedlock, and Western women are endlessly seductive. The concept of a woman's sweet pleasure in the sexual act is unknown to them. Can you wonder a woman like you incenses them?' She listened quietly. His words and the wine were beginning to make her head spin. He saw her quiescence and pressed his advantage. Raising his glass he said, 'To us, my dear friend. After this delightful dinner,

I will show you the Arab night as you have never seen it before.'

Joelle did not really want to go to the west bank at night. It was a formidable, barren place, a fitting site for the tombs of the great pharaohs. It was impressive by daylight but the mystery of the place would seem ghostly and sinister at night. No Westerner was permitted to go there after dark but Felix roamed as he pleased. His limousine swept through barriers with instant recognition. When they arrived, it was after midnight and bitterly cold. As they got out of the car, the darkness was absolute. The slim moon and canopy of stars pricked the black sky with piercing intensity. Their shoes crunched on the thick red sand as he held her closer to him and named the stars.

'Orion was the inspiration for the great pyramids. Do you know,' he added, 'these people discovered longitude thousands of years before your greatest sailors? Admiral Anson sailed for three months the wrong way round the world as late as the seventeenth century . . . You see, at least I learned something at that English school,' he laughed, taking her by the arm. 'Inside the tomb of Tutankhamen you will see that they were a seafaring people. Here in this arid land they were navigators. We know nothing of these great mysteries. We can only go by instinct, the same instinct that tells me your destiny is wrapped with mine. The gods are watching us here, Joelle.'

They were alone, or so it seemed. They had walked a little way from the car and the only reminder of the presence of the other two men was the smell of Egyptian cigarette smoke on the cold night air.

He reached for her chin and, raising it a little, he kissed her. His mouth tasted aromatic, and his saliva was warm. She wanted to melt into his body. He felt her mould her form to his.

'I will take you home before you catch cold,' he said gently.

As they drove back to Crocodile Island, Felix talked formally about the latest archaeological finds. He explained how the temple in Luxor, only recently uncovered beneath the urban chaos of the modern-day city, was having to be underpinned because of subsidence. The great dam, he added, was in many ways a menace; years of flooding of the Nile delta were a way of life.

The car slowed as they reached her hotel.

'I will see you to your bungalow,' Felix insisted.

As they entered the room, she was struck by the erotic smell of roses. She was about to turn on the light when he put his hand over hers and stopped her. 'I will pull back the curtains. The light from the garden is enough,' he said. She saw in the dim light the room was full of roses — white, pink and red.

'I don't believe it!' she gasped.

'I knew you would like them,' he said, pulling her to him. He sat on the bed and she stood still as he slowly undressed her, his mouth exploring each part of her as her clothes slithered to her feet. When she stood completely naked, he pulled her on to his lap and then lay her on the bed. He parted her legs with his hands and gently let his mouth savour the secret musk. She squirmed in pleasure.

'Stay there,' he said.

He took his clothes off, folding them immaculately as he did so. His movements were perfect, as if he had rehearsed the scene a thousand times.

7

It was the Wednesday after the Easter recess and parliament had returned the previous day. David had had a busy afternoon. As PPS to the Environment Minister, he had been responsible for arranging some helpful supplementary questions about water authorities, the worst figures on wastage coming from his own constituency, and still no end to the drought. His mind had not been as focused as he would have wished. He had slept badly for the last two nights. The phone call from Joelle had been a catalyst for some unwelcome thoughts. This morning he had been summoned to the Whips' Office. At first he thought he might be in trouble for missing a vote, but the Chief Whip, Jeff Roberts, had been all smiles and cups of coffee. To David's astonishment he had been offered a job in the Whips' Office.

'We've been watching you for a while, and we think you could be very useful,' Jeff said, dropping sweeteners into his coffee. 'My weight, you see — chest pains, got to lose some,' he explained. David was not surprised. Jeff had put on at least two stone since taking the job as Chief Whip; endless late-night sittings and chatting up members in the bar had taken their toll. The Chief Whip's job never ended and the Whips' Office was more or less a prison. Gone was the hurly-burly of rushing to committee meetings and outside engagements which kept a Member fit.

David's response to the offer was ambivalent, so much so that Jeff could hardly disguise his displeasure. 'If you turn this down, young man, you may not get another chance,' he said as he rose to his feet to end the meeting. David thought he heard a fart. Upsetting the dregs of his coffee on his blotter, stifling an oath, Jeff dismissed David with a cursory, 'Get back to me in twenty-four hours then.'

David had been considering all this during the afternoon. To his surprise he had done a good job on his brief and the minister gave him a nod of thanks as he resumed his seat on the front bench.

But now it was four o'clock and David was awaiting the arrival of his father in the Central Lobby. He wanted to show him his new office and this would be a useful opportunity to ask his advice. David felt he was at a watershed in his life, and he couldn't get Anna Frazer out of his mind.

He wished he could. It was ridiculous to be falling victim to a kind of schoolboy crush on a red-headed opera singer when his life was poised critically on so many other fronts. Such irrationality could do nothing but undermine his capacity to make the right decisions.

He saw his father come along the thickly carpeted corridor which linked the Lords and Commons. He would have recognised him by his walk alone. Charles Lovegrove was a tall man, and despite his age and his tendency to slouch, he still stood above his colleagues. His gait had a casualness about it that spoke of generations of intellectual breeding. Half-glasses on the end of his craggy nose gave his chin a tilt. He looked like a batty professor hunting for butterflies. In his years as a High Court judge, this batty quality had made him what the press called 'the people's judge'. David found it hard to believe he had one of the finest legal brains in the country. It was his work on legal reform which had got him to the Lords. Charles was that rare thing, a man popular and universally successful without seeming to try at all. David admired him and loved him, but he knew the public facade hid the sadness of his private life. Charles's problems stemmed from a reluctance to face the issues in his domestic life. David could hardly remember an occasion when his father had stood firm and confronted Lavender. In a way, he himself had been complicit in this. They had developed a way of making a joke of Lavender's ineptitude and selfishness. It was Meg who had really suffered.

David and his father greeted each other with their usual embrace, a kind of enthusiastic chest bump. They went up in the Members' lift to the second floor to David's new office, one of a number of rooms that had only been discovered in the last few years. The area had been a forgotten maze of unused rooms. A small corridor had been inserted through a dividing wall to give the House of Commons access to the wasted space above Speaker's House. Members walked down a labyrinth to the north side of the building, past the Northern Ireland Office and into David's attractive new domain. He had waited five years to get it and it had transformed his life at Westminster. Prior to that he had shared an office with two other MPs in Abbey Gardens across the road from the House. It had meant many journeys along the road and through the busy traffic each day in all weathers for votes and committee meetings in far-flung rooms at the end of miles of corridors. David had never ceased to be surprised by the distances he must have walked by the end of each of his eighteen-hour days. Now he felt he had his finger on the pulse. He had put up some pictures and brought in a couple of nice lamps and generally made the place feel comfortable. His father looked around approvingly.

'I congratulate you, my boy. This must be one of the best offices in the place,' he said, and flopped into the comfortable armchair opposite David's large desk. He noticed a picture of Polly and Joelle on the filing cabinet, a model of loving mother and daughter. He found it hard to believe that a woman could be so cool about her child. Joelle was a strange mother. Lavender seemed positively broody by comparison. But at least his children had always had a well-run home, thanks to Mrs Duvver. She had been housekeeper, nanny and cook for them all her working life. He looked at his son now and could see the telltale signs of neglect. His shirt was worn about the cuffs and collar and his suit looked slightly creased. He looked tired and fraught and there were shadows under his eyes.

David left Charles alone in the office for a moment while he went to fill the kettle from the tap in the cloakroom. He darted a look at his reflection in the mirror above the washbasin. He looked awful. He must get a grip, find time to take his suits to the dry cleaners and sack the au pair — she was useless. So many things piling up . . . He leant briefly over the basin and closed his eyes. He could feel a headache coming on. This place provided the only bit of calm he had; the rooms were cleaned, his secretary smiled and helped, things ran according to a strict routine. He had begun to dread going home to find Polly sometimes in tears, the au pair on the telephone, the house stinking of cigarettes although she knew she was not allowed to smoke, and Ross getting thinner. He knew the dog wouldn't eat when the au pair fed him, it was a matter of pride. She had said she hated dogs.

David settled down in the armchair opposite his father. Loosening his collar a fraction he looked at the steam coming off his cup of tea. 'I need to talk to you, Dad. One or two things are happening and I need your advice.'

'You say what you have to say, and then I have something I need to speak to you about,' Charles said gravely, lifting his cup to take a long drink of refreshing tea.

'Well, firstly, I've been offered a job in the Whips' Office.'

'But that's wonderful!'

'Well, is it?'

'Of course it is. We all know if you have been spotted by the secret police, as it were. This is a stepping stone to a ministerial position. It's tremendous, dear boy, I'm pleased.' Charles raised his cup of tea slightly from the saucer in a toast.

'Well, yes, Dad, but hang about. I'm not at all sure I want to go to that particular monastery when I've got quite a few interesting things going on the back bench, and I don't relish the idea of spying on my friends. The quickest way to become one of the most disliked people in Westminster is to go into the Whips' Office.'

'Well, one thing you have to get absolutely clear in your mind is this. If you do not take the job, you will remain for ever on the back benches. You don't get a second chance. This is a kind of trial to see if you've got what it takes.'

'Dad, I think I need to tell you the other thing because the two are interconnected.' David got up and walked to the window. He could see Big Ben. The hands were at four thirty. He thought of Polly alone in the house in Battersea with the au pair and felt a surge of anger.

'It's Joelle. I can't go on like this. She rang

from Luxor. She's staying on another two weeks. To be quite frank, Dad, it's a sham of a marriage. We've nothing in common any more, she doesn't seem to give a damn about Polly and, to put it bluntly, I can't cope.'

Charles stared grimly at the carpet for a moment. He had been expecting something like this. If David had not brought the matter up, he would have done so himself. Polly was obviously disturbed by the situation at home. Her clothes had been filthy when she had come to stay, Mrs Duvver had had to wash everything she brought, and even Lavender had expressed concern.

'I think you have some decisions to make on the home front, David. You will have to call the shots and force Joelle to decide what she wants out of life. I mean, she obviously isn't going to turn into a stay-at-home wife, but maybe she would be willing to compromise.' He hesitated. He wanted to put something to David without seeming too intrusive. 'Are you quite sure Joelle doesn't have someone else?'

David looked at his father in amazement. Such a thing had simply never occurred to him. 'That's the last thing I would have thought of, Dad. I might as well tell you, Joelle is not very interested in the physical side of marriage.' He sighed heavily. 'It's not exactly easy for me, Dad. I'm a young man, I do have certain needs. I mean, she had a bad time with Polly and nothing has ever been the same in that department since.'

Charles was mildly embarrassed by these disclosures. He was no prude, his years in the Family Court had not left much to the imagination, but he didn't want to get into a discussion about sex with his son. He remembered the time he had heard David and Joelle making love soon after they were married. They had all been staying in Scotland on a stalking holiday. The walls were thin. There had been something unnatural about the noises Joelle had made. The feral ferocity of the woman did not bode well for a lasting and happy sexual relationship. Lavender had never been able to feel the same way about her daughter-in-law after that. Charles felt dreadfully sorry for his son. He said nothing, just nodded in an understanding way.

'She's wedded to her work,' David continued. 'She's far too bright to be content to be a parliamentary wife in the background, I can see that now. But she has given up on even making a pretence of trying to sort things out at home. I don't see how I can possibly take a job in the Whips' Office at the moment. I mean, who on earth would look after Polly then? Getting everyone on side for votes is the worst job in terms of hours. I've known whips stay up all night tracking people down.'

'I could help, if that means anything,' Charles said earnestly. 'I would love that. I get quite lonely sometimes. Polly is great company and Mrs Duvver would come into her own again, so if you want to take the job we, as a family, can pick up the tab.' Charles was beginning to like the idea; it would give him a new lease of life. He looked expectantly at David.

'Well, as far as the job is concerned, Dad, it's a little more complicated than that. Frankly, I'm disillusioned with politics and with the party. We're full of sound bites and rent-a-quotes, driven by apparatchiks, not policies. If my private life is a mess, I would at least like to think I'm doing something worthwhile elsewhere.'

'Fair enough, David. I always had my doubts about you following a political career. It was your mother who set her heart on it, as you know.' Charles thought for a moment. 'But I do think you would be unwise to make any drastic career changes until you've sorted out your marriage and your domestic life.'

'You're right, Dad. I shall have it out with Joelle when she gets back. I don't think she

71

realises that a man can only take so much of this sort of thing.'

'There is an old Chinese proverb: 'If your children are no better than you are then you have lived in vain.' All I can really offer you in my old age, dear boy, is love, of course, and a little wisdom based on my own mistakes. If I had been firmer with your mother — I mean, made it clear what I was prepared to live with, or not, as the case may be — we might all have been a lot happier. This business about staying together for the sake of the children, it's bunkum. Don't let your conscience turn you into a martyr, my boy.'

'Let me ask you something. Do you regret your marriage to Mother? Would you have been happier with someone else?'

'I'm very fond of your mother, David. I don't claim to have been the perfect husband. We've jogged along well enough and now that we're older, we have an understanding. There comes a time when it is too late for great upheavals. We don't have the same responsibilities any more, just two elderly people making the best of the time we have left and trying not to be bitter about the time we have had. As we're being so frank, I feel there is something you should know about your mother and me. I've had someone else in my life for many years. I'm not going to tell you who it is. I'm fairly certain your mother knows all about it, but we never discuss it, we're quite happy with the way things are. It has saved our marriage. She knows I will never leave her because, believe it or not, David, your mother is quite frail inside and she would go to pieces if I deserted her. All that bossy hard stuff, it's a cover. I've played along with it and it works in its way, whatever you and Meg think.'

What David loved so much about his father was his capacity for discretion. Often he had observed the way Charles had skilfully kept the many and diverse strands of his public and private life separate. Not once, for instance, had he heard him react or be drawn on his work, even when he was involved in a particularly high-profile case. David looked at him now and thought how typical of him it was that he had managed a longstanding affair for all these years without any of them ever suspecting a thing.

David respected his father's confidence. He would never mention the matter again. He thanked him for his friendship, and over another cup of tea they chatted about the Prime Minister's latest bombshell, the reduction of benefit for the third child, and speculated about the old chestnut of abolishing fox hunting, which was still a controversial parliamentary issue following the first failed attempt in the previous parliament. Charles was all for it. He was disgusted by the government's U-turn on the subject. David did not agree but he kept his own counsel. The last thing he wanted, after such a good discussion, was for it to end on an acrimonious note.

He bade his father farewell in the lobby. Charles was off to do some more work on the Bill for Conjugal Rights for Prisoners. 'I expect you've seen Baroness Stewart on the TV. She is very impressive. We've been working together on this for a long time.'

Something about the way his father divulged this information gave David food for thought as he made his way back to his office.

8

As Anna drove down the M23 on her way to stay with Meg in the Lovegrove family's cottage in Sussex, her spirits soared. The sun shone brilliantly and the countryside looked fresh and green; the very air had the promise of renewal. Her good spirits were not solely on account of the weather. She had made a concerted effort to get her life in order. Her career was blossoming. The chorus master who had first noticed her was rightly proud of his decision to put her forward to play Cherubino, and she had now been offered two small parts for the next season — Flora in *La Traviata* and Kate Pinkerton in *Madame Butterfly*. This morning had been her first rehearsal for *La Traviata* in the Terrace Bar. It had gone well — until Justin put his head round the door.

The previous night Anna had finally finished their affair, or so she thought. As principal conductor for the company and undeniably attractive and charming, Justin was unused to being given his marching orders. In fact, his sexual life operated according to a kind of 'droit du seigneur', much as in the plot of *The Marriage of Figaro*. The fact that he and Anna had been lovers for some time was of no particular significance in their hothouse world of opera companies or indeed to his wife Felicity, who lived in Surrey with their two children. Anna was just one of many women, mostly singers, who had occupied her husband while he waited for the evening performance. There were some, of course, who saw Anna's meteoric rise to be not wholly unconnected with her friend in high places.

Justin had a shock of dark curls and favoured long jackets and cravats. He cut a somewhat Byronic figure. His reputation as a conductor was growing daily and he had been a great help to Anna. He gave good advice about her career and was extremely supportive, at no time more so than when she found out she was pregnant. Neither hesitated about the abortion. He had booked her into the clinic and handled everything.

To Justin, the murder of her baby — for that was how Anna began to see it after the event — was purely a medical procedure, but to Anna, with her roots in the dour Church of Scotland, it was a passport to hellfire and damnation. She did not discuss this with Justin, but she cried on Meg's shoulder and Meg had sent her to her own therapist, a beautiful Austrian called Frieda who looked like Queen Nefertiti. She helped Anna to rid herself of the mantle of guilt which her violent father had woven for her. Gradually the bad dreams stopped and her mind resumed its customary clarity, and it was this new resolve which had enabled her this morning to be unshaken by Justin's 'bite of lunch around the corner?', delivered with a particularly suggestive tilt of his handsome head as if to consign Anna's ending of their relationship to the lovers' tiff department.

Anna reviewed her life as she sped down the motorway and said a quiet 'thank you' to Frieda who had listened as good therapists do. She had gently coaxed Anna into identifying her negative areas and finding her own solutions and then helped her to think them through. Frieda had, of course, identified the two men as the negative forces in Anna's life and she knew there was a great deal more work to do in ridding Anna of the spectre of her father. There were things that Anna had buried somewhere in the recesses of her psyche. One day she would be able to deal with them, but not now. As for Justin, Frieda had simply said, 'You don't want to feel like a piece of cake in the deep freeze which he takes out and has a slice of when he feels like it.'

Anna still worried terribly about her brother Shamus, but at least Aunt Jeannie was there to keep an eye on him until he took his exams and moved to London. On the seat behind her, Anna had the details of several small flats and houses in the Kennington area she thought would be worth following up.

Anna was looking forward to the weekend. She had been told that David would not be there as his wife was expected back from Egypt, and Meg was having Polly to stay to give David and Joelle time alone as 'they had one or two things to sort out'.

When Anna eventually got to the little Sussex village she had to ask the way. 'Oh, you mean the MP. It's up the hill and nearly at the top of the Downs that way,' an aged gentleman on a rickety bike told her.

Built of Sussex flint, the cottage nestled into a fold of the Downs, embracing the full evening sun. Some of the white painted windows were open and she could see snatches of interior; bright coloured walls and flowery curtains, oil lamps on the windowsills, a trellised porch clad with early white clematis. There was a small front garden surrounded by a white picket fence. On the right of the front door were a lawn, a craggy apple tree laden with pale pink blossoms, and a child's swing.

Anna parked the car on the grass verge at the edge of the lane. As she did so, Ross rose lethargically from his afternoon siesta on the brick step and stood waiting for her to come up the path. He wagged his tail slowly in wide sweeping movements and Anna met his gaze. His eyes dropped slightly at the corners, giving him a look of almost human wisdom. Anna half expected him to offer her a cup of tea.

'The opera singer is here, Auntie Meg,' called an excited child's voice from somewhere inside the cottage. 'She's very pretty. Shall I go out to say hello?'

'Yes, darling. I can't go, I have to get the cake out of the oven.' It was Meg's voice.

A small girl appeared at the front door. She wore pink dungarees and a white T-shirt. Her mass of very fair hair was tied in two bunches either side of her head and her eyes were the brightest of blue and completed the resemblance to her father. Anna was struck by her beauty. The girl ran down the path, jumping up and down with excitement, words tumbling out in a kaleidoscope of plans and questions. 'Have you sung for the Queen? Will you sing to me? Will you come for a walk with Ross and me? I did the flowers in your room and I helped make the cake. Can I have your photograph?'

Anna was unused to children and she was struck by the infectious joy that seemed to radiate from this little girl. In an instant Anna had a flash of something she had missed in her own childhood, something in one of the dark rooms to which her therapist had alluded.

The child took her hand quite naturally, as if they had always been friends. Anna knelt down and looked into her face.

'You must be Polly,' she said solemnly. 'I'd heard you were very pretty and you are. It's very nice to meet you.'

'And you are the most beautiful lady I have ever seen,' said Polly seriously.

Anna looked up as Meg appeared in the doorway. A very different Meg — one wearing a long denim skirt and sandals, and her hair flying about her head.

'Meg, darling. I hardly recognised you! You look so different out of your power-dressing kit.'

Meg looked at Anna's smart designer jeans and pristine luggage and remembered that she and Anna had never been together in the country.

Inside the cottage there was a smell of burning apple wood and polish. The front door opened straight into a large living room with a red brick floor, at the far end of which was a huge inglenook fireplace with a faint glimmer from a hissing log. Opposite the fire was a battered sofa upholstered in brown hessian. At each of the windows, two of which had uninterrupted views of the Downs, white sailcloth curtains swept to the floor from fat wooden poles.

'Just dump your things here while we have tea,' said Meg, pointing to an area below the staircase which wound enticingly upstairs. Below it was a highly polished dark oak chest with a copper jug full of lily of the valley; above it hung an imposing set of antlers draped with an astonishing selection of sporting items and hats for every pastoral occasion. Through a door at the end of the room, Anna saw a rustic kitchen containing an antiquated Rayburn cooker, a big pine table, and a Welsh dresser laden with odd coloured china. A smell of baking filled the air.

'Auntie Meg, can I take Anna to her room? I want her to see my surprise. We'll only be a minute.' Polly took Anna's hand and led her up the creaking stairs. At the turn, a grandmother clock proclaimed five o'clock with a loud regular clanging.

'I hope the clock doesn't keep you awake.

Mummy won't come here, you know. She says the country is noisy and the clock is as bad as the birds and, of course, Ross snores and she can hear him through the floor.' Polly prattled on as they crossed the tiny landing into the prettiest room Anna had ever seen.

The floorboards had been painted shiny white, the walls also, with a bright blue stencil round the ceiling. There was a tall brass double bed with a thick white cover, and blue flowery curtains rustled softly, framing the Downs. There was very little furniture — a white-painted chest which served as a dressing table, a cane armchair and a hat stand with some blue satin hangers.

'Do you see the flowers? I picked them for you this morning. We can get some more after tea.' Polly pointed to a china jug full of primroses and a little note propped up beside them. Anna picked up the note and read it slowly. 'To Auntie Meg's friend from Ross and Polly.' There was a childish drawing of a dog, presumably Ross, and a child, Polly, and a woman with a large crown and wings. 'That's you,' explained Polly shyly.

Anna thanked Polly and gave her a hug.

'Can I help you unpack?'

'Later,' said Anna, hearing Meg's call from downstairs.

'We're going to be friends, aren't we?' asked Polly eagerly.

'Brownies' honour,' said Anna.

'What's a Brownie?'

'I will have to tell you all about them,' replied Anna, patting Polly's head.

After tea, Polly insisted on taking Anna for a walk up on the Downs. Meg stayed behind to get on with the supper. As the two started to climb the path, they heard Meg's CD player wafting on the evening air.

'Is that you singing?' asked Polly.

'No, darling, that is the most famous singer in the world. I wish I could sing like her.'

'Auntie Meg says you will be famous one day. She says you sing like an angel. She says you have a gift from God. Do you believe in God?'

They had reached the top of Firle Beacon. The larks swooped gracefully about them, catching evening gnats. Anna spread her sweater on the grass and they sat looking down on the village below, still and silent in the calm evening air. There was a purple veil of mist over the trees on the opposite Downs. A gaily coloured hot-air balloon moved silently above them, the silence and peace only interrupted by the odd roar of the balloonist's blast of hot air and the occasional cry of the evening larks.

Anna and Polly sat quietly together in perfect harmony. Anna answered Polly's question about God with care and with the same deference she would have afforded an adult. Consequently they fell into a profound discussion of the nature of their particular God, in the course of which Anna found out a great deal about Polly. It was clear she was not popular with her school mates and that her loneliness at school was an extension of her isolation at home. She was touchingly in need of friends. Her mother, while very fond of her daughter, seemed to regard motherhood as something which could be done by people you paid. It was clear Polly had a wisdom beyond her years and she was evidently used to surprisingly adult dialogues with her father, Meg and her grandfather. Her mother had taught her to play backgammon and she could beat all her family. She spoke French fluently, thought her lessons boring and stupid, refused to do maths and wanted to be a doctor.

'You won't be able to be a doctor if you don't do maths,' commented Anna firmly, remembering how difficult she had found the subject and how she had had to overcome her innumeracy in order to read music. 'Why don't you learn the piano?' she asked, remembering seeing an upright in the sitting room of the cottage.

'Will you teach me? Can I have a lesson tonight? I have a book of tunes. Funny thing is, Grandpa said the same thing. He can play the piano but Granny doesn't like music so he can only play when she isn't there. You wouldn't like Granny Lavender. She smells of fish because she's always boiling revolting things for her cats, huge dead fishes' heads with eyes and things. Granny Lavender can't cook, at least Auntie Meg and Daddy say so. She has a lady who does the cooking. They have terrible quarrels about the cats' fish. Mrs Duvver thinks it's disgusting and the cats should have tinned food like other cats. She says if it goes on she's going to make it into pâté and give it to Granny Lavender for supper without her knowing. Kill or cure, she says. I don't think she likes Granny. She only stays because she likes Grandpa.'

They heard the noise of a car approaching the cottage below them.

'Come on,' cried Polly, 'we've got visitors! Let's go and see who it is.' She leapt up from the grass and, pulling Anna's hand, set off running down the steep grassy hill. Anna tried to keep her footing but lost her balance when she tripped on a clump of gorse. She felt her ankle wrench with a sharp pain which made her cry out. She toppled to the ground, nursing her injured foot. Full of concern, Polly fussed about her. Ross decided a good wash was the ideal treatment, nuzzling Anna's face with his wet nose.

'I'm going to stay here for a minute,' said Anna faintly. She knew she had a bad sprain and would find getting back to the cottage a painful process which she would rather tackle on her own.

Polly ran on down the hill like a gazelle. 'I'm getting Meg. She can bring a bandage,' she called over her shoulder.

Anna lay back on the grass and closed her eyes. She was waiting for the pain to pass. She smelt the fragrance of the evening, the spring flowers of the Downs and she thought she could detect salt from the sea. Presently she heard voices, Polly's and a man's. She sat up. Approaching her up the hill were Polly and her father, David Lovegrove.

'We've got a bandage,' Polly called out. 'Daddy is here! Isn't it wonderful? Auntie Meg said she had a surprise for me.'

David Lovegrove looked quite different, almost burly. He had on an open-necked blue checked shirt and jeans. Anna's heart missed a beat as he bent down and inspected the ankle. The feel of his hands on her foot made her tingle. He looked up with very blue eyes from a tanned face, his sandy hair thick and curly. She thought he looked at least ten years younger than he had when she met him after her performance.

He helped her to her feet. She tried to put some weight on the ankle, wincing with pain. He supported her for a moment and then swept her off her feet. With her face on his shoulder, she inhaled his fresh male smell. If it had not been for the running commentary from Polly she might have felt embarrassed. As it was, she surrendered to David's strong arms. She dared not look into his face, afraid her eyes would betray the heady and disturbing feelings running through her as he carried her down the hill to the cottage.

* * *

It was still twilight when they finished their supper. 'Why don't you and David go for some fresh air while I put Polly to bed?' said Meg firmly.

'Oh, can't I go with them? I bet Daddy is going to take Anna to see the big house. No one ever lets me go there. It's not fair!' whined Polly. She ensconced herself in her father's lap and upset the remains of his red wine on to the table-cloth. Anna leapt for some kitchen roll and began mopping it up, wondering what Polly meant by 'the big house'.

Meg was surprisingly firm with her niece on the subject of bedtime and Anna, Ross and David set off on what was something of a mystery tour since David would not be drawn on where they were going. Concerned about Anna's foot, David announced he was going to wheel her to the house on his old bicycle.

The evening held the promise of summer. The air was still and the silence was broken only by the squeal of darting bats diving for gnats. The lane to the village consisted of six cottages, a rectory and a small post office. The cottage windows were still open to let in the last shimmers of evening. Anna and David wheeled silently past. The end of the road veered sharply to the left and the vista that confronted Anna took her breath away. It was so unexpected it had an almost surreal quality in the fading light.

The house stood at the end of a winding drive edged by an avenue of budding pink chestnut trees. The pale sandstone building was what the guide books would describe as early Georgian, but Anna guessed it had a much earlier provenance, judging by the chimney stacks. The front door stood in the middle of two rounded bays which continued up the three floors. Behind the flat roof was a discreet mansard where Anna suspected house servants had been billeted in a more prosperous era. The building was faced in honey-coloured stucco, and an ancient wisteria defied the lack of attention apparent in the rest of the garden, except for the sweep of mown grass round the house. There was evidence of a ha-ha at the south side of the small park; on the other side, sheep jostled for position under a magnificent oak tree, and on the sweeping terrace the occasional white and pink rose picked up the last glimmers of the bright day. Anna got off the bicycle and stood still as she took in the timeless beauty of the scene before her.

Laying down the old bike, David started to pick his way over the cattle grid on to the drive, holding his hand out for Anna to follow.

Anna had an instinctive dislike of interfering with other people's privacy. 'You shouldn't, David! The owners might see us!' she hissed under her breath.

'We are the owners,' said David flatly. 'Come on, it's empty. The roof leaks and there is only one room habitable but the power is on. I want to show you. I told

Meg and Polly not to tell you about it. I wanted to surprise you. Meg has some plans and she wants your opinion,' he said confidentially, taking her hand and helping her over the grid.

He fished a bunch of keys out of his pocket and unlocked the front door. Wisteria blossom blew about their feet as they entered a cool marble-floored hall. In the dim light Anna saw a winding stone stairway. A huge window lit the hall and the last shafts of evening light settled on a double doorway. One door stood half open. Anna saw a parquet floor. She thought she could hear a clock ticking. David walked swiftly to the half-open door and went into a room. With a click of the ancient brass lamp switch, all was suddenly bathed in light. He threw open the doors and beckoned Anna to follow.

The room smelt of hot summer afternoons and country house musk. It was almost empty; two tattered brocade sofas stood either side of a handsome ornate fireplace, and on the mantel an ornate gilt clock proclaimed nine o'clock. The walls were covered in faded pale green silk, its original colour evident where pictures had obviously been removed. At the far end of the room a gilt mirror picked up Anna and David's reflection under a dusty crystal chandelier.

Anna noticed the glass was cracked and scarred.

'This is a wonderful place. I can hardly believe it belongs to your family. Meg has never mentioned it. I simply don't understand,' said Anna in genuine bewilderment.

'It's a long story and one which makes Meg and me very sad. That's why she hasn't mentioned it, but there have been some developments in the last few months.'

'Well, please explain. I long to know the story,' said Anna eagerly.

'The house belongs to my father's side of the family, but there is no money to support it and very little land. It was requisitioned in the war for the Admiralty. Even then my grandparents found it impossible to keep up. My father was actually born here at Loverstone. After the war it was turned into a school. It wasn't a bad school, as schools for rich young middle-class girls go. But last year it began to get into financial trouble and in September the bank called in the debt and all the young ladies had to be shipped off to another school in Ascot. The lease reverted to us and the trustees have been selling off all the old school furniture. They got nothing for it, of course, and then a few months ago some men came and took some of the lead from the roof — it's now covered in tarpaulins. My parents want to sell the place. I expect someone would like to turn it into an hotel. Some of the original furniture was saved, and the family pictures. They're in Scotland now, in my brother's house, mouldering in his cellar. This room is known as the salon, I don't know quite why. Perhaps because my great-grandmother fancied herself a poet. She used to have literary weekends here at Loverstone. They were quite famous, I believe.'

'How can you bear to think of it going out of the family?' asked Anna.

'Meg and I have been thinking. We, at least Meg mostly, could turn it into a small money-making concern. There are masses of stable buildings at the back which could be holiday homes or something and the main house would be the perfect venue for a small arts festival. We're already thinking about trying to raise money to restore the roof. What do you think?'

Anna was thinking so many things she didn't know where to start. The Lovegrove family were beginning to intrigue her. Coming as she did from the solid middle-class professional background of her parents' families, this world, with its wonderful country houses and crumbling estates in Scotland, was wholly unknown to her. It was clear the Lovegrove family had very little cash and certainly not the wherewithal to enjoy the sort of life their ancestors had lived in this house. But they were the type of people her father despised. Not so her gentle mother who would have sympathised with their predicament, sandwiched as they were between a past they had been bred to and a future where there were no safety nets, a world of what you are instead of who you are. She could tell David was his own man — he had told her over supper about his offer of a job in the Whips' Office and how he was unsure about the political life. He seemed to be poised at some sort of crossroads. It was part of what she found so attractive about him; she felt he was involving her in his thoughts as if she was an established friend.

David walked to one of the rounded bay windows and flung it open, letting in the smell of acacia blossom. 'Just imagine it. A grand piano here in one of the bays and concerts every night, dinner in the garden perhaps, workshops for young musicians. We could bring children down from London to do children's theatre. There are fifteen bedrooms upstairs. Come, let me show you.' He took her hand and led her into the hall and up the winding staircase. Seeing him here in his family home, she thought she was beginning to understand him a little better, but at the same time she couldn't match up this David with the one who sat in Westminster. It just didn't fit.

9

Jeff Roberts, the Chief Whip, did not get up when David entered his office at nine o'clock on Monday morning. He was not best pleased. He did not like the whiff of arrogance which had surrounded David's request for more time to make up his mind about working in the Whips' Office. 'Bloody nerve!' he said to the Prime Minister when he saw him at Chequers at the weekend. He had been all for telling David to stuff it but the Prime Minister had been adamant.

'We need young men like David,' he had said. 'He must be given time.'

Silently Jeff had disagreed. The David Lovegroves of this world were precisely what the party didn't need; keeping them in line was the devil's own job.

David noticed the room smelt of boiled eggs. He wished he could open a window before he sat down.

'Warm in here, Jeff, isn't it?' he said pointedly, running a finger round the collar of his shirt.

Jeff didn't take the hint; instead he unwrapped an indigestion tablet and unashamedly broke wind.

'Stomach playing up again,' he growled by way of explanation. He eased himself a little in his swivel chair and David thought the smell of eggs intensified. He made a note to avoid the Chief Whip's room on a Monday morning. No doubt Jeff's digestion suffered after a weekend's wining and dining. He knew the Prime Minister had been entertaining the German Chancellor at Chequers on the Sunday, and the WAAFs who did the catering specialised in foreign food. The papers had been full of the effects suffered by the guests after the visit of the Japanese leaders. It was rumoured live goldfish had been consumed from the PM's aquarium. Questions had been asked in the House. The PM had vigorously denied any such thing. *Private Eye* had had a field day — it had become a sensitive issue, especially with the rows about fishing rights.

'That German food is far too rich. The wife was up half the night.'

'How did it go at Chequers?' David asked politely.

'Bloody disaster, between you and me,' said Jeff, munching angrily. 'But you haven't come here to talk about that. Have you made up your mind yet?'

'I've decided to accept.' David couldn't

quite decide if the expression on Jeff's face was glad or sorry. He thought about the Members he would be expected to keep in order, all surrounding his own patch, and many of them preoccupied with events far removed from the inner city problems they should be addressing. But then he reminded himself how the reverse was so often true. He thought of his brother living in glorious isolation on his Scottish estate and as often as not pontificating about the dangers of the immigrant population in the inner cities, about which he knew nothing at all.

'Delighted, young man.' Jeff shuffled some papers on his desk. 'But I warn you, you may have a rough time with your brief. We are giving you Greater London, and blood sports, or what's left of them, will be top of your agenda because we are putting you on environment.' Jeff fixed David with a menacing look.

David went visibly pale. Of all the jobs in the Whips' Office, environment was the nastiest. A nightmare of revelations about his family background flashed past him — Lavender's latest wind farm venture with his brother Jamie on the estate in Scotland, pictures of him as a boy deer-stalking. Even his father's passion for fly fishing would not be immune from attack by the campaigners who were successfully dispatching the fox hunting brigade. He felt decidedly gloomy. It would all be the same disastrous hash it had been in the last parliament.

'One thing I do need to cover with you. Something has come up about your personal life which I think I need to mention to you.' Jeff was beginning to enjoy himself.

David looked at him, unable to disguise the startled look on his face. He wondered if the legendary powers of the whips' secret police had read his thoughts every time he looked at Anna or seen the passionate kiss he had given her as they said goodbye last night.

'Oh?' he replied guardedly.

'It's about your wife. Attractive woman, clever too, but not quite clever enough to deal with the sort of thing she seems to have become involved with. It won't do, David, it won't do.' Jeff puffed out his cheeks as he spoke. David thought he looked like a hamster storing up nuts for future consumption.

'I don't quite follow you,' replied David, genuinely baffled.

'We make it our business to know what wives are up to. The Foreign Office is concerned. Part of her job, I know, and she is good at it, but this man Felix

Khamul . . . very powerful . . . a coup for her to interview him . . . sort of unofficial roving ambassador to the president . . . Your wife has his ear . . . pops up everywhere with him . . . ' Jeff's words hung in the air. Unfinished sentences were a trick of his. People liked to finish them, and in doing so let slip things Jeff wanted to know, but in this case he was disappointed.

'And?' said David blankly.

'What do you mean, *and*?' said Jeff with thinly disguised irritation. 'The man was nearly blown up by a fundamentalist the other day. He's a Muslim but rather in the same way as some people embrace the Labour Party, taken out of the deep freeze when it suits them.' Jeff paused and looked pointedly at David before continuing. 'Sort of Sunday Muslim, you might say, women all over the place. I wouldn't have my Peggy risking life and limb in that sort of work, however much I needed the money. Besides which, you have a young kiddy, don't you? Needs a mother, especially with you taking on this job.' Jeff glanced affectionately at a photo of what David assumed must be Peggy. He tilted it proudly in David's direction. It showed an enormous woman dressed in a nurse's uniform. 'Chairperson of the local Red Cross,' he explained. 'And this is our Shirley.' He pointed to what looked alarmingly like a picture of Jeff in drag dressed as a drum majorette.

'Your only one?' asked David, feigning interest. He wanted to get out of the room as quickly as possible. He pushed his chair back.

'Yes. Peggy had a bad time with our Shirley, she weighed twelve pounds. She's been quite enough for us. Strange creatures, women.' Jeff looked pensively somewhere above David's head. Then abruptly he got back to business. 'Heritage questions this afternoon. Nothing like plunging in at the deep end. See you later by the Speaker's chair. And good luck.' As David left the room, he muttered under his breath, 'You're going to need it.'

10

'That fish pâté you left out last night was delicious, Mrs Duvver,' said Charles from the doorway.

Mrs Duvver's normally rosy face went ashen. 'It wasn't for you, Lord Lovegrove. I thought you were out. It was for her ladyship,' she stammered, wiping her floury hands on her apron.

'Well, I ate it. I deserve spoiling too, you know,' quipped Charles. 'Lady Lavender had to go out unexpectedly.'

'Well, if I'd known you were in I would have done your favourite. I thought you were out, seeing as how them flipping tarts for prisoners is taking so much of your lordship's time. Though in my opinion they have it far too good. Your lordship always did have a soft heart.' Mrs Duvver looked at him closely. She hoped he would not suffer any ill effects from the cats' fish pâté.

Mrs Duvver adored Charles; he had given her a chance all those years ago when she had applied for the job of housekeeper with no experience or references. Her loyalty to him was absolute. He was, as she constantly told her daughter Janice, 'a perfect gentleman'. But Lavender was a different matter. A cold war raged between them, but at least Lavender never strayed into Mrs Duvver's territory. The kitchen in Vincent Square was Mrs Duvver's personal domain.

'Mrs Duvver,' said Charles, 'once again I must ask your advice. May I sit down?'

Mrs Duvver's mouth creased into a good-natured smile. She did not look her sixty-one years; her skin was unlined and firm, and she still had a full set of teeth. She had bright laughing eyes, the more so for the fairness of her lashes. Her fair-to-grey hair was not permed in the ubiquitous frizz of her peers but secured neatly at the base of her neck in a tidy bun. Many years ago, when Charles had first met her, she had been extremely pretty. In his eyes she still retained much of that wholesome, reassuring attraction.

'Of course,' said Mrs Duvver. 'I'll make us both a cup of coffee.' She pushed one of Lavender's mangy cats off a kitchen chair then furiously brushed hairs off the seat with her large capable hand.

Charles sank gratefully into the chair. This was the nicest room in the house, all in perfect order, unlike the rest except for the drawing room which was also Mrs Duvver's responsibility, and of course his study, when she could get into it. There was a large dresser which had come from his mother's old house at Frinton-on-Sea, and Charles had found a table and chairs to match on one of his circuit judge assignments. The fittings had been replaced a few years back, chosen by Meg. The morning sun streamed in and picked out the china on the dresser shelves. The room held many happy memories. When the children were young and Lavender was, as usual, absent, this room had been the centre of their lives. They had shared Mrs Duvver with her own daughter Janice. Homework and all family meals took place here, except Sunday lunch, the one meal Lavender graced with her presence in the gloomy dining room. But Sunday lunches were now a thing of the past since none of the family would voluntarily undergo the dreary ritual.

Mrs Duvver made the coffee, removed her floral crossover apron and sat down expectantly.

'I don't quite know where to start,' said Charles. 'It's about little Polly.'

'Poor mite,' Mrs Duvver mumbled disapprovingly.

'Yes, well, that's just it. I'm afraid things can't go on as they are. David can't cope. He has been offered an important job, and he will have even less time to be mother and father. I — '

'Shocking it is!' Mrs Duvver interjected. 'I never approved of that girl, never. She's foreign and full of hoity-toity ways, and besides, her eyes are too close together. It's a disgrace the way she neglects that child. I don't know why Mr David stands for it, and him such a lovely man, like his father, your lordship, if you'll pardon me. He could have anyone. He'd be better off without her.'

'Well, that's for David to sort out, and until he does, I have offered to help with little Polly, which is where you come in. You know Lady Lavender doesn't get on too well with children. I think between us we could cope; after all, the school is just round the corner.' Charles paused and looked hopefully into Mrs Duvver's kindly eyes.

'Well, of course we can manage. The child is a dear thing. We could do up the room next to the study for her.'

There was a clatter of feet on the staircase. Charles stiffened and Mrs Duvver raised her eyes to heaven.

'I'm just off but I would like a little something before I go. Do you have anything in the fridge?' The question was directed at the room in general and nobody in particular.

Lavender wore a floppy dark-brown twinset and a baggy tweed skirt. Her thin varicosed legs were encased in thick lisle stockings ending in curiously anachronistic black high-heeled court shoes. Her once fair hair, now pepper and salt grey, was cut in a severe pudding-basin bob. Despite its nondescript colour, Lavender's hair was the one vigorous thing about her appearance.

She waited while Mrs Duvver rustled something up which Lavender could take upstairs to her den to eat. Lavender's den was an untidy corner on the half-landing, strewn with files and stacks of magistrates' magazines, a battered old typewriter, and petrol stamps way beyond their expiry date stored in a biscuit tin on the floor in which the oldest and most incontinent of the cats frequently defecated. Mrs Duvver did not protest at being forbidden to enter this squalid corner with her new bagless vacuum cleaner. Occasionally Lavender emptied her ashtray into a large wastepaper bin under the rickety card table which served as a desk. The disorder she created about her had once been part of her attraction to Charles in the days when they had spun round the dance circuit; now he tried not to let it overwhelm him. He was above all a kindly man. He had seen too much of what was truly base in human nature to condemn his wife for her domestic ineptitude.

'What about that lovely fish pâté?' he suggested, helpfully opening the fridge door. Mrs Duvver's face reddened as he peeled back the tin foil from the dish. To Mrs Duvver's astonishment it was completely untouched save for a tiny dent in one corner. 'Just the thing, wouldn't you say, Mrs D?' said Charles with a wink.

11

The House of Lords clerk backed courteously towards the thick mahogany door of Baroness Stewart's office. The room was momentarily silent. Behind Veronica Stewart's head of blonde hair, a large barge sailed serenely down the Thames as he spoke.

'Baroness, Lord Lovegrove, it has been most interesting,' said the clerk with the slightest of bows. 'There are one or two things I will have to check, but I am impressed, yes, most impressed. I only wish most Bills were so well drafted. I wish you both good luck with it.'

'Thank you so much, Dennis,' crooned Veronica with her usual charm. 'I could not have done any of it without Lord Lovegrove's help.' She smiled towards Charles who had risen from his chair opposite her desk, acknowledging both the departure of the clerk and Veronica's thanks with a nod of his head.

The door closed behind the clerk and Veronica stood up and moved towards Charles. 'Thank you so much,' she said softly, gently placing an appreciative hand on the shoulder of his dark tweed jacket. He could smell the fulsome richness of her skin and her distinctive perfume as she stood beside him. Her bosom, upholstered in a cyclamen designer two-piece, brushed his cheek.

'I would do anything for you, Baroness. I am your slave, as are all the other gentlemen who pound in and out of this office,' he said teasingly, giving her firm behind a quick pat. He had never admitted to her that he didn't really think her Bill on conjugals for prisoners had a constructive future; there were too many anomalies. They had already run into difficulties about gay prisoners, and the Home Secretary was definitely trying to stall. But Veronica genuinely cared about the subject and if anyone could see the Bill through, she could. Veronica had an impressive record.

Charles's mouth showed the faintest of smiles as he recalled last night when he had seen Veronica in a very different setting. They had spent the evening in her large and comfortable flat in Battersea. It was in an upmarket block in Prince of Wales Drive, overlooking the park. They had drunk champagne in the pale, well-furnished drawing room and then the two of them had retired to her kingsize bed with a takeaway supper and a video. They had made love in the same gentle, uncomplicated way they had done for twenty years.

They didn't talk as they made love and they didn't think much either, but occasionally Charles remembered how, as a young man, he thought sex stopped somewhere in a man's forties. He certainly didn't think his own now adult children would believe the feelings he still had, the reassuring continuity of his sexual and cerebral dependence on Veronica Stewart whom none of them had even met.

But lately, as David approached the age Charles had been when he had first fallen in love with Veronica, he had felt the need to tell his son more of the relationship which had kept him sane over the last years. In a sense, it had also saved his wife from what would have undoubtedly been an unimaginable wasteland, for, bossy as Lavender seemed, Charles knew that underneath she was still as unsure about everything as she had been when he met her. She was utterly and totally dependent on him. Charles was a rare breed. A man whose loyalty and courage does not first seek a witness, he would never let Lavender down.

Lavender knew about the affair, Charles was pretty sure she did. She seemed only too pleased to let someone else fill her husband's bed and relieve her of her painful marital duties — without, of course, being a threat. She knew Charles would never desert her.

Veronica's husband had died of cancer, the very illness from which he had saved so many of his patients. Veronica had embraced her widowhood with characteristic fortitude. She had become Chairwoman of the Regional Health Authority, a path which had led her to the Lords and to Charles.

He had first noticed her late at night when both the Lords and Commons were working well into the small hours of the morning. Veronica was addressing an almost empty chamber on a clause giving customs officers more powers to search. There was much use of the words 'rectum' and 'concealed condoms'. Charles was dozing happily, dreaming about swimming in a stream surrounded by water nymphs, when he was roused by a question sharply directed at him personally: 'Would My Lord not prefer to be searched by trained personnel on embarkation rather than be conveyed to hospital? The rubber gloves would be sterilised,' the voice had insisted.

Charles travelled back into the full glare of the present to find himself fixed in the unflinching gaze of Veronica's blue 37-year-old eyes. He had suppressed an irresistible desire to burst out laughing. Later, over a brandy in Veronica's flat, he had kissed her. Hardly a day had passed since that time when they had not met or spoken. Veronica's life suited her perfectly; marriage was the last thing she wanted. She and Charles went away regularly on painting holidays to remote parts of Europe where English was hardly spoken and they would not be discovered. They worked together and they played together but they did not live together. Their relationship was perfectly balanced; neither asked what the other could not give and each gave what the other asked.

12

The black taxi drew up outside the house in Battersea. As Joelle got out, she looked apprehensively at the upstairs windows. It was late, but there were no lights on. The au pair's bedroom was at the front of the house. Why wasn't she in? Someone must surely be there to look after Polly.

The driver unloaded her expensive Louis Vuitton luggage while she unlocked the front door. The burglar alarm was on and the door pushed against a pile of unopened mail on the doormat. Joelle noticed a musty smell, as if the windows had not been opened for some time.

She turned off the alarm, switched on the light in the hall and thanked the driver for bringing in the luggage. As the cab drew away in the empty street, she walked tentatively upstairs to Polly's bedroom. The door was open. She switched on the light. It was strangely neat and tidy, and some of Polly's toys were gone, including her fluffy animal. Wherever it was, Polly was with it. Joelle felt a surge of fear. What the hell was David playing at? She had faxed him the day before to tell him when she would be getting home.

She opened the main bedroom door and stamped her foot in irritation. Obviously this was not Beatrice's day for cleaning. A shirt and a pair of socks were on the floor and the linen basket in the corner was overflowing with unwashed shirts. The bathroom wasn't much better. She carefully straightened her special white initialled towels and screwed the top back on the toothpaste tube. She decided to go downstairs and unpack in stages. She had hoped David would at least be in attendance to carry her cases upstairs. She felt terribly depressed. The poky little house in Battersea seemed a long way from the luxury and space she had been enjoying in Egypt. The only thing she had looked forward to was seeing Polly and she wasn't here.

The slam of the front door made her jump. It was followed by an eerie silence. She called down the stairs. 'David?'

'Well,' said David flatly from the hallway where he was absent-mindedly glancing through the pile of mail he had picked up off the floor. His face appeared gaunt and tired. He looked up as Joelle slowly came down the stairs.

'Where's Polly?' she asked.

113

'So you noticed your daughter was not in her bed, did you?' replied David quietly.

'What do you mean?' said Joelle sharply. 'Of course I noticed.' She felt a pang of alarm. Why was David being so cool? It was quite unlike him. And he never dissembled. 'Something hasn't happened to her, has it?' Her voice rose in alarm. She stood still, halfway down the stairs, dreading the answer.

'No. As a matter of fact she's on great form, no thanks to you, Joelle. I simply can't believe the way you behave. You don't deserve to have a child.' David had had a glimpse now of what life could and should be like. For all her beauty, Joelle didn't care about making people happy, not him, not Polly, not even herself. During the last two weeks Polly had seemed like a different child. She had moved in with his parents in Vincent Square, in the little room next to Charles's study. Even Lavender had entered into the spirit of the plan, getting Meg's old school desk down from the attic. And Ross had gone too, despite the initial difficulty with Lavender's cats, but they had soon learned to keep to the top of the kitchen dresser, out of Ross's way. Charles took Polly to and from school each day, and at four o'clock Mrs Duvver gave her tea. Later each evening

Charles took Ross and Polly to the park — the weather had been glorious. David had been sweating it out in the Whips' Office. His only consolation as the long evenings spilled into the small hours was that Polly was being properly cared for.

'What are you talking about? Where is my daughter?' Joelle shouted. David noticed she had gone pale under her expensive tan; it made her complexion look sallow. He suddenly had a flash of Anna's peaches and cream skin, and the realisation hit him that his love for his wife had died as suddenly as it had kindled when he had first met her. There, under the harsh electric light, he saw her for what she was. He knew now that she had not cared for him for a long time. He suspected she had been hedging her bets until something better came along. She had denied him the pleasure of mutual desire, and on the rare occasions they had made love in the last few years, it had almost been as if she was doing him a favour. He had even found himself thanking her as she had got up and on with her day as though she had finished a tiresome chore. After a while he had given up trying to make love to her. It was demeaning.

Joelle decided to change tack. She knew something seriously unexpected had occurred.

David seemed so cool and in control, it was almost attractive. She walked calmly down the stairs towards him. He betrayed no emotion as she came close to him, so close that their bodies touched. He could smell her perfume, see the sheen on her black hair as she stood beneath the light. She wore a cream silk blouse, the top buttons undone to reveal her tanned skin, the small hard breasts so different from Anna's.

'Darling, it is lovely to be home,' Joelle lied. 'But, please, don't tease me. Where is my daughter?'

'That wretched girl Karen is out on the town all the time. She doesn't respond to my notes. Polly has gone to live with my parents for the time being. I have her for weekends, when I try to be both mother and father to her,' he said icily.

'Gone to live with your parents?' Joelle shrieked disbelievingly. 'What are you saying? Have you gone mad, David? I shall go and fetch her right now!' Joelle reached for her bag on the hall table and started fumbling for her car keys.

David calmly grabbed her hands and held them still, pulling them towards his chest. She had forgotten how strong he was. She was unable to move, and she could feel his

116

heart beating through his blue and white striped shirt.

'We have to talk, Joelle. You have been away for nearly a month. How do you think Polly feels about that? Someone has to look after her. She is staying at Vincent Square. I mean it, Joelle. Don't think you can ride roughshod over us. Things will have to change.'

Joelle began to cry, tears of anger more than anything else. 'You don't mean it, you can't!' she shouted furiously.

David was momentarily overcome by a mixture of emotions, guilt mixed with regret and sadness. He had hardly ever seen Joelle cry. She suddenly looked pathetic, frail and thin in the harsh light of the hall.

He took her hand, the one in which she held the car keys, and bending her fingers open, removed the keys and put them on the table.

'Calm down,' he said quietly, getting a handkerchief out of his pocket and handing it to her. 'Let me make you a drink, Joelle. We're both tired. If we could at least be honest with each other, perhaps we could avoid hurting not only us but both our families.'

'I don't have a family, David. You've never understood that. It's never been you and me, it's been me and all your family, and they all hate me. They don't know what I'm about. The work I'm doing now, it's so exciting ... it's ... well, it affects all our futures. Polly's, our children's. But your family lives in their own cosy world ... you're part of that ... I ... ' She put her hand to her brow and pressed it, closing her eyes. 'Oh, what's the use? You wouldn't believe me anyway.' She turned to walk back upstairs. 'I'm tired, David. I think I'll go and lie down.' Her voice had become subdued.

David mixed two strong vodka and tonics and took them upstairs. Joelle lay on the bed with her eyes closed. She had taken off her clothes and wore a dressing gown. Her sudden change of mood had taken him unawares. He didn't quite know what to do so he erred on the side of kindness. His motto had always been, 'When in doubt, be nice.'

'Why don't you tell me about it? What exactly have you been doing in Egypt? I don't underestimate you, Joelle, not like you think. I know you feel your work is important. After all, it's come between us and it's taken you away from your child. Please try to explain. I don't want to feel bitter, I want us to be friends.'

David took a slug of his drink and began

to feel better. He hated confrontations and he wanted above all to be gentle with Joelle if she would allow him to be, but she had never invited tenderness, something he had so longed to give.

He reached out a hand and took hers, which lay feebly on the bed. To his surprise she took it and moved closer to him.

'Hold me, David,' she said simply.

They came together as friends, from a desire for comfort in their unhappy state, much as people look for companionship in a strange city. She began to tell him about events in Egypt.

'They've elected a woman president, as you know, but the extreme fundamentalist groups are dedicated to destroying everything she stands for. There are many women who wear Western clothes under their black veils, who have the benefit of a good education and in some cases lead almost Western lives, working with men and holding down jobs, for instance in the tourist industry. Yet they are devout Muslims. For these women, a fundamentalist regime would mean no more jobs, no more education, no more freedom of any sort. I used to think the extreme groups should be involved in the democratic process, but I know now this is not possible. I've been invited by the president to make a documentary. I'm going to follow her for several weeks. It's the most fantastic opportunity.'

'But where will you stay? Surely . . . I mean, for God's sake, Joelle! What about Polly?'

'I'm making plans, David. I shall stay with my mother. She plans to let her flat in Paris and rent a small apartment in Cairo. She wants to be in Egypt for a few weeks in the summer, see some of her old friends. Perhaps Polly could — '

'Polly could what, Joelle?' David's voice was grim.

'I've been thinking about Polly, but first I want to finish explaining to you why I am so fired up, how important this is, so you will understand how it transcends family things.'

David began to wonder whether Joelle had been contaminated by the very fervour she was trying to expose. How could fundamentalists in Egypt matter more to her than her own daughter?

Joelle's face became animated as she described the political consequences if the Muslim extremists gained control in the Middle East, and how the movement was gathering a terrifying momentum. 'Can you imagine the effect on the Western world if the supply of oil fell into the hands of these people?' she said. 'I've made some powerful friends. I meet all the most important people now at diplomatic parties. You begin to hear things. I know the names of the most dangerous groups, how they operate. People get careless at parties. Some of the most Westernised high-ranking Egyptians are really fundamentalists. They use Western culture for their own ends, which are to plunge the entire Arab nation into the Dark Ages. They hold the West in complete contempt.'

'Oh, come on, Joelle. I've met these people too. Take the Saudi royal family, for example. They know their own people, the way they think. What would be the point of overthrowing them? They're Muslims too, and they want to negotiate with the West.'

'Don't be stupid, David!' retorted Joelle angrily. 'I'm talking about extremist fundamentalist groups who don't want to negotiate at all. They might be small but they are disciplined, highly organised and very dangerous. Look what happened in Algeria. Men, women and children were slaughtered. This is much bigger. I tell you, David, I have a mission. I'm getting the channel to finance the documentary. We've started the script, but it's all deadly secret. You're the first person I've told about it.'

David began to feel real alarm. 'Do you realise just how dangerous all this is, Joelle? You're getting yourself into something very frightening. Has it occurred to you that you will have been monitored by all the agencies? I expect the CIA already have a file on you, if what you tell me is true. And has it dawned on you that you are married to a British politician? That is not without its significance. It sets you apart from other reporters. For example, Joelle, you know all MPs' phones are tapped as a matter of course, and all the recordings go to GCHQ, although God knows what they make of most of them! But ours must be of special interest. Do you think the Foreign Office are not aware of everything you do? You know I have to inform them every time you go to one of these sensitive areas. Remember the fuss when you went to Northern Ireland? Just think, you could be kidnapped. Fanatics will try anything. Your life is worth nothing in the power game.'

Joelle leapt up off the bed and stood angrily staring at David from across the room. She wound her dressing gown tightly about her and, seizing a brush from the dressing table, began to stab at her short dark hair.

'That's typical!' she snapped, her voice

rising a decibel. 'Mr bloody Big. I should have known not to confide in you. Don't you see? I'm committed. I care about this and I can do something about it. The power of the media, David, that's what I have in the palm of my hand and I'm good at what I do — very, very good — and all you tell me is that I should realise I am married to a rising Member of Parliament. Bugger the bloody British parliament! Its members can't see the wood for the trees. They have their heads up their arses, David, just like you do. I thought for one brief moment you might understand, but you don't. We're from a different planet, you and I. This is beyond my own personal safety.'

'Reason and calm have never been your strong points, Joelle, but I certainly didn't mean to be patronising. Nevertheless, you are Polly's mother and you are still my wife. I have a responsibility for both of you and always will have.'

'Talking of Polly, I want to take her to Cairo with me,' she blurted. 'She can go to the French Lycée where I went myself. I'll pay the fees at the London school to keep the place open. It's just for two terms until I finish the film. Whatever you may think of me, I care about my child and I want her to be proud of me — and I don't want her to think that this little smug, self-satisfied island is all there is. After all, David, she is half me and — '

'I think you must be slightly mad, Joelle,' David interrupted. Joelle had been about to say something he did not want to hear. She had a look of terrifying vengeance on her face. Her anger was beyond him, beyond anything he could begin to understand. He didn't want to be part of it. 'Polly stays here in the safety and security of her home with her family and friends. You do not take her anywhere, do you hear? On this I give you my word.'

He left the room swiftly and shut the door. He went out into the silent street and sat in his car. He phoned his father on the car phone. He had to talk to someone. Joelle watched him through the darkened window and rang Felix.

13

'Can you keep a secret, a very important secret?' Joelle asked Polly. She had fetched Polly back from Vincent Square and they were having lunch out together, which Joelle had suggested as a treat to celebrate her homecoming.

'Well, yes, I suppose, if it's very important, but if it's bad I would rather not. I don't want to know any bad things at the moment and anyway, I don't have secrets from Daddy, we tell each other everything,' said Polly hesitantly. 'So you see, it wouldn't really be a secret, would it?' Polly cupped her chin in her hands and looked at her mother across the table.

Joelle pushed her plate of uneaten pizza away irritably. Polly didn't look at her mother now. Her antennae were up. Her mother was planning something serious and she sensed it might cause disruptions, and this frightened her, just when things were beginning to be so wonderful, like other people's families — well, almost. The best thing about it was that she had begun to look forward to going to school. It was ever since Granny

Lavender had said, 'Why don't you ask some friends to tea?' Grandpa had been there and he had organised some brilliant games and everyone had thought the whole thing was really cool, even Melissa who had always made Polly's life such a misery. And then yesterday Melissa had solemnly invited Polly to become one of her group. They had a ceremony at break time and now she had a badge. The other girls no longer moved away when they saw her, they went about together in a tight gaggle.

It wasn't just the tea party that had changed things. Polly was aware that she herself had changed. The routine at Vincent Square and the lovely food cooked by Mrs Duvver made her feel good, and Mrs Duvver washed her clothes all the time so she didn't look a mess. Granny Lavender had taken her to have her hair cut and now she wore it in an Alice band instead of silly plaits which people pulled and teased her about. One of the best things was sitting with Grandpa while they did what he called 'their' homework, and he was teaching her the piano. It was lovely getting home and having everyone smile at you and ask about your day. Polly was happy and although she loved her mother because people should love their mother, there was something alarming about her. Her father didn't alarm her at all, he was the best friend she had ever had, and he only told her nice secrets about birthdays and things, but this secret wasn't like that.

Polly sucked the last dregs of her banana milkshake noisily from the bottom of her paper beaker and then looked up guardedly. She could tell her mother was cross. She didn't want her to be.

'Well, why don't you tell me the secret, as long as I can tell Melissa?'

'Melissa? Who's Melissa?' asked Joelle impatiently.

'Mummy, you weren't listening. I told you about Melissa, she's my new best friend.'

Joelle's face softened a little. She smiled and patted Polly's hand. She hadn't noticed before what nice hands Polly had; she had stopped biting her nails. Joelle looked up and was struck for the first time by how much her daughter had changed, and a vague unease about what she was planning to do filled her. She wondered if the venue was perhaps responsible for this unusual lack of resolve. The Pizza Parlour had been Polly's idea of a treat; it was where all her school friends liked to go on their birthdays, 'just like in America' she had claimed importantly. Joelle looked uncomfortably around the neon-lit tables and had a sudden urge to go home

127

and raise the matter again, to show Polly some photographs and tell her about the school she herself went to in Cairo.

'Polly darling, let's go home now and perhaps we can talk about the secret another time,' she said brightly, looking at the bill and getting her wallet out of her bag.

'No, Mummy, I want to know about it now. Grandpa says things shouldn't be hidden from children because they always know something is going on and then they think it's worse than it actually is. Does it have to be a secret? I mean, if it's very important, everyone will have to know one day, won't they? Or is it a surprise? Like when Melissa's mother told her that she was having a brother or sister?'

Joelle struggled to conceal the irritation she felt at this reminder of the cosy predictability of the world of which her daughter so obviously wished to be a part. She decided to come straight to the point.

'All right, darling. It is a sort of surprise. How would you like to come to live with me in Egypt for a while? Just while I finish some very important work I have to do. We could have a house with a swimming pool . . . you could have Melissa to stay. Your other granny, my mother, wants to get to know you. And you could see wonderful things, like the pyramids, and we can sail on a great big sailing boat . . . ' Joelle faltered. Polly had begun to tear her paper napkin into little bits, her face contorted.

'No! I don't want to come!' she said vehemently. 'I don't want to go anywhere! I want to stay here. I want you and Daddy to be like other people's parents. It's a bit like that at Granny and Grandpa's, that's why I like it so much. And if you go away again, I want Daddy to come and live at their house too, and when you come home you can come as well. I'm never leaving Daddy, or my friends and Ross and my room at Vincent Square. I'm learning the piano, and next year Melissa said I might be vice form captain.' Polly's lower lip started to tremble. 'I hate . . . I hate . . . ' She began to cry quietly into the remains of her napkin. 'I hate Egypt. I hate your work. I hate not having you at home. I wish I could find another mother if you won't stay with me. I am never going to be like you, never. I don't want to be famous, I just want to be happy. I'm more important than your work. Does your work know about me?'

Faced with the defiance of her daughter, Joelle felt unaccustomed fingers of self-doubt start to tear at her agenda. She had had it all so perfectly planned: a chance to catch up on her relationship with Polly, start making a new life, send Polly to her own school, show her some of her own roots, ones that she, after all, had given to her daughter. She wanted to be a good mother but in the only way she knew how, to rear Polly into an equal. She was surely past the babying stage now. She could come into her own as her mother prepared her for real life, taught her all she knew. She thought to herself as she looked at her daughter's anguished face, she is not old enough to know what is best. As her own mother had said, 'Children are very adaptable.' But Joelle didn't say it. She just got up from the table and hugged Polly as they walked into the street. Polly didn't pull away from her as Joelle feared she might, she walked close to her, holding her hand, not speaking. Her mother could not even guess what she was thinking.

14

David had made up his mind about two things. Firstly he would have to go and see the Foreign Secretary. Joelle's life had become a distinct worry. He couldn't make up his mind whether she was suffering from some kind of *folie de grandeur* or if she really was living in the wash of world-shattering events. The appointment with the Foreign Secretary was this morning and Jeff Roberts would be there. The second issue was what to do about the danger of Joelle taking Polly out of the country. Charles had advised him to apply for a court order to stop her, but David baulked at this. All semblance of civilised behaviour would evaporate if war was declared between himself and Joelle. He had decided instead to confront Joelle with his own ability to pull strings in high places. He had pointed out to her the trouble he could make for her through his diplomatic connections, and the consequences this would have on her work. A high-profile battle would do her no good at all; the doors she had opened in the upper echelons of Cairo society would soon begin

131

to close if she became an embarrassment. Joelle had been outraged and had accused him of blackmail. Her shrill tones still rang in his ears. The row seemed to have gone on for days. She seemed more determined than ever to take Polly to Egypt, and with a sinking feeling David realised he would probably have to take his father's advice after all. Since then she had been unpredictable and moody. He couldn't make out what her overall game plan was at all. He had made up his mind to wait until the day before her next departure to have it out with her and suggest they both accept the marriage was effectively over. He had often heard of couples waking up in the same bed on the day they moved from the marital home to embark on separate lives. He used to find this totally incomprehensible, but his own life recently had taught him there was no such thing as 'normal' when two people were experiencing the death throes of a long relationship.

'Would you like a cup of coffee?'

David looked up from his desk. He had been miles away from the stuffy office he shared with three other junior whips.

'Oh, thank you, Gloria. I really need it this morning.'

The Whips' Office was proving as onerous

as he had feared it would be. Every day he slogged into the House of Commons and then out to the constituency for evening engagements. One of the disadvantages of having an inner London seat was its proximity to the House, leaving no excuse for unavailability. Last night it had been a fundraising dinner with the Deputy PM as the guest speaker and then a rush back to the House for a close vote on the fox hunting issue. He had finally got to bed at one in the morning.

The vote had gone through on its second reading despite the many grey areas in the small print. David would have liked to abstain, but in view of his new job in the Whips' Office he felt he had to give it his support. He knew it would be a long time before it became law because it had all been too hastily drafted. It would be the same shambles as it had been in the last parliament when it had been abandoned as unworkable. A law is not a law if it cannot be enforced, his father had remarked gleefully at the time.

'Can I get you anything else? Yesterday's letters are in the blue folder ready for signing, and your father rang.' Gloria wore a canary yellow jacket and a very short black skirt. The jacket fitted tightly, somewhat too tightly, in fact. It was only recently that David had noticed how attractive Gloria was. She cheered him up, and she was a marvellous secretary. It wasn't that he wanted to tear her clothes off and make love to her; she just reassured him of his masculinity in some way. It was like looking at a menu; it whetted the appetite before you selected what you wanted. He wanted Anna Frazer.

He knew his father would have rung to ask about Polly. None of them had the right to stop Joelle removing Polly from Vincent Square and taking her back to the house in Battersea, but he couldn't blame his father for being worried. Still, Joelle seemed genuinely happy to be with Polly again, and sometimes life in the Battersea home appeared almost normal, except for the night when he lay awake, conscious of the bizarre fact that he still shared a bed with this woman he wanted to divorce. Last night he'd woken up and hadn't been able to get back to sleep. He had wandered about the house and then gone into Polly's room. She had been sleeping peacefully, her thumb in her mouth and her fluffy animal under her cheek. He had gently pulled the thumb from her mouth and kissed her smooth forehead. He had a sinking feeling as he watched her.

Joelle would do whatever suited her. She might well take Polly away. He didn't think he could bear that.

'I'm just popping out to ring my father,' he said to Gloria who was busy at his filing cabinet. He couldn't talk to him in the office, he wanted privacy.

He found a quiet spot in an empty committee room and dialled Charles on his mobile phone.

Lavender answered. 'David, thanks heavens you've rung.' His mother sounded agitated and upset, which was unusual for her.

'Hello, Mother. What's wrong? Actually, I'm returning Dad's call.'

'I haven't slept a wink, David. That poor child. I shall never forget the way she cried. Grandparents have rights, you know. I shall do something . . . Charles and I feel responsible. I . . . we are all upset, including Mrs Duvver.' There was a catch in Lavender's voice, and David could hardly believe his ears. He could have sworn his mother was stifling a sob.

'Are you all right, Mother?'

'It doesn't matter whether or not I'm all right,' Lavender replied crossly, sounding more like her old self. 'It's Polly we have to do something about. We had such a lovely time while she was here . . . she's put on

135

weight, David. I've tickets to take her to the ballet. She wants to start dancing classes, did she tell you? I . . . ' She faltered, and there were sounds of nose blowing. 'Your father has something to say to you. He's on the other phone. I'll put the receiver down.' There was a click on the line and his father's voice came on.

'David, your mother and I are very concerned. We must act quickly as a family. As you know, the scene when Joelle came to fetch Polly was most distressing. Of course we tried to smooth things over, encourage Polly to go back home with her mother, but the child seems very disturbed. I fully expect her to come back here of her own accord — she knows her own mind, that child. Your mother has become very close to her.'

'Just what are you trying to say, Dad?' asked David.

'We are genuinely worried, David. I think your wife is mixed up in something quite dangerous. I suspect she doesn't know quite how dangerous. You must impress on the Foreign Secretary how concerned you are. I don't think you should underestimate things. Your mother and I think Polly should come to us for the time being.' Charles's voice finished on a firm note which left no room for argument.

'Bear with me. I have my meeting with the Foreign Secretary today. Things may be clearer after that. I'll call you at once.'

'A word of advice. Read their lips carefully, David. They will know more than they let on. They will be watching you and recording everything you say. They will be deciding what to tell you and, more importantly, what not to tell you.'

At eleven o'clock David set off through St Stephen's Hall to talk to the Foreign Secretary. He pushed his way through the crowds waiting to gain access to the Public Gallery; some of them were obviously intending to get into the House of Commons early to be sure of a seat for Prime Minister's Question Time this afternoon.

Parliament Square was the usual mass of tourists. He thought how happy they all looked, having normal holidays together, and thought wistfully how his life had never been like that with Joelle. He wondered if he would ever reach the calm waters of a safe, trusting relationship, a planet away from the events he was about to discuss with two comparative strangers who were now privy to the sad intimacies of his dysfunctional life. He looked at his watch. It was seven minutes past eleven. His appointment was at eleven fifteen. His heart sank as he realised he had not rung Anna this morning as he had promised. The fact was he couldn't really cope with his feelings for Anna at the moment. The exhilarating freshness of his feelings for her was jumbled up with foreboding about Joelle and anxiety about her plans for Polly.

He went into Whitehall and into the Foreign Office, showing his pass at the entrance, and took the lift to the Foreign Secretary's office. The building was palatial in design, reminiscent of the colonial splendour over which its earlier occupants had reigned supreme. A plethora of marble-decked ante-rooms and corridors into which the sun seldom strayed put the visitor in a suitably respectful frame of mind. As David approached the inner sanctum marked by a plush plum-coloured carpet, it was exactly eleven fifteen. He was shown into Maurice Whitaker's office at once. The room was, by contrast, comfortable though still impressive. Maurice and Jeff rose together as David entered the room.

Maurice Whitaker was a tall, slim man of about fifty-five. He was handsome by any standards. His dark, intelligent eyes were accentuated by a shock of almost blue-black hair which showed no signs of grey, and his regular features gave him a look of order which inspired confidence. His manner was both charming and assured, but those who knew him well were aware that this superficial veneer of affability belied the true nature of the man. He was a cool and ruthless tactician, a fact which made him eminently suitable for the post he now occupied.

'My dear David,' he exclaimed beneficently, taking David warmly by the arm and gesturing to him to sit where he and Jeff had dented two capacious armchairs in the separate seating arrangement reserved for less formal interviews.

Prior to David's arrival Jeff had been acquainted with the contents of a large file on the life and loves of Joelle Lovegrove. Jeff had read the contents with a mixture of disapproval and concern. 'Poor bugger. Do you think he knows?' he asked Maurice when he got to page twelve.

'No, I don't suppose he does,' Maurice replied slowly. 'I've always liked David Lovegrove. I think he is a thoroughly decent man and it's not our job to enlighten the man about his wife's extramarital arrangements as such. What concerns us is whether there is a risk to security, if her activities endanger the life of a Member of Parliament, and how seriously we should take the information she has given her husband. Why would she be so indiscreet?' he added thoughtfully. 'Ask yourself that, Jeff. Ask yourself that,' and he tapped the side of his nose conspiratorially.

The file was now safely back under lock and key. Jeff looked sympathetically at David as he stammered his way through a rerun of the story Joelle had confided. He had got to the point where Joelle's information had become somewhat more detailed when coffee appeared. David had a sense that the timing had been orchestrated for some reason. Cups clinked and sugar and milk were distributed. Maurice appeared deep in thought.

'Now, David, let me tell you what I think,' he said eventually. 'That wife of yours is doing some valuable work. We all know the march of fundamentalism is a very real concern and not as far-fetched as some would have us believe. But in Egypt, popular opinion does not support Muslim extremism. Moreover, fundamentalism is not compatible in any way with the life of the Egyptian ruling classes who want a secular modern state. Nevertheless, an assassination attempt on leading political figures could well destabilise the country. We cannot officially respond to the information you have brought us, but we have a solution, don't we, Jeff?'

Jeff sat forward in his armchair. 'Yes, we

do. We think we should plant a question in the House and the answer will register our concern. We thought to hang it on the recent concessions made to terrorist demands.'

David sat silent for a moment. He half wondered if he was going to be asked to put the question.

Maurice, as if alerted by osmosis, pre-empted his concern. 'We thought Peter Hacket would be the right person,' he announced decisively.

The merits of Peter Hacket's credentials were briefly explored while David plucked up the courage to mention his personal problems.

'Maurice, this may not be entirely relevant but I thought I should make it clear that I have decided to begin divorce proceedings. It has all been a little difficult and, well, we, the family, are concerned about our daughter. She is very young . . . well, we . . . ' David shuffled awkwardly in his chair. He was beginning to regret mentioning this until Jeff gave him a reassuring pat on the knee.

'Don't worry, David, your Polly won't be leaving the country.' He paused and looked at Maurice Whitaker's inscrutable face.

'No, that's absolutely right. Give my regards to your father, David. I was only talking to him this morning. Baroness Stewart

141

is my wife's sister. She and your father are working on a Bill at the moment. Fine man, your father. Now, if you will forgive me . . . '

The meeting was over. Jeff and David left and made their way to the lift.

'Couldn't have the kiddy upset now, could we? Take my advice, the sooner you find yourself a nice English girl, like my Peggy, the better,' said Jeff warmly through a slight whiff of boiled eggs. 'Now, how about a bite of lunch?'

'Love to, and thanks, Jeff,' said David sincerely.

15

Anna arrived at the Coliseum at ten o'clock. She would have overslept this morning if the telephone hadn't rung at eight thirty. She had been dreaming about her mother and her home in Scotland, the Laurels. At first she hardly recognised the voice and then she realised it was Shamus. His voice had started to break.

'Aunt Jeannie has given me the fare. Can I come down to stay with you for Whitsun? I have a week off and I want to go and see some colleges,' he squeaked, and then plunging into a deep bass he said he had all her dates and could he come to her performances at the Colli.

'That's brilliant,' Meg had said when Anna told her. 'We can take him down to the cottage. I have Polly every weekend, as you know, and if David comes, we'll be one big happy family.' Meg had gone off into a spiral of plans, barbecues, walks on the Downs, a visit to the big house. 'And,' she informed Anna, 'I've found a grand piano someone wants to store. It's going into the salon next week.'

Meg was planning a series of concerts to try and raise enough money to restore the roof of the big house. Anna knew she had been working every weekend clearing debris from the salon. Anna was helping her find a group of young musicians who could get a programme together.

All these happy plans were buzzing around in Anna's head as she swiped her card through the pass door of the Colli.

She made her way up to the Balcony Bar where she was to meet Jason, the young pianist who would coach her in the small parts she had been offered in next season's productions. She wondered briefly if Justin had had anything to do with her recent run of good fortune, and then dismissed the thought. After all, Justin's affairs with other singers hadn't done them much good. She thought with a shudder about Justin's wife down in Surrey, calmly going about her life bringing up their two young children, and felt even more resolute in her determination not to resume their affair. Apart from anything else, although she had not intended to regard David Lovegrove as other than her flatmate's brother and a married man at that, from what she had learned he was a lot less married than Justin was. According to Meg, David's marriage was all but over.

Meg had made no bones about her matchmaking intentions, and fate had played into her hands because David had been offered the government position on the council of the Coliseum. 'Now he will be able to watch you rehearsing,' Meg said with a broad smile. He was due here today and would be having lunch in the boardroom after the rehearsal for *Butterfly* in which Anna was to sing Kate Pinkerton. She wasn't on until the last act so she had plenty of time to run through her part, but she was so excited at the thought of seeing David she found it hard to concentrate.

Anna passed the administrative offices on her way to the bar and didn't hear Justin come up behind her.

'I miss you.' He pressed his body against hers. She felt his breath on the nape of her neck and his lips moved on her skin as he spoke.

She turned and met his eyes.

'I don't have a performance tonight. Let me give you a lovely dinner, somewhere quiet. We need to talk.'

She made as if to decline the invitation. He put his fingers to her lips to silence her.

'I do understand, darling. It's not all about sex, you know. I want to help you with your career. We should stay friends. This is a small world, it doesn't do to have quarrels.'

'I'll let you know later,' she said lightly.

Anna had to admit that when face to face with Justin's attractiveness, she did miss him. She missed the love-making, she missed the excitement of his company, the heady high she got on stage when her eyes met his as he stood in the orchestra pit, his eyes glinting in the cosy light of the conductor's desk from where he exercised his control over the musicians and singers, the sensual knowledge of the intimacy between them as he mouthed her words . . . It was a glamour and allure which surpassed anything she had dreamed of. If she did have dinner with him, they both knew they would end up in bed together. She felt an uncontrollable excitement at the thought. He would pick her up at seven thirty, and she would wear the dress he had brought for her from Florence the previous month . . . And then she thought of David.

'You look a bit flushed. Everything OK?' asked Jason. He had been watching the exchange through the glass door as he tinkled with the libretto for *Der Rosenkavalier* — he had just been given it for the next season. 'My thoughts are of you alone,' he sang, an octave lower than the score. 'Recognise it?' he asked.

'Yes, of course,' replied Anna. It was

Octavian, she knew every note; she almost sang it in her sleep.

'Well, his nibs has just given it to me. I suppose you know we're doing it next winter? Has he talked to you about it? Probably not. I expect you two have more important things to see to.' Jason embarked on a theatrical examination of his immaculately manicured nails as he continued to tease Anna about Justin. He had seen it all before.

Jason liked Anna. He thought there was something refreshingly down-to-earth about her. In a way she reminded him of his own family with whom he had only lately had a rapprochement after years of non-communication. He was genuinely devoted to them, but when he had been taken up by the homosexual group of musicians he had met when he auditioned for a summer job at Glyndebourne, they just couldn't cope with it. He had realised, after a while, it was no use trying to explain to his parents that it wasn't just a sexual preference. It went far deeper than that. For the first time he felt among friends. They showed him a way of life that pleased his artistic and fastidious and, in a way, very domesticated nature. He went to live with a conductor who had a beautiful house not far from London. He discovered interior decoration, French and Italian food. They had elegant and interesting friends who all dressed beautifully and laughed at his wit. They talked about things his parents knew nothing about. Guy took him to Italy where they rented a villa in Tuscany. He felt as if he had come home, found himself. He loved Guy in his way. Guy's elegant, tanned body was beginning to show signs of his forty-seven years but it pleased Jason in a way he had never experienced with the girls at his school who had sold uprights behind the staff garages. They smelt of BO and menstruation whereas Guy smelt of Tiffany's For Men and Floris bath essence.

Anna put down her bulky leather music bag and slumped into the chair next to Jason. He wore a spotless pink poplin shirt carefully rolled up at the sleeves. It suited his lightly tanned skin and thick hair which, on a woman, would have been described as mousy but on Jason seemed almost the colour of pewter. It tended to flop over his forehead when he was playing. He would flick it back into place with a quick twist of his head. His trousers were immaculately pressed and a folded cashmere sweater lay neatly across his knees. He always removed his gold signet ring when he was playing, and it now sat on top of the piano in a leather presentation case. Anna knew the ring was a present from Jason's conductor friend; he had shown her the entwined initials of them both engraved upon it. Jason emanated a sense of order which spilled over into his work. 'It's logic,' he would explain to a particularly stupid singer, and he would lead them gently down a path of discipline until they found themselves automatically counting crotchets and quavers as they spoke. He could teach harmony and counterpoint to the dimmest of the company members. He took them back to basics, to the tonic solfa. But not Anna. She was of the old school, music was in her blood. She had learned doh ray me before her ABC. They would often fool around together on the piano at the end of a session. In fact, it was on just such an occasion that Justin had first noticed Anna. He had heard them and, intrigued, had put his head round the door — musical skills of this sort were an aphrodisiac to Justin. One look at Anna, after hearing this simple example of her skills, made his testosterone surge. Jason had known Justin would bed her but he suspected the dalliance would last longer than most. Anna Frazer was different.

Jason's powers of organisation were far-reaching. Anna usually found the sessions with him developed into a therapy. He had the capacity to analyse heterosexual relationships with searing accuracy.

'Darling, I know what's going through your head. We're all tarts in the end. Your friendship with his nibs hasn't done you any harm, you know. Don't let a misplaced conscience make a martyr of you.'

'It's not my conscience that's bothering me. It's just that I'm so weak. I finished it, you know. I don't want to be the other woman in someone else's marriage. People like Justin are always more married than they say they are. I bet when he's at home with his wife in Esher he's a model father and husband. Besides which, I want to have someone around, a friend. With Justin, you only have some of him for some of the time. Even all of him some of the time would do, but I get the feeling he's on to the next page of the Filofax address book the moment we say goodbye.'

'How do you think he files you all? I hope it's F for Frazer and not something else.'

'You have the foulest mind, Jason. I'm happy to say I don't get half your jokes.'

'Oh yes you do, darling, and that's what makes you such a wonderful singer. Remember what your teacher used to say, women sing from their private parts. I know it sounds better in a Yorkshire accent — forgive the newly acquired Sloane speak, Guy is giving me elocution lessons.'

'Oh God, Jason, do you think I'll have to get rid of my Scottish accent if I want to get on in polite society? Talking of which, one of the reasons I could kick myself for falling for Justin's fatal charm again is that I've met someone else.'

'Two things, darling. Firstly, if you dare lose that lovely lilt of yours you can find another accompanist, and secondly, make sure this one isn't married. There's enough trouble out there without going looking for it,' said Jason, thumping the piano lid to make his point.

He looked directly into Anna's face and thought that if he ever did decide to make love to a woman, it would be Anna. She had a lightness about her, as well as divine looks. Jason had often wanted to touch her auburn hair; it had a mind of its own, like Anna herself. Jason had no doubt she could make a success of any life she cared to follow. Above all, he knew she was a true and loyal friend, the sort you could ring up in the middle of the night when you felt like topping yourself. But he hadn't felt those feelings recently, not since he had decided to throw in his lot with Guy.

'Well, come on, who is he then?'

Anna hesitated. 'I can't tell you.' She wanted to confide in Jason. Apart from Meg, he was the best friend she had, but the whole thing was a little too close to home. Gossip was rife in a company like this and Meg would be sure to get to hear if she gossiped to Jason. Anna knew that if she and David were seen having dinner alone, people would soon hear about it. They had kept their relationship very discreet but recently they had risked dinner in an Italian restaurant round the corner from David's house. She had gone back to David's house and they had listened to music. Yesterday they had met at lunchtime and then gone to an exhibition at the Tate. She had been down to the cottage with him and they had been for long walks on the Downs. The more she saw of him, the more she realised how much they enjoyed each other's company. She had not slept with him, he hadn't expected her to, but she found him increasingly attractive and the connection with his family was a welcome change from the uneasy, compartmentalised contact she had with Justin. Anna had become fond of Polly, who had promoted her to the status of goddess. But still there was something about David, as if he was frightened of his sexuality.

Anna didn't feel she could let herself go.

'So this one is married too, then?' Jason's voice sounded vaguely disapproving.

'How did you guess?'

'Well, obviously he is or you would be able to talk about it, wouldn't you?'

'Yes, he is, but he's different from Justin. He confides in me, and his wife isn't interested in him. But there's a child, a lovely child. I feel terribly sorry for them both.' Anna's voice faded a little as she thought about Polly.

'You are one for punishment. Out of the frying pan and all that. You might as well stick with his nibs. Enjoy your dinner tonight. They still haven't cast Octavian.'

'I'm not going,' she replied defiantly.

'Oh yes?' he said, as she opened her score.

16

'I can't believe it,' said Lavender over the phone to David.

'Yes, after all that, she's gone.'

'Do you mean for good?' asked Lavender guardedly.

'I hope so, but I'm not sure. Typical Joelle, she just announced she was going back to Egypt and off she went.'

There was silence at the other end of the telephone. 'Was Polly upset?'

'Not really, she took it all in her stride. She seems to have grown up in the last few weeks. I hate to say it because a child needs her mother, but she has become very philosophical about Joelle. In fact, she puts me to shame. I wish I could be as calm.'

'Well, when is she coming round? You can send her things even if they are dirty. Mrs Duvver and I will wash everything and I still have the tickets to the ballet.'

David still couldn't believe this transformation in his mother. She made no attempt to hide the excitement in her voice when she talked about Polly and the enthusiasm for doing Polly's washing was so out of character as to render him speechless.

That morning he had felt wonderful as Joelle's minicab swept down the street. Karen, the au pair, stood challengingly in the kitchen, in a red track suit, the usual fag hanging out of her mouth.

'I've asked you not to smoke, especially when we're trying to eat our breakfast,' he said, impatiently.

'Joelle doesn't mind, she told me so,' she said coolly, putting the fag in her coffee saucer and pouring milk on a bowl of muesli. Polly stood in the corner of the kitchen watching this exchange. David knew what Polly wanted him to do.

'Pack your bags now. You can have a week's money when you hand me your key. I have the number of the Sisters of Mercy from whom you got this job. They will give you accommodation until you find another job, or better still, go home, for I won't give you a reference. You have half an hour while Polly and I have our breakfast. And I know what you've been smoking in your bedroom, it's here in my pocket,' said David, fingering the Cellophane packet full of cannabis that Beatrice had found the previous day. 'If I have any trouble from you at all you know where you'll end up.'

Polly advanced towards the table from her

quiet corner. 'And I hope when you're born again you come back as a dog and get treated the way you've treated poor Ross who never did anyone any harm.'

The au pair rushed out of the room, leaving a fetid disturbance of air.

David watched her go with relief. He didn't want another scene like the one he'd had with Joelle last night.

'Can I go back to Vincent Square now, Daddy,' Polly asked eagerly.

David sat on the big Windsor-backed chair by the kitchen table, a remnant from his bachelor days. He pulled Polly on to his lap. Ross, seeing a chance for a communal love-in, lumbered up from his basket and nudged his head on to David's knee. David held the two of them, child and dog.

'I'm so sorry about all this, Polly darling.'

David wondered if she had heard the terrible exchange between himself and Joelle the previous night when Joelle had announced she was leaving for Egypt in the morning. 'If you go this time, I hope you don't come back!' he had shouted.

'So you've suddenly grown some balls, have you?' she sneered.

'No, but it wouldn't surprise me if you had,' he answered. Dressed in a khaki designer outfit, her hair cut shorter than ever, she looked like a young boy. To David she was suddenly sexually anodyne. 'And if you are still thinking of having Polly with you in Cairo,' he went on quietly, 'I have already applied for a court order to prevent you taking her out of the country.'

Joelle's face had drained of colour and she threw her wedding ring at him. He picked it up, wrapped it in some kitchen paper and flushed it down the lavatory.

'You bastard!' Joelle had screamed at him.

And that was exactly what the au pair said now as she bundled past the kitchen door with two large suitcases. She threw her key on to the hall table and slammed the door behind her. It was as if she had never slept in their house, drunk from their cups and shared the intimacy of their domestic lives.

David gave Polly a squeeze. She had not mentioned her mother's leaving. Not once.

17

'This time I'll drive you down,' David said emphatically. He and Anna were having a quick lunch near the Coliseum. 'Can you be ready by nine o'clock?'

Anna hesitated. She was singing on the Friday night and she had to do a few domestic things around the flat. Recently she and Meg had let things slide. They were both so busy, especially as Meg seemed to have Polly every weekend. One weekend they had had Polly to stay in London and Meg had brought her to a rehearsal.

'Make it ten,' she said, 'then I won't keep you waiting.' The prospect of two days in the country with David made her feel very happy, especially when he went on to inform her of the latest developments with Joelle.

'Joelle has left me,' he said bluntly. But as he explained what had happened, Anna felt sure Joelle would be back when it suited her.

'For instance,' she commented reasonably, 'what has she done about her things? A woman who is genuinely leaving a man works that sort of thing out and Joelle

158

doesn't sound like the sort of person who would leave anything to chance. She'll be back, David,' she warned, hating the sound of her words. She wanted Joelle to let go of this man whom she found so attractive. But one thing she had learned about David was that he had a streak of obstinacy in him. It was both a strength and a weakness, and part of the reason he had remained in an unhappy marriage for so long — a kind of dogged determination to make it work. But now, clearly, he had made up his mind that the relationship was over, and it was war as far as Polly was concerned. Nothing could bring hope back into that marriage. As Jason liked to joke, 'You can't put the cock back, darling.'

The drive down to Sussex was slow and hot, the traffic was bad, and when they got to the cottage, Meg and Polly had left for the beach with Ross. A cold lunch awaited them on the kitchen table, salmon and an onion tart, a crisp green salad and strawberries and cream. They took it outside and ate it on the scratchy lichen-covered table on a little terrace made of a mosaic of old bits of broken china. They drank some cool white wine from the fridge and Anna wanted nothing better than to fall asleep in the hammock in the orchard. But David

159

was eager to show her Loverstone again. He pulled her to her feet and together they set off through the village to the house.

As they walked, a soft breeze enriched the air with the smell of roses from the cottage gardens. Anna was slightly behind David and she found herself admiring the back of his neck. His thick sandy hair curled on to the collar of the blue and white shirt he had chosen, which she had once admired, saying it brought out the blue in his eyes. She found herself wondering what sort of children they would have if they married and lived the sort of normal life she had always expected. This was what she daydreamed of at school on long summer mornings, sitting at the back of the classroom in the middle class girls' school where her father had insisted she go instead of the local State school where her mother taught music.

Soon they were through the village and David took her hand to guide her over the cattle grid. As they reached the other side of it, he put his hands either side of her waist. Her skirt had parted from the white linen blouse and his hands were on her flesh. There was no need for words between them. She raised her arms about his neck and he kissed her, at first gently but then, as their passion rose, more urgently.

160

When they drew apart, they smiled almost secretly to each other and turned to walk faster up the drive to the cool house. David had been here earlier, just after they arrived, and the front door was unlocked. Anna followed David inside but they didn't go into the salon. He led her purposefully up the winding stone staircase and along the creaking boards of the galleried landing.

One of the mahogany doors stood slightly open. David pushed it and led Anna inside.

The room was at the back of the house and faced southwest. The first thing Anna noticed were the long casement windows which were wide open. Faded cream sun blinds moved lazily back and forth in the breeze. She looked slowly about the room. It was as if she had walked into the private world of someone from another age, who had just slipped out for a walk round the garden.

A four-poster bed faced the windows. Its curtains, though faded, were still richly coloured and picked out the tones of a wardrobe, dressing table and bedside cabinets painted in the Venetian style with swathes of flowers and beribboned mandolins on a soft green background. There were two large, old-fashioned trunks standing open by a painted screen and on the screen hung several pleated silk dresses. Anna walked over to them, her steps silent on the rug. She picked up the hem of one of the dresses and held it to her cheek. It had a musky, aromatic smell which reminded her of something, and then she remembered her mother's clothes which she had had to deal with after her death.

'David, whose dresses are these? You didn't show them to me when we were last here.'

'This is my grandmother's bedroom, the one room in the house which is left intact. The school never used it and the Navy weren't allowed in as we stored some of what little we had left in it. It's a beautiful room, isn't it? And my grandmother's dresses are still in perfect condition. Meg has been airing everything. I think that's why it feels as if this room is still lived in. Odd, isn't it?'

'Odd and wonderful at the same time. Is that a picture of your grandmother?' asked Anna, pointing to one of a group of faded pictures on the dressing table.

David picked up the sepia photograph. It showed a woman in her mid-thirties holding a smiling baby who stared besottedly up at her, its tiny fist holding the long string of pearls which hung from her neck.

'Yes, that's her, and the baby is my father. She was very beautiful. People say your mother is the first woman you fall in love with. In my father's case, perhaps it was the first and the last. He fought hard to retain this room as it was, through all the ups and downs.'

'Surely he loved your mother once. He sounds a very special person, but you hardly ever mention your mother.' Anna saw a shadow flicker over David's face.

'I'm never sure about the past,' he said evasively, 'how much we should hold on to it. My father never wanted to do anything to disturb his past but Meg takes the opposite view. We'd both like you to sing here, to help raise money for the roof repairs. As you know, Meg's been working on it and the locals have been very helpful. But I don't want to talk about that now. You're a beautiful woman, Anna. You know I've fallen in love with you, don't you? I want to lie with you on my grandmother's wonderful bed.'

Anna did not resist. They went quietly to the soft welcoming bed. Anna lay down and David unbuttoned the front of her light summer shirt. She wore no bra and he cupped her breasts in his hands and kissed them.

He felt Anna's nipples harden between his lips and he almost thought he could taste milk. He experienced a sublime eroticism as he revelled in the warm, sweet smell of Anna's aroused body. And then he was aware of her slowly unbuttoning his shirt. He felt for the softness under her navel and at the top of her thighs. He pulled at her underwear. She did not need to guide him as he began to make love to her with an assurance which both surprised her and took her quickly to the place where she and Justin sometimes, but not by any means always, went.

Justin's lovemaking was a selfish form of self-aggrandisement which often left her unsatisfied and forced her to lie to satisfy his urgent need for reassurance about his performance, much as he expected about his conducting. She was glad, now, that she had refused his dinner invitation.

As David lay with Anna in his grandmother's bed, where his father had been conceived, he knew he could never make love to Joelle again.

Eventually they fell into a deep sleep until Anna heard the church clock strike five o'clock. They woke slowly, revelling in the thrill of their lovemaking. Anna didn't want to wash. She wanted to keep the reminder of their passionate embraces with her for the rest of the evening until David, as she knew he would, crept into her bedroom in the cottage.

'Anna. I'm going to divorce Joelle. Will you move in with me? Ross needs a mother, you know,' he joked. 'Polly thinks you're the answer to everything. And there's me. You've made me the happiest man in the world.' Between kisses he went on, 'Your body, your breasts, your smell . . . and your heavenly voice. I cannot bear the thought of any other man coming anywhere near you. I love you passionately, Anna. I knew it the moment I saw you on stage. Say you will think about it, please.'

18

It was difficult for the people around Lavender to take on board this astonishing bond she had developed with her grand-daughter Polly. 'So unlike her,' they all said. Somehow Polly had touched Lavender deep in her heart and the bond was all the stronger for the emptiness it had replaced. Charles was delighted for his wife and today was to be just one of the days that Lavender had begun to enjoy so much.

She had been looking forward to it for some time. She felt a little foolish when Charles teased her about it. 'You look like a teenager going to her first dance,' he said as she fussed about what she and Polly should wear.

'I'm only doing it for the child,' she retorted.

Charles smiled wryly knowing this was not true and glad that his wife, so long a prisoner of her own past, had attached herself to the slipstream of Polly's never-ending flow of wonder and enthusiasm.

It wasn't that Lavender had not wanted to share in her own children's childhood.

She had wanted more than anything to compensate for all the things of which her own mother's premature death had deprived her. But when she married Charles, nothing turned out as she had hoped, least of all what went on in the bedroom. Then came their first child, Jamie. He had been born after a long and agonising labour. She had the baby at home and the worst thing about it was that Charles was there. He saw it all, the mess, the pagan nakedness, her cowardice — she had cried out terribly. And then there was the monthly nurse. Everyone had one in those days. She, of course, was there too, along with the bad-tempered family doctor who kept offering her an aspirin. 'Goodness me, we are making a noise. You must stop it, you're hurting the baby,' the nurse kept saying and then the doctor had pressed a black, foul-smelling mask over her face and the next thing she knew a baby was crying. They didn't let her hold him; he was too frail, they said, he needed a rest. And she wasn't allowed to feed him. She was told she didn't have enough milk. The nurse fed him from a bottle. Every morning she would wake Lavender at six and bring Jamie in with the bottle. Lavender had surreptitiously tried to put him to the breast. He had screamed indignantly and his whole body went stiff with fury until she put the rubber teat in his mouth and he sighed contentedly.

The next two babies had been Caesarean. She had a fear of anaesthetics after the black mask, and when Meg was born they gave her a very light one and she felt pain the whole way through. She felt them cut her open and she tried to call out at the dreadful pain as the knife went in. Nobody believed her, but years later many such cases came to light and the victims were awarded damages.

Lavender felt it was dangerous to love anything too much. You would always be disappointed — and then Polly came to stay.

Polly needed her and it was nice to be needed. Her parents hadn't needed her, Charles didn't need her; Mrs Duvver serviced his domestic needs and 'that woman', as Lavender thought of Veronica, serviced his bed. And her own children had always gone to Charles when they needed something, so much so that when Meg had actually asked her for help with buying a flat, she had said 'no' without really thinking it out. The one place she did feel needed was on the Bench but she was soon to be retired. She had contemplated the future with a sort of isolated depression, almost as if it wasn't happening to her.

Polly had changed that. Polly asked her things no one else had ever asked her. Lavender even found herself talking about her own childhood. Polly would sit gazing intently at her as she spoke. This odd, brave little girl aroused some fierce, protective instinct in her. There were times when she felt something similar about one of the many dysfunctional delinquents who filed past her Bench. She would make them stand up straight, hands out of pockets, no smirking in the back of the court, no gum-chewing — the usher would come with a saucer to collect it. She would see them begin to focus on her. She had the power to lock them away, after all. She liked them to expect the worst and then she would say, 'This is your last chance. Take it.' Sometimes they did. In a way she felt Polly was her own last chance, and she was going to take it. She hoped Joelle would never come back. She prayed every night that she wouldn't, down on her knees by the bed. Once Charles had watched her, eyes shut, silently mouthing the words. He had asked her what she prayed for so vehemently and she had been ashamed to tell him.

Today they were off to the ballet, just the two of them. It was half term, and Polly had been with them all day, every day, for

169

three days now. Lavender had taken her to Harrods to buy a new dress for the occasion. She had been surprised when Polly chose an old-fashioned dress in sprigged cotton with puffed sleeves and smocking. She had helped her wash and dry her long fair hair. It was lovely hair, not a bit like poor Meg's hair which was dark and straight and never looked clean no matter how often she washed it.

Now Polly stood to attention in the drawing room at Vincent Square while Lavender tied up her hair. She caught a bit of it up in a black velvet bow and the rest hung about the child's shoulders. The afternoon light from one of the long casement windows caught the white-gold lights in it as she twirled to be admired by Lavender, Charles and Mrs Duvver. The arrival of Polly had brought a harmony to the relationship between Lavender and Mrs Duvver rather in the way a new pet can do in a failing, aged marriage when the children have fled the nest and the conversation has no focus. Their dialogues about Polly and the mendacity of 'Mr David's wife' had a great present and a great future.

'I wish I had a camera. She looks a picture, a really pretty Polly, as they say,' said Mrs Duvver affectionately.

Charles could hardly believe what was

happening to his domestic life. There were flowers in the gloomy drawing-room, a huge arrangement of peonies on the grand piano which had had its cloth taken off. It now stood open and music sat on the stand. The dark, dreary table which stood in the window sported a bright flowery cloth and was covered in children's games and colouring pens. There was a breeze across the square and the curtains fluttered merrily. Meals, too, had taken on a different aspect. Four people now sat down to lunch round the kitchen table instead of snacking furtively in different parts of the house. Today they had eaten shepherd's pie and baby broad beans, followed by rice pudding and syrup, which Polly said was the 'yummiest thing' she had ever eaten. It was as if his wife was enjoying a second childhood. But there was something very frail about it all, as if it were too good to last. A photo of Polly was taken by Lavender's trembly hand.

'Anna takes pictures,' piped Polly.

'Anna? Who is Anna?' asked Lavender sharply.

'Oh, she often comes to the cottage with Daddy,' answered Polly.

19

'Grandpa, this is Shamus.' Polly was clutching the hand of a solemn-looking youth of about sixteen or seventeen. The boy had Anna Frazer's chestnut-coloured hair and bright eyes. Charles noticed that he and his sister were very alike except for the expression on their faces. Instead of Anna's confident, smiling demeanour Shamus had a watchful, agitated look. A good-looking lad, thought Charles, honest and clever. He liked the way he allowed Polly to parade him round the room. Charles recalled Meg telling him something about the boy's mother having died and he realised, from the brief meeting he had had with Anna, that she had taken on the role of mother. Meg had told him very little about the Frazers' father.

'So, Shamus,' said Charles seriously, 'I hear you are an up-and-coming musician as well. You must be very proud of that sister of yours. She is quite a celebrity. I'm looking forward to hearing her sing again. I loved the rehearsal. She has a beautiful voice.'

Shamus's face lightened up considerably. 'Yes, I am proud of Anna, she deserves success. She's worked so hard. Our mother always said Anna had a great future as a singer.' Charles noticed the seriousness of Shamus's reply, his high forehead puckering slightly as he spoke. He suddenly felt very concerned for him. There was something about Shamus that confirmed his first favourable impression of the woman David was now so patently in love with. Charles liked family loyalty. It had kept him with Lavender all these years. He was constantly pained by the way Jamie, their firstborn, seemed to have so little in common with his siblings. He had mismanaged his affairs to a point of ruin but Lavender wouldn't have any of it, the truth was never discussed. But tonight one of Charles's great concerns, Loverstone, was beginning to be sorted out.

David had borrowed money and bought out Jamie's share and was now hell-bent on restoring it. It was one of the various strands that had recently come together to unite and restore his family. Anna Frazer and this boy were part of it all. He felt as if there was magic in the air.

'Well, my boy, we're all very grateful to your sister for helping with this evening,' he said. 'I know she has made it all possible.' He put a hand on Shamus's thin shoulder and noticed the grey suit he wore was much too small. His wrists protruded and the cuffs of his shirt were worn.

'Tell me why your sister thought of doing a Handel opera. Let's sit here.' Charles indicated the front row of the room full of shining gilt chairs.

'Actually, it was my idea. I once saw *Acis and Galatea*. It's very simple and light and perfect for a summer evening. Of course it's really an oratorio. Anna loves the music and it only needs a small orchestra. Galatea is really for a soprano and Anna is a mezzo, but we are experimenting. The singers are all doing it for free and the musicians are mostly students and they just want a small fee, so I suppose it has worked out well.'

As Shamus went on to explain the plot, Charles looked about the room. The last time he had entered the house was when it was a school. He had hated the smell of ink and rubbers and hot teenage girls and the shabby state of the place. Pubescent girls had rampaged up and down the curved staircase and down the long gallery. The room in which they now sat had been used as a gym. He had vowed not to go back, and to leave it up to the next generation to sell the house when the school's lease ended. But how delighted he was that things had taken such an unexpected turn.

The far end of the salon had been turned into a summery bower. A small dais emerged from a mass of cow parsley and dog roses and honeysuckle. He could smell their fragrance as Shamus continued his vivacious account of the plot.

The magnificent parquet floor he remembered so well had been cleaned of the ink stains from years of school use. He remembered the bossy headmistress informing him this room used to double up for exams and evening studies. It had been rewaxed by a team of volunteers from the village. Meg had managed to get the room repainted and the glass in the broken mirrors replaced. She had found the original chandeliers in a box in the stables and now, with the gilt chairs and candlelit tables set in the big hall and on the terrace for dinner, this part of the house looked as lovely as at any time in its long history. And as for Anna Frazer . . .

Charles and Lavender had arrived in the middle of the afternoon rehearsal. Confusion had reigned. The flowers were still being arranged, teams of people were busy preparing the tables for supper. The orchestral players, dressed in a colourful selection of clothes, looked hot in the heat of the afternoon, despite the open windows, and the girl he assumed to be Anna Frazer was in full song, her head covered in a silk turban under which her hair was obviously in large rollers. She wore blue denim jeans and a loose cotton shirt which he recognised as one of David's. He had given it to him the previous Christmas.

She had stood very still and commanding, her beauty evident despite the curlers. As she sang, she lifted her head, revealing her fine slim neck. Charles's breath had caught in his throat. Several of the helpers had stopped their work to listen. 'As when the dove laments her love,' she sang. 'When he returns no more she mourns . . . billing cooing panting wooing.' The sensual words struck at the centre of Charles's being, and just for a brief moment he wished he was young again and could take such a girl in his arms, and then he noticed she was singing for one person alone, and he turned and saw David standing at the back of the great room. His gaze was steady and the message passing between him and Anna was palpable. After a brief moment of jealousy, Charles rejoiced for his son and knew David was experiencing something which few people in life probably do, a moment of sublime happiness, one he would always remember. Charles looked at Lavender. She had sat down on one of the gilt chairs. She, too, was looking at Anna, her expression rapt.

And then Polly had sidled quietly into the room. She sat beside the stiff figure of Lavender and held her hand. Lavender had pulled Polly's head to her shoulder and as they listened together, Charles saw a tear slowly trickle down his wife's cheek.

20

David watched Anna sleeping. He had as usual woken early, about six o'clock. Anna was tired after the weekend so he let her sleep on. This was the first time she had stayed in his house. She had refused to take such a risk before but after the weekend and the successful meeting with his parents, who obviously knew everything, she had willingly fallen asleep in the spare room bed after they had made love. Polly had gone back to Vincent Square, and Shamus had returned to Scotland on the overnight sleeper.

David almost had to pinch himself to get used to the idea of such complete happiness. Whatever Joelle did, nothing would stop him divorcing her. He was sure now that she was having a serious affair with someone in Cairo. He assumed it was Felix Khamul. Jeff Roberts obviously thought so.

Being with Anna had given him a new perspective on life. Whereas with Joelle he had frequently had the feeling that disaster hovered in the wings, Anna exuded a calm serenity which pervaded everything around her. Last night, coming home in the car, he had asked her about her family. He had been impressed by the way she had got on with his parents, even charming the initially hostile Lavender, and the way Shamus had taken Polly under his wing and sat at the piano with her, teaching her endless varieties of chopsticks.

Anna had at first been wary of discussing her family, but having met David's parents she decided to tell him all about her father. David had listened in astonishment as she described the events leading up to her mother's death. He simply couldn't understand how a father could have such feelings about a daughter and especially one like Anna.

She had been terribly upset when Shamus had gone back to Scotland. She had confided her anguish at her inability to do enough for him while he finished his schooling. And she was worried about how he would manage financially when he started music college. She did not think her father would contribute anything towards Shamus's pursuit of music.

David wanted more than anything else to marry Anna. He would help her with Shamus, and he could come and live with them in London when he got into music college. Their lives would dovetail beautifully. While Anna was singing in the evenings, he himself would be at Westminster. They would live in a wing of Loverstone at the weekends, and Meg could run the music festival there and give up her job in London, which she was beginning to tire of anyway. He would ask his father for his grandmother's engagement ring; he had never wanted it for Joelle. It was not the sort of thing she would have liked, a hoop of diamonds in a Victorian setting. Yes, he thought with a thrill, he would ask her when she woke up.

It was now seven thirty. He would go and make a cup of tea.

As he put the kettle on, the phone rang.

'May I speak to Mr David Lovegrove?' said the educated male voice somewhere down a rather bad line.

'Speaking.'

'Mr Lovegrove, my name is Miles Anderson. I'm the Consul at the British Embassy in Cairo.' The voice sounded breezy and efficient.

David had an immediate feeling of foreboding.

'Is something the matter?' he asked, sitting down slowly on the kitchen chair by the telephone. Ross had got up from his basket, his nose now firmly pushed into the palm of David's left hand, ready for his morning stroke.

'I don't suppose you have seen the news yet, but there has been an explosion here. An assassination attempt on one of the president's most trusted advisers.'

'You mean a bomb,' said David blankly.

'Yes. It was left in Mr Khamul's car, although he wasn't in it at the time. It was an inside job, the car was locked up in a security garage. The driver was killed instantly when he turned on the ignition.'

'What has this got to do with me?' asked David, almost knowing the answer.

'Well, I'm afraid I have some bad news. It's your wife. She was in the car.'

'My wife in the car? Is she dead?' David asked. He felt sick.

'No, but she's in a very bad way. Burns, you know . . . ' The voice trailed away as if embarrassed to continue.

'Where is she? Is she having the best treatment? Can you fly her home? She has insurance,' David blurted frantically.

'She's too ill to be moved. She's in hospital in Cairo. They are doing all they can to make her comfortable. I don't think she's conscious which, frankly, is a blessing.'

'I'll come at once . . . I — '

'Mr Lovegrove, I took the liberty of booking you on to the next flight to Cairo from Heathrow. It leaves at ten thirty. I'll

181

have a car at the airport ready to take you straight to the hospital. I hope you don't mind. It's just that this is peak holiday time and all the flights get booked. I was lucky to get one. I am so sorry about all this. You will of course stay at the Embassy.'

David thanked Miles Anderson and wrote down the flight number on the kitchen notepad. Joelle's writing was still there. He slowly replaced the receiver. It was some sort of list; among other things, it said, 'Ross, kennels'. Ross's nose pushed into his lap. He felt numb.

21

'Will you come this way, Mr Lovegrove? The doctor would like to speak to you before you see your wife.'

The pretty nurse looked Mediterranean. She could have been Italian. She wore a smart white uniform and a stiff starched cap. As David followed her down the long corridor, her white, rubber-soled shoes squeaked on the polished linoleum floor. The sound reminded David of a trapped animal and he felt a surge of horror at what had happened to Joelle, trapped in a burning car. He dreaded seeing her perfect body disfigured, suffering. After all, she was Polly's mother, the woman he had once loved.

The office looked clean, workable — not very up-to-date. A fan lazily rotated on the ceiling to supplement the inadequate air conditioning. The doctor was small and dark; he looked very young for such a position.

He came straight to the point. 'She does not have long. All we can do is try to make her comfortable.'

David felt he was going to pass out.

He was taken to a small room off the side of a bigger ward. There was a peculiar smell, almost sweet, as they pushed through the swing door into the room. It contained only one bed. David wore a gown and mask which made him feel unbearably hot. As he approached the figure on the bed, the smell worsened. The nurse saw by the expression in his eyes he was finding it hard to bear.

'It's the burns,' she said gently. 'They have become infected. We are doing all we can to make her comfortable.' She pulled forward a chair and placed it by the top of the bed and steered David into it.

It was not Joelle, the thing on the bed. She had left that shattered and burned body, though something still breathed. He saw the bandages expand regularly in little shudders. Almost the only part of her body visible were her hands lying very still on the edge of the bed. He didn't know quite why but he twisted his wedding ring off his left hand and, gently lifting her right hand, placed it on her middle finger. And then he cried silently.

'I'm a Coptic Christian. Shall I get you a minister?' asked the young nurse. 'She doesn't have long. I'm sure it would help.'

Later he prayed over Joelle's still body and then he left the hospital. He didn't look back. Miles Anderson drove him to the smart apartment block where Joelle had been living. Her mother would be coming from France to see to her things but perhaps there was something David would like to take home. In the event, he took nothing.

* * *

Meg, Charles, Lavender and Polly sat at lunch in the dining room in Vincent Square. The mood was one of artificial normality. Lavender had resorted to a strange kind of forced gaiety when talking to or in front of Polly. Polly herself had withdrawn into silence since hearing of her mother's death. Charles had been the one who told her after David had rung with the news. Charles had thought he sounded confused and evasive, the story was garbled, and there was something about David's voice he didn't like at all, as if he was not quite there.

As for Lavender, she had been down on her knees in her bedroom, not so much praying for Joelle but for her own guilt in wishing, and even praying, for her to disappear for good, and leave them to bring up Polly. But not like this. The horror of such an event was unimaginable in the protected environment of Vincent Square. The sordid side of life that Lavender came

185

into contact with through her work on the Bench paled into insignificance beside the violence that had ended the life of her grandchild's mother.

'We can give her a lovely send-off,' said Mrs Duvver once she had recovered from the shock. She liked nothing better than a 'nice funeral'. She was disappointed when Charles told her it was Joelle's wish to be cremated and that her ashes were to be scattered on the Red Sea. 'It's not right,' was her final comment on the situation, before she returned her attention to domestic affairs.

'You're a brick, Mrs D,' said Charles as she bustled into the dining room with roast lamb, and fresh peas and new potatoes from her brother-in-law's allotment in Streatham.

'Got to keep your strength up when there's trouble in the family,' replied Mrs Duvver.

'You go home now, Mrs D. I'll put the dishes in the machine and clear away, if you leave the pudding on the table,' said Meg.

Charles knew things would not stay quiet for long. Soon the press would be at the door; the death of an MP's wife in a terrorist attack had already been announced on the news. There had even been footage of a distraught David leaving the British Embassy in Cairo where he was staying. Then some recent archive pictures of Felix Khamul, for whom the bomb was intended.

They had decided to keep Polly away from school for the time being.

'So, Polly darling,' said Charles, 'you're off with Aunt Meg this afternoon. What are you two going to get up to?'

'Taking Ross for a walk, that's what we're doing, and then . . . ' Polly paused, holding her spoon aloft. 'And then I want to go to a church or somewhere with Anna and I want her to sing a song for my mother. Anna is magic, she's like that person Orpheus in the Underworld. I think that's where Mummy is and I know Anna can sing to the bad spirits and Mummy can go to heaven, like Anna's mother did.'

This was the first and last comment Polly was ever to make to them about her mother's death.

'All human beings are special, Polly,' Charles responded, 'and your mother particularly so, and if Anna can sing to the spirits and help your mother to find God, that is an excellent idea. I don't know why none of us thought of it.'

Meg took a handkerchief and blew her nose; she didn't want Polly to see she had been crying. She didn't understand it herself. It wasn't as if she had liked Joelle very much. But such a brutal end to Polly's mother's life was something none of them could quite accept. She feared for the consequences the truth would have on so young a child and Polly would know it all one day, however much they tried to keep it from her. She was surprised to feel her mother's hand softly patting her knee. She glanced at Lavender and wondered if it was too late for her to start being the mother she had wanted her to be. As she looked at her funny bobbed hair and the curve of her neck, she suddenly saw how alike she and her mother were. They had the same straight hair, the same almost tubular thinness, the same fears and insecurities. Perhaps even the same inability to express their feelings, even when so much was poised delicately on the hope that they might. But they were bound by all they had been and would be together, good and bad. It was never too late, absolutely never. Meg stretched out her hand and put it on her mother's, who took it with a slight, embarrassed smile and held it, just for a moment.

Meg and Polly went to the church where Jason sometimes played the organ. 'Poor kid. Of course I'll come and play for her,' he had said when Anna explained the plan. There were just the four of them, Anna, Meg, Polly and Jason.

The church was empty. Evensong was to start in an hour. Anna sang 'Orpheus and His Lute' in an arrangement by Vaughan Williams, and then 'The Lord Bless You and Keep You' by John Rutter. A few people came in from outside when they heard the music, and discreetly applauded and asked for more.

'Yes, please do,' said Polly. 'We must make sure she gets to heaven.' Anna sang some Handel she and Jason knew by heart.

'I know she's there now,' Polly said finally.

They went home and collected Ross for an evening walk before Meg dropped Polly back at Vincent Square.

22

David hadn't told the family when he would be back. It was a question of getting a flight and there had been formalities to attend to. Everyone had been very kind.

Joelle's mother, Regine, had offered to pack up her things and send them to London, but David had looked at the closet full of smart women's clothes and decided they would be of no use to anyone in the family. He had tactfully suggested Regine dispose of them as she thought fit. She said she would pack up the laptop, the cameras and the mobile phone, together with all Joelle's papers, and bring them over to London herself in the next few weeks.

They didn't talk to each other much, there was a restraint between them. Regine didn't meet his eye or his heart. It was only on the day of the hastily arranged cremation that she showed any real emotion. It was a stiflingly hot day. When he and Joelle had made their wills, Joelle had said she wanted her ashes to be scattered at sea. Regine was adamant it must take place here, in the country of her birth. The family could gather for a

190

memorial service later. 'It would,' she said, 'in the sensitive circumstances be better, particularly for Polly, to keep the disposal of the ashes very private.' And so they had. They had boarded a small cruiser and sailed out on the Red Sea, accompanied by half a dozen people from the agency Joelle worked for, Miles from the Embassy and the priest from the Catholic church she used to attend when she lived just outside Cairo.

The sea got up a little as the priest said the necessary words and then David and Regine held the urn containing the ashes and tipped the grey powder into the choppy water. David threw in a dozen red roses and Regine, to his surprise, produced a child's patchwork doll.

David could only guess at her feelings as she bade farewell to her much loved daughter. The doll bobbed defiantly on the water and as they watched it a member of the crew dropped a wreath of stephanotis over the side. The wreath bore a note from Felix Khamul. By chance it fell round the doll. Caught by a sudden eddy, the little doll, now wreathed in flowers, bounced resolutely away from the boat and out to sea.

'How fitting,' came Regine's anguished voice. 'Flowers from the man who murdered my daughter and they sail away with the only thing I had left from that happy youth.' She turned to David. With a catch in her voice, she said, 'And it was so very happy, David. She was so full of promise, she had so much life. One day I must tell her daughter how much joy she gave her father . . . she should know.'

★ ★ ★

As David let himself into the house in Battersea, his spirits rose just a little. Soon he would see Polly, be able to comfort her. And then there was Anna. Beautiful Anna, so far removed from the scene in Cairo. Anna, his hope for the future — but he knew he mustn't let himself think about that with Joelle's death so raw. And Polly had lost her mother, she would need time to come to terms with it. She must be feeling very confused. She had been forced to choose between her mother and a life of stability with her father and her grandparents, and in a sense she had rejected her mother. David knew he would have to help her get through that; they would need time together and they would be each other's consolation.

He dumped his luggage in the narrow hall, turned off the alarm and opened the drawing-room door. The late afternoon sun filled the room. Beatrice had obviously been spring-cleaning, the room looked wonderful. Someone had washed the covers on the sofas. He noticed at once because Ross had taken to sitting on them and they had become a dull grey. There were flowers on the table in the window. The desk in the corner had been tidied and Joelle's filing cabinets had gone — they had always been an eyesore in the pretty room. And then he noticed the wedding photograph had gone. Obviously someone had been tactfully purging the house before his return. There would probably be a note on the hall table where Beatrice sometimes left barely intelligible communications.

A pile of unopened mail awaited him, much of it, he suspected, about Joelle's death. He dreaded the prospect of reading it. As he shuffled through it, an airmail envelope caught his eye. His stomach contracted. It bore Joelle's handwriting.

He walked slowly back into the drawing room. His hands shook as he sat in the chair by his desk and slowly broke the seal. It opened easily. He unfolded the paper and began to read. The letter was dated the day before the accident.

The letter was handwritten, unusually for Joelle; she preferred to use her laptop. The neat, well-ordered hand gave the letter an added impact. David felt for a moment that she was in the room with him, but the contents spoke of something unimaginable and alien, something so unexpected, it was almost worse than the events he had already had to accept.

Darling David

There are some things which cannot be said politely or kindly. Trying to dress them up in acceptable terms would not help to diminish the pain and shock of them. So I will not insult you by trying to trivialise what I have to tell you.

Whilst I was back in London I had some blood tests. I found out that I am HIV positive. This is why I left so suddenly to return to Cairo. When I first found out, I can honestly say I felt like killing myself. But I have begun to come to terms with it. I do not intend to let it change the way I live my life, but I realise there are serious things you and I have to discuss, and I can only imagine how this news will affect you.

Before we embark on the painful process of sorting things out, I only ask one thing of you, and that is that you don't tell Polly about this, not for my sake but for hers. I want her to be proud of me, I want her to have her innocent childhood. She would not understand it anyway.

Of course this speaks volumes to you about our marriage and about things we should have discussed long ago. I am coming home in the next few days, probably soon after you get this letter. I am so very sorry, David. We loved each other once, and it is the good times we should remember. I have not been what you wanted me to be, but I could not have been any different. I only wish things had not turned out this way and that we could have parted friends without such a dark cloud hanging over me.

Joelle

David was stunned. After all that had happened, he simply could not take it in. His mind seemed paralysed. He couldn't even bring himself to ring his parents and Polly to let them know he was back. He crawled upstairs to bed and fell into a comatose sleep.

When he awoke, he plunged into a frenzy of activity. He rang the family doctor, Desmond Lane, to arrange to have blood tests as soon as possible, and then he contacted the help line Dr Lane suggested. They were cautiously reassuring. He decided he must try to find out where and, more importantly, when Joelle could have got the virus. He tried to contact Felix Khamul through the Foreign Office but he couldn't get hold of him. He had apparently gone to ground, and nobody knew where he was. He had booked a flight to the USA shortly after the bomb explosion but had failed to show up. David had not seen or heard from him while he was in Cairo, for which he had been thankful at the time. Now he wondered at the lack of contact. Simple courtesy demanded some sort of communication, surely, from the man for whom the bomb had been intended. But then perhaps not if he was sleeping with Joelle.

The Foreign Office advised him not to get involved with the circumstances of Joelle's death. It would only hamper their inquiries. Much better, they said, to let things progress through the proper channels. David was only too happy to let them get on with it.

He rang Regine. She said she would be coming over and would let him know her dates. She agreed that there were many things they needed to discuss but they were too important to talk about on the phone, and must wait until she came over.

His mind turned to Polly. He must go and see her, but first he had to get a grip on himself. Neither Polly nor his parents must be burdened with the contents of Joelle's letter. There would be time enough to tell them if, God forbid, his blood tests proved positive. And what about Anna? His mind froze at the prospect of telling her.

One step at a time, he told himself firmly. Right now his priority was Polly.

23

David and Anna drove to his home in Battersea in an awkward silence. They had had dinner at their favourite Italian restaurant, but David had been distant all evening. Anna had known the moment she saw him that something had changed. He wouldn't touch her, he wouldn't meet her eyes, he wouldn't really talk to her. She had known he would be in shock after all that had happened, perhaps even be feeling full of guilt, but this was something more.

David preceded her into the house, turning off the alarm and throwing open the sitting-room door. Polly was still at Vincent Square. As Anna turned to shut the front door, there was a flash. David came running back down the hall and just as he reached her, there was another flash.

His mood changed instantly to one of blind rage. Bounding down the steps, he gave chase to a young man in jeans who leapt into a waiting car and sped off round the corner.

'Fucking bastards!' said David furiously, bundling Anna back into the house. 'I need a drink. Can I make you a gin and tonic?' he asked.

'Yes, please. What on earth was that all about?'

'You'll know soon enough if you buy the papers tomorrow. I've had them on the phone all day. At least they didn't probe too deeply into Joelle's relationship with Felix Khamul. I think they're showing some restraint about digging up dirt on Joelle because she was one of them. After all, she had a lot of friends in the press and they look after their own. I'm fair game, however.'

Anna put down the drink David had handed her and put her arms round his neck. She thought she felt his body stiffen but then he relaxed and put his head down to hers. She was counting the minutes until he slowly removed her flimsy Indian sundress from her eager body and made love to her.

'Darling, beautiful Anna,' he said gruffly into her hair. 'I've missed you so. I wish we could just go away somewhere together, be alone. I want to hold you in my arms. I . . . ' He loved the feel of her warm skin under the fine cotton of her dress. It made her feel romantic and sensuous. She moved away from him a little and reached up her mouth to find his.

'Don't, Anna. Please don't,' he said

desperately, seizing her arms and pushing her away. She stood bewildered, her lip shaking as she tried to hold back her tears. 'Darling, I'm so sorry,' he said. 'There are things I have to sort out, terrible things I can't tell you about. Can you be patient with me, Anna? I couldn't bear to lose you.'

'Let's go into the other room,' said Anna abruptly, trying not to let David see she was crying. She turned and walked into the sitting room. 'It looks much nicer in here. Have you changed something?' she asked brightly.

'Meg and Beatrice have done a number on the whole house. I'm very grateful. Meg is the best. She's even offered to use some of her annual leave to take Polly to stay with Jamie in Scotland until the press lose interest in us.'

'I know, she told me,' said Anna, getting out her compact and reapplying her lipstick.

'Don't do that, I like your lips with nothing on them,' said David.

'It would seem it won't make much difference at the moment,' Anna blurted.

'Oh, don't say that, darling. I want you so much. It's just . . . ' David broke off and banged his fist on to his knee.

Anna decided to change the subject and let the temperature between them cool a little. David seemed to be under terrible strain and for some reason he was keeping something from her.

'I'm going to Scotland soon myself,' she said. 'I need to sort out my mother's effects. I've put it off too long.'

'That'll be nice,' said David vaguely, clearly only half listening.

'Not really.' Anna tried to keep the edge out of her voice. 'I'm not looking forward to seeing my father again. But the good news is that while you were in Cairo, I found a house I like. It's in Kennington and my offer for it has been accepted. I can't wait to show it to you.'

'Good, I'm glad,' said David dully. He seemed to be finding it an effort to speak, much less express enthusiasm. Anna had to curb her impatience and remind herself just what he had been through lately.

'Poor David,' she said gently. 'Do you want me to leave? You're so far away, I feel I'm talking to a ghost.'

'I am sorry. I feel in a kind of haze, it's all so awful. But you're a great help, you know, and I'm very grateful for what you did for Polly. She told me all about how you sang for Joelle while I was away. But I feel so guilty about Joelle . . . She was obsessed with image and with her work. She really needed a man with a lot of money and I . . . well, you know I don't care about that. I suppose I failed her, drove her into someone else's arms because I just couldn't deliver the things she wanted.' David stared sadly into his glass as he cupped it between his hands.

'Joelle knew exactly what she was doing and you aren't exactly some pathetic little failure of a man. She could have had a great life with you.' Anna took David's hands in hers and looked intensely into his eyes. 'If a woman loves a man, she will follow him to the ends of the earth, David. It's as simple as that.'

'I suppose you're right. She just didn't love me enough I suppose. But then I don't really know what love is. Take my parents, for example. My father has been having an affair for years. My mother knows all about it and she also knows he will never leave her. Is that love? Or is it just duty that has confined him in a less than happy marriage all these years?'

'Look, David. You're just terribly upset by what has happened. Who wouldn't be? You loved your wife once, enough to marry her, and you have a little girl by her. Nobody would want a thing like this to happen even to their worst enemy. You're bound to have conflicting feelings and, as for your parents, don't get into all that. They've made their own choices, and from what Meg tells me, there is more there to bind them than you think.'

'Maybe,' he said doubtfully. 'That's one of the things I admire about you, Anna. You always manage to see the positive side of circumstance. You would make a go of anything, even life with me. But I . . . I can't ask you to . . . I mean . . . don't bank on me, Anna. I don't know . . . ' David stammered into silence.

'What are you saying? For God's sake, David, we've fallen in love with each other, at least I thought we had. Joelle's death doesn't change that, it should make our love stronger. Don't shut me out, David. I thought we had made a commitment to each other. I came out of a longstanding relationship because of you, because I thought you were different. But you aren't. I suppose that's the truth of it. I was just another affair while you were married and now that the obstacle of a wife has been removed, you're going to play the field. I just can't bear it.' Anna burst into sobs.

David came to her at once and put his arms about her. 'None of what you say is true, Anna, none of it. I adore you, surely you know that. There will never be anyone like you, never. Trust me, Anna. I don't mean to shut you out. Just give me time and I'll tell you everything, I promise.'

Despite himself, his lips found hers. They kissed lovingly and slowly, and then she broke gently away from him and said goodbye. They had restored a kind of calm, and a knowledge that what they had together was indeed something they had both yearned for, but Anna's certainty about David had been badly shaken.

24

Anna sat on the train to Glasgow a few days later. The journey seemed to pass more quickly than usual because she had so much to think about, so many imponderables, not least her feelings for David, and then Justin had asked her to sing in the festival in France to fill in for the soprano who had found out she was having a baby and had been ordered to rest or she risked a miscarriage. In a way it couldn't have come at a better time. August was approaching and Anna was faced with an empty diary. She and David had planned to spend some time together, perhaps at the cottage. Meg was full of ideas for Loverstone and work had commenced on the roof, at least to stop the worst of the damp before the autumn. But these plans had all been made before Joelle's death and they had now been cancelled. Anna was terribly disappointed.

Two days before her departure to Scotland she met David for lunch. She told him about the possibility of a trip to France, and he had seized on it. 'Yes, you must go,' he urged her, although he knew it was with Justin. 'I shall be very busy. There's a lot to see to after . . . ' His voice trailed off and he changed the subject, asking her brightly about her programme for the winter. She told him she had been given the part of Octavian. He wasn't really listening. 'How nice. You must be pleased,' he said in that vague way of his that was becoming all too familiar. She noticed he hadn't touched the food on his plate.

He said goodbye to her in the street, giving her a peck on the cheek, avoiding her mouth. He quickly walked away while she unlocked her car. When she turned, he had gone. She had wanted to lie down in the road and scream, ask someone, anyone, how this could have happened; pinch herself and find she was just having a bad dream. Things didn't happen like this, not to people she knew. They weren't blown up by bombs, shattering their own lives and everyone else's dreams.

Later, she had cried and told Meg about it. Meg said she thought David would take some time to get over what had happened to Joelle. Perhaps she should go to France and when she got back in the autumn, David would have sorted himself out. But Anna knew Meg well enough to know that she herself was worried sick about David. She was unclear about David's plans but she promised to ring Anna while they were both in Scotland. 'After all,' she said brightly, 'we'll be less than two hours away on the train. You and Shamus could come to Bonniemoor while you're up with your father, couldn't you?' Anna thought she sounded as if she was trying to look for a way of keeping channels open between their two families.

As the train journey approached its end, Anna wondered what she would find at the Laurels. She hadn't seen her father since just after her mother's funeral, well over a year ago. She was dreading going home; in fact, she didn't really have a home. The Laurels belonged to her past, and held nothing for her now except memories of her mother and the few remaining personal items of her mother's which she had come to sort out.

She had somewhere to put them now. She had liked the small house in Kennington as soon as she saw it, all clean white paint and sanded floors with a south-facing patio garden. It was in quite a rundown street and as a cash buyer she was able to knock the price down. Her salary had secured her a small mortgage and if things went according to plan, she could complete by the end of August, just after her return from France.

Her spirits lifted a bit as she thought of her mother's grand piano on the wooden pine floor of the little house which would now be home to herself and Shamus. She would put it by the garden door, and the room would be a haven for her to practise in. Life would be transformed. Jason could come to the house sometimes to help her with the practice she would have to do for Octavian. She was worried about Jason. He looked very thin. She would enjoy feeding him up when he came round.

As the grey roofs of the outskirts of Glasgow came into view, it started to rain. Anna suddenly felt very tired. The prospect of the next few days appalled her, but then she thought of Shamus. He must be her priority now. He, too, must start making plans for London; an offer from one of the colleges might have arrived in the last few days since she had been in touch.

When the train drew to a halt in the station, she clambered down on to the platform and looked eagerly towards the barrier. There were Aunt Jeannie and Shamus. He was holding something up as he ran towards her. It was a letter from the Royal College of Music in London, offering him a place. Anna hugged and congratulated him. She kissed Jeannie and the three of them headed for the car park.

'Who's learning to drive?' asked Anna,

noticing the L plates as they approached Aunt Jeannie's Ford Escort.

'Who do you think?' replied Shamus as he took the car keys out of his pocket and unlocked the passenger door for Jeannie.

'You're never teaching the boy to drive, are you?' asked Anna, looking again at her brother who had grown several inches since she last saw him. He had been slow growing up, so small for such a long time. As he got into the driving seat of the car, he seemed suddenly to have become a man.

'Shamus spends his time with us now,' Jeannie informed Anna on the way to the Laurels. 'And if you want to do the same while you're here sorting things out, you're to think of our place as home.'

Anna caught her brother's eyes in the driving mirror. She knew him well enough to read his expression. Something was going on, there had been some sort of development. 'So how is Father?' she asked.

There was a short silence. Anna thought Shamus's neck went a little red.

'Och, it didn't take him long to get over his grief, Anna. Shamus and I think you should find out for yourself. Things have changed a lot at the house. You had better prepare yourself for a shock.'

The car pulled up outside the Laurels,

an imposing Edwardian villa in the west side of Glasgow where many prosperous professionals lived.

'Why don't you leave your things in the car until we've had a cup of tea?' suggested Shamus.

As they opened the stained-glass front door to the house, Anna sensed at once that things had indeed changed. The first thing that struck her was the smell, some kind of air freshener, and then she noticed that the red polished tiles of the hall were covered by a cream shagpile carpet. The brass rods were gone from the staircase and the shagpile continued up it, replacing the dark green Wilton her father had given to her mother on her last birthday.

Anna recognised nothing in the hall. Even the family pictures which had once hung on the stairs had gone. The Victorian picture of her grandmother no longer hung on the upstairs landing. There was a marble table where her mother's old linen press had been, and a louvred cupboard stood where a jumble of coats had once hung from a mahogany hatstand.

Anna nervously bent to smell the perfect pink roses in an ornate glass urn which graced the marble table. They had no smell and she noticed they were made of silk.

'You'll be wasting yer time with those. No fresh flowers in this house any more,' sniffed Jeannie.

'I'll make us a cup of tea,' said Shamus quickly, 'and find Father. He must be at home, his car is outside.'

Anna opened the door into the sitting room and gasped. 'Jeannie, what on earth has happened?' she cried.

'Here's Angus, he can tell you himself,' replied Jeannie firmly.

Angus Frazer came slowly into the room. He looked sheepishly at his daughter. 'How are you? It's been too long,' he said gruffly, giving her a peck on the cheek.

Pulling away from him Anna asked furiously, 'What on earth have you done with our things? The house, this room? It looks like a doctor's waiting room.'

'Are you ready for tea now?' asked a voice from the doorway.

Anna turned. The face she looked at was familiar but she couldn't immediately place it.

'How are you, Anna? I haven't seen you since you went down to London. You don't remember me, do you? I'm Joan, your father's receptionist.'

Joan stood behind a smart gilt tea trolley set with tea things Anna had not seen before.

211

There were sandwiches and a Dundee cake and starched linen napkins.

'Did your aunt not tell you?' said Angus. 'I don't see NHS patients any more, just private here, and yes, this room doubles as the waiting room. Joan has done a grand job, don't you think?' It was more a statement than a question.

Anna looked round the room; it was unrecognisable. Her mother's pale green striped wallpaper had been replaced by magnolia emulsion, the parquet flooring was covered with carpet, the pine fireplace had been painted white, and the open fire replaced with a gas fire. None of the original furniture remained except for a round gate-legged tea table which now stood in the window, neatly piled with glossy magazines. No grand piano, instead a two-door cabinet which obviously housed a large TV. The old velvet sofas had gone and been replaced with an expensive floral three-piece suite. New curtains made of blue silk swagged the big Edwardian windows. It was not unattractive, but it was the sort of room you would expect to find in one of the second eleven glossy women's magazines. The faded charm of her mother's drawing room, so full of warmth and character, had been totally expunged. Anna felt terribly angry.

She didn't answer her father. She didn't have to, Jeannie intervened.

'I won't stay for tea. I've some errands to do in town and Shamus has to fetch his flute from the repairer. If you'll excuse us, I shall be back later after you and your father have had a chance to talk. The cake looks nice, Joan,' she added as an afterthought.

'I'm sorry you won't stay,' said Joan nervously.

Anna had so much to take in, she hardly knew where to start. Joan was acting as hostess behind the teacups, and Anna would have felt instantly resentful of her had she not looked rather frightened. She wore a cream trouser suit and high heels and her hair framed her round, comfortable face in a thick dark-brown bob. She looked quite young, probably in her early forties.

Anna sat silently on the new floral sofa, balancing a fluted plate on her lap, on which lay a cucumber sandwich.

'Shall I fill your cup?' asked Joan.

'Oh yes, thank you,' replied Anna awkwardly.

'Now, if you will excuse me, I have some work to finish in the office and I expect you two will have a lot to catch up on.' Joan picked up her cup of tea and left Anna and her father in a palpable silence, but not for long.

Anna's feelings had been gathering momentum. She felt like a kettle about to boil over. 'Father, what is going on? Where are all Mother's things and what is Joan doing here? No wonder Shamus has gone to live with Aunt Jeannie. This isn't Mother's house any more.' She felt hot in the stuffy room, and longed to open the window. She noticed it had new double glazing. She wiped her hands on the side of her denim skirt; her palms always perspired when she was tense.

She could feel her father staring at her. She felt apprehensive but then suddenly it was as if her mother had come to stand at her elbow, strengthening her resolve. Anna and Shamus no longer had any ties here; there was nothing in this dreary, clinical room which had any connection with their past or future.

She jumped up from her chair, tipping her teacup into the saucer. A little tea spilt on to the pale green carpet.

'My God, girl, you've ruined the new carpet!' The mask had slipped. Angus Frazer reverted instantly to the father Anna feared, the one from whom Shamus had been removed by the loyal and indomitable Jeannie.

214

'It's only tea, Father. I'll get a cloth.'

'Only tea, you say? With you, girl, it's always only something.' Angus pulled a handkerchief out of his pocket and leant down to rub the two spots off the carpet. Anna noticed two strands of hair fall away from the bald patch over which he had carefully brushed them. He stood up and faced his daughter, his face now flushed and angry. The strands stuck out from his head, giving him a demonic look as if he had grown a set of horns.

'That's your trouble, Anna. No responsibility for your sins, however small. It's a pity you don't read the Good Book. It would show you how to be a good woman. Just look at you. Who do you think you are? Too busy to look after yer grieving father. Yer place was with me, but you left home to live a Godless life and now you come back full of airs and graces. I'm ashamed of you, ashamed, do you hear?' Angus's voice had risen to a shout, and his expression was menacing, but as Anna looked at her father, she realised that she no longer feared him. Instead, she felt a kind of dispassionate anger, and she knew exactly what she must do.

'Don't you speak to me like that, Father! You're a sham and a fake. You have a nerve preaching to me when you have the gall to move another woman into my mother's house when she is hardly cold in her grave. And then you preach to me about my duty. What about your duty to your bereaved children? And where were you when Mother was ill and I had to come and nurse her? With Joan, I suppose, or some other woman. That is why my mother was so unhappy. I should have guessed.'

Angus raised his arm as if to strike Anna. She stood her ground.

'Well, why don't you hit me, Father? But if you do, by God I'll hit you back!'

'Like your brother, you'd strike yer own parent. Well, I can tell you one thing, miss. He who calls the piper calls the tune. I know what your game is with that wimpish pansy brother of yours. You want to take him down to London to prance about with your fancy friends at some godforsaken music college. Well, you'll not get a penny from me. Not a penny, d'you hear? He's coming back here to live with me and Joan.'

'Oh no he's not, Father! Shamus has got into music college and he's coming to live with me. I'm buying a house with the money Mother left, in spite of your attempts to delay probate by every possible means at your disposal. There is absolutely nothing you can do to stop us.'

'So you think my son will be sleeping under the same roof as the father of your murdered baby, do you?' Angus bawled, making for a shining new tantalus on the table in the window and slopping whisky into a tumbler.

There was silence in the room. Anna heard a shuffling outside the door. She suspected Joan was listening. She didn't care. Joan was not her concern, and she would probably never see her again.

'I don't think you deserve to be called a father! You're disgusting and cruel. The fact that I had to have an abortion was my own private sorrow. You couldn't begin to understand any of it. My mother was dying, my life was in turmoil. I needed a parent, a father. Where were you? And while we're on the subject, how did you find out?'

'I went through your bag and read your letters, and I'm not ashamed of it. I needed to know what I was harbouring under my roof, and you haven't changed, Anna. Yer mother was too soft with you both, and I'm telling yer now, if yer take Shamus, he goes for good and so do you!'

Anna heard the front door slam and Jeannie and Shamus's voices outside in the hall. The door opened. Jeannie came in first, followed by Shamus. Joan sidled round them and began to collect the teacups.

Angus caught her arm roughly. 'Stop doing that, yer stupid woman! They won't be long, yer can do it when they've gone.'

Joan began to weep quietly. She blew her nose in one of the napkins.

'By the looks of the two of you,' said Jeannie, 'your father hasn't been a fountain of human kindness. I think we should be off, Anna, unless there's anything more you want to say to your father.'

'I've told father that Shamus is coming to live with me, if that's what he wants.'

Shamus looked very pale. He stood very close to his aunt as he addressed his father. 'I want to go with Anna, Father. It isn't as if I've been living with you much. Anyway, all my things are at Aunt Jeannie's. I'm sure you and Joan . . . well . . . ' He ground to a halt and looked at Joan.

'Yes, well, dear, perhaps it is for the best,' faltered Joan, twisting the napkin awkwardly.

'Silence, woman, this is not your business!' said Angus furiously.

'I was only trying to help,' she said miserably.

'Stand out from behind your aunt's skirts and be a man, boy!' commanded Angus.

Jeannie stepped forward. 'Don't speak to the boy like that, you idiot! He made up his mind long ago. He has his mother's gift, the one your daughter has too. Until the day I die, Angus Frazer, I will never know why the Lord saw fit to give you two such talented, charming children. You've never done anything but try to crush them in the same way as you did my sister. Mercifully they have the strength to get away from you and your bullying. You're a stupid tyrant, you deserve to end your days alone and miserable. Why anyone should want to spend more than five minutes in your company, I will never know. Those two will be just fine without a penny from you. I'm not short of a penny or two to help my sister's boy. You keep your money, much good it will do you.' Jeannie rearranged her large handbag on her arm to indicate she was ready to leave.

Angus stared at the three of them. The only sound in the room was Joan sniffing into the twisted napkin.

'Stop yer snivelling, woman, and open the door!' Angus bawled. 'Violet's children are leaving. I have nothing to say to any of you. Get out, the three of you, before I throw you out!'

'There is just one thing before we go,' said Anna quietly. 'Where is all Mother's furniture? It didn't belong to you, it was carefully listed in her will.' She dreaded the answer, but it came from Jeannie.

'It's in store for you, child — but that's another story, isn't it, Angus?'

'Just go!' he replied harshly. 'You were always against me, Jeannie Barraclough. But don't think you've got the better of me. This isn't the end of the story.'

Shamus took Anna's hand and with impeccable politeness he formally said good-bye to the now weeping Joan. Then he looked at Angus steadily.

'Goodbye, Father. It's not quite what you think, you know. It's not going to be my sister looking after me. I am going to look after her, like you should have done, and one day I will pay Aunt Jeannie back every penny, you can be sure of that.'

Silently Jeannie hustled them to the front door. As it opened, Anna thankfully breathed the cold fresh air of early evening and left the Laurels feeling a mixture of triumph, relief and sadness.

25

Bonniemoor House, Jamie Lovegrove's Scottish home, was in sharp contrast to the Laurels. It had been built by Lavender's grandparents for shooting and fishing on the site of a much earlier house in the middle of two thousand acres of moorland in the Rannoch Hills. The estate included two small tenant farms struggling with a collection of livestock, a keeper's house and two cottages.

Bonniemoor House sat high on an incline and was approached by a winding road bordering an expanse of water which looked either threatening or welcoming, depending on the weather. On cloudy days the water took on a steely-grey hue and the house rose beyond it in tones of granite grey. Its architect had had a fondness for turrets and imposing baronial carvings unsuited to the wildness and natural beauty of the terrain, with its pines, spruce and firs. The forbidding aspect of the house was softened by plantations of silver birch at the edge of the loch. On sunny days their graceful shadows danced on the reflection of the sky in little eddies of water lapping on to the bank where David, in his youth, had kept a small sailing boat. The loch was always icy cold, even on the finest of August days, but as children the Lovegroves had often swum, and picnicked in the heather.

Meg had told Anna all about these happy childhood days and Anna relayed them to Shamus on the journey from Glasgow. Shamus was familiar with the countryside, as Bonniemoor was only a short distance from his boarding school, but he could hardly control his excitement at the prospect of a few days in such a grand house with perhaps a little rough shooting before the grouse season began. Meg had established that Shamus could handle a gun and that the keeper would be glad to take the boy for the odd day out on the estate. Anna thought gratefully it was just what Shamus needed to help him come to terms with the fact that he no longer had a home in Scotland and was now dependent on Jeannie and Anna for family and security.

Anna had decided to forget about the scene with her father for the moment. They all needed to cool down. But she knew those things had needed saying and she felt as if a weight had been lifted from her shoulders. There had been too many hard feelings festering; it was better to have got it all out in the open. Now she could get on with her life.

Meg met them at the station. She looked windblown and prettier than Anna could ever remember. The last few days had seen fine weather and Meg had been out on the loch fishing. She had told Anna to come equipped for some outdoor pursuits and it took several minutes to load the luggage. Shamus had brought the gun and fishing rod which had belonged to his uncle but which he had never used before. Meg had told Anna he could have some lessons with the gillie and the keeper.

'I wish the sun was out,' said Meg, as she swung the battered Land Rover up the long drive to Bonniemoor. 'The whole place would be transformed, even the house, which I personally think is a monstrosity.'

Anna silently agreed with her description as the house loomed out of the fine drizzle of rain and wisps of mist. But once inside, it offered a pleasant surprise. Although faded and shabby, it bore the imprint of accomplished planning with the accent on comfort. The flagged hall gave access to three reception rooms, a dining room, a study and a large drawing room complete with billiard table and grand piano. The kitchens were situated at the back of the house through a green baize brass-studded door. The wooden floors were covered with thick Persian rugs. Plump sofas and chairs abounded, so deep that if the occupant sat right back, feet would protrude at right angles.

In the centre of the hall was a large round table covered with a floor-length tapestry cloth. On it was a blue and white china jardinière and a luscious-smelling jasmine reached towards the light from tall stained-glass windows at the top of the turn in a mock-Tudor staircase. The staircase directed the eye through a forest of stags' heads and crossed swords to a gallery of bedroom and bathroom doors. The house felt surprisingly warm and welcoming. As Anna later discovered, all the downstairs rooms had fires, even in midsummer. Baskets of logs were constantly refilled by a silent, apparently nameless man in shabby tweeds and gaiters.

Jamie Lovegrove was not there when they arrived. They were told he was out with Polly, somewhere on the moor.

Meg took them into the drawing room where tea was laid. Shamus consumed a pile of toasted tea cakes. 'Watch where you put your cup,' said Meg, as Shamus placed his on a large drum which served as a coffee table. 'That's a family heirloom. A young drummer boy was sent with a peace offering from a warring clan. My ancestors declined the terms and the little boy was hung out of the old castle window in the drum until they agreed.'

'What happened to him?' asked Shamus warily.

'He died. They couldn't come to an agreement,' replied Meg casually. Shamus looked nervously at Anna who gave him an encouraging smile. They heard Polly in the hall, back from her walk. She burst into the room full of plans to have a candlelight dinner alone with Shamus, then watch a video instead of joining the boring grown-ups. Shamus was tired and willingly agreed.

Later, Anna bathed in a claw-footed bath so large she could not lie down without putting her feet on the brass soap rack to stop herself from slipping under the water. She was tired after the train journey and had a short peaceful sleep before going down for dinner. She dreamed of David. When she woke she couldn't quite remember what the dream was about but it left her feeling good, and being in this house, where David had spent much of his youth, made her feel part of him. She felt suddenly confident, as if she belonged, as if this was the first of many visits to a place which would be significant in her future.

She still had that happy, unaccustomed feeling of belonging as she sat in the dining room, halfway through a dinner for ten, an occasion for which Meg hd prepared her with a potted biography of the neighbours who comprised the usual guest list. Anna had not taken it all in, but she smiled politely, and said she was looking forward to meeting them all, especially since it would be fun to talk to David about them on her return to London.

She had been placed on Jamie Lovegrove's left, under the beady eyes of several ancestors, the fixed stare of a variety of stags' heads and the rapt attention of her host. The soup plates were cleared by Meg and a thin man in a green velvet suit, introduced as Peter. He was the token spare man, Jamie later informed her, an expert on rare birds. Anna was glad she had brought a long silk skirt and blouse and a magnificent Florentine shawl given to her by Justin. She had almost left them behind when she packed. Meg wore a long tartan skirt and white shirt which, elsewhere, would have seemed incongruous for the time of year but here the air had a distinctly autumnal feel by six o'clock.

Anna thought Jamie looked almost handsome in the light from the two candelabra on the long baronial table. He didn't have David's fine features but his face had a craggy charm. His thick hair had gone prematurely grey but the remaining black traces matched the darkness of his eyes which bore the mark of permanent humour. He obviously spent much of his time outdoors, and his florid complexion was assisted by what was clearly a preference for the whisky bottle.

The men in the party wore velvet smoking jackets and Jamie had on the regulation tartan trousers. Before dinner there had been a long conversation about tartans and Anna had, under fierce interrogation from Lady Strathwade, admitted to being a Lowlander without claim to the banner of the Highland clans. 'Your father, an ear, nose and throat specialist, you say,' her interrogator had declared before dinner. Without waiting for further information about Anna's credentials she moved on, addressing the room in general on the evils of the European Community's regulations on deer farming.

Meg had pointed out that the practice by local landowners of culling does in the breeding season and removing the living foetus was worse than anything suggested by Brussels.

Lady Strathwade continued the discussion at dinner, just as the aged cook brought in the marinated venison in cranberry sauce.

'My husband will not allow the culling of does in the breeding season and, what's more, it is quite unnecessary. The whole thing is a disgrace. The population estimates are all based on some research into the animals' droppings which do not take into account the drought, and the fact that the droppings remain intact from one month to the next.' Lady Strathwade took another gulp of claret and was about to continue, but Jamie turned to Anna, offering her some gravy from a silver sauce boat, slopping a little on the white damask cloth.

'Oh, I am sorry. That's what comes of burying yourself in the Highlands on a wind farm. Completely forgotten how to behave,' he said with an engaging smile.

Anna was grateful he had so deftly distracted the talk from the subject of culling and droppings.

'Silly man. Don't listen to a word of it. He's chased by all the spare ladies in the country,' explained Lady Strathwade through a mouthful of mashed potato.

'None so bonny as you, my dear,' Jamie

said, raising his glass to Anna. Lady Strathwade gave an impatient shrug of her shoulders and turned to the neighbour on her right, leaving Anna and Jamie to themselves.

'So, you live with our Meg, do you? Wish you could find her a husband. Mother is getting quite fed up with us all, me still unmarried and Meg thinking she's an old maid. And then this bad business with David.' Jamie's face clouded with concern. Anna wondered if he knew about her and David. He and Meg were obviously close. She had been surprised to see how close, since Jamie had always been painted as the black sheep of the family, but now that she had met him, she understood why he was such a favourite in the family. He had a charm that was irresistible. Anna had discovered he had started his adult life in the Army, where he had developed his loud guffawing laugh and over-the-top right-wing sentiments. In fact, he seemed like a dyed-in-the-wool Conservative, which Anna found quite at odds with the liberal ethos of the Lovegrove parents. She wondered if half the things he said were tongue in cheek. It was difficult to tell as he had a permanent twinkle. Earlier he had complained about the daily papers' extensive coverage on the latest expedition to Mars, asking why they couldn't give greater space to more important subjects, like the proposed abolition of blood sports.

Meg had told her he had taken a grip on his drinking and was courting a wealthy widow in the neighbourhood who might well be the answer to Bonniemoor's financial difficulties. Jamie was clearly no businessman. Anna had noticed an attractive woman of about thirty-five, one of the last guests to arrive. She guessed that, of the ten people at dinner, she might be the one who had caught Jamie's eye. But he showed no sign of this as he gave Anna his undivided attention.

'Tell me about the wind farm,' said Anna.

'Well, it seemed like a good idea, although I've got into a lot of trouble with the locals. The noise from the turbines they say is like a hundred helicopters. I thought no one would be near enough to hear, but when the wind is in the wrong direction, it disturbs the tenant farmers.'

'I must say I sympathise. Being a singer, for me noise is one of the worst kinds of pollution.'

'Well, the fact is, it will probably have to go. The idea was to sell the electricity it makes to the National Grid. But frankly, it doesn't make enough to pay for itself.

In this case, however, I was not entirely responsible. It was largely Mother's idea. She doesn't approve of blood sports, and the grouse have been declining. I used to let the moor and it paid very well, but the last few seasons have been a disaster, so the wind farm seemed like a good idea. It appealed to environmentalists, too, but as usual they got it wrong. Not to the manner born, you know,' Jamie added with a loud laugh.

Lady Strathwade swung round. 'What's that?' she inquired imperiously.

'I was just telling our beautiful singer how our futures were not to be trusted with a lot of trendy townies who think driving grouse means conveying birds to the moor in Land Rovers,' replied Jamie.

'I'm glad to see we're fighting back. Our people are planning something very nasty in the autumn. Did any of your people go to the rally last week?' she asked briskly.

Anna assumed they were talking about the recent demonstrations against the banning of blood sports. She herself was not at all clear on the issue, but it seemed to her that life on a factory farm represented something far crueller than anything she had seen on the hunting field. She remembered that one of David's tasks as a whip had been to gather the views of the Party on what was clearly a thorny issue.

'Why don't you ask the local Members of Parliament to dinner and discuss the issue as seen from the countryman's point of view?' she asked brightly.

'You must be mad!' Jamie exclaimed. 'I wouldn't even ask them to the Keepers' Dance!' he exploded with a broad grin.

'And make no mistake, the Keepers' Dance is a very lively affair,' chipped in Lady Strathwade.

'But I don't understand,' Anna ventured. 'Wouldn't it be better to get them on side and try to get them to see it from the point of view of the constituents? I mean, they are there to represent their views, aren't they?'

'One would hope so, but the Labour Party think of blood sports as part of the old class war.'

'Yes. Nothing has escaped the march of the revolutionaries. Even the army is full of a lot of charlies. Not like your day, is it, Jamie?' volunteered Lord Strathwade from across the table.

'Quite right. Look at the regiments. I mean the Life Guards are all nouveaux and the Blues are only just acceptable,' said Jamie loudly.

'What I would like to know is where

your brother stands in all this,' said Lord Strathwade, giving himself a full facial wash with his table napkin.

Anna noticed Jamie dart her a look before he answered, which confirmed her view that Meg had told him about her relationship with David.

'My brother is a whip, he has to keep abreast of the wishes of the party. I don't know what he feels about hunting personally, but after the failure of the Bill in the last parliament, feelings are running high. I suspect most Labour MPs would support anything that continued the decline of what they perceive as the upper classes.'

The whole table now fell into a discussion about blood sports. Anna caught Meg's glance. Meg rolled her eyes to heaven and placed a finger on her lips as though to warn Anna against getting involved in what was clearly an old chestnut.

Anna tapped Jamie on the hand gently to attract his attention. She wanted to talk about other things. He took the hint and asked about her singing. He said he would love to hear her and would she sing after dinner.

Meg hastily told her brother that Anna was trying to have a break before starting on an arduous singing tour, but Jamie was not to be put off. He told Anna that he could play the piano, after a fashion, and would accompany her on some old Scottish ballads.

Soon the whole table joined in to persuade Anna to sing. She thought for a moment of this mob in pursuit of the fox and realised they would not let her get away. She agreed to sing just one song. Jamie was delighted and after dinner he led Anna to the grand piano in the drawing room.

As he played the first bar of 'Jeannie with the Light Brown Hair', Anna realised he was quite a good pianist. But their combined talents did not appear to be of interest to everyone, despite the earlier pressures. The Strathwades were talking excitedly and loud laughter came from a couple by the window.

Meg was sitting with Jamie's widow friend, to whom Anna had spoken briefly over coffee. Her name was Elizabeth. She had fine classic features and a warm, unaffected way of coming straight to the point. Anna liked her and had thought, for a brief, happy moment, that all these people might well be part of her future life with David when the traumatic upheaval of the last few weeks had settled down. She wished David was here. He had rung her only once since Joelle's death. She had told him that Meg had invited her and Shamus to Bonniemoor, hoping he would come and join them there, but he had hardly seemed to be listening. Their conversation had ended with no firm arrangements about when they would see each other again.

Elizabeth now rose to her feet and gestured to Jamie to stop playing. She clapped her hands and the room quietened.

'Anyone who doesn't want to listen should go into the library where you will find a fire and drinks.'

Meg caught Anna's eye and gave her a surreptitious thumbs up. The room came to an orderly, respectful silence and Jamie began playing again. Anna's mellifluous voice filled the room and spilled into the hall and up the stairs, where Polly and Shamus were watching TV in what the family referred to as Nanny's sitting room.

Hitherto, Anna had felt largely ignored by the other guests. She was not, after all, one of them. They had been polite, but only just. The moment she spoke with her slight regional lilt, she saw their eyes glass over and their attention stray. But now their attention did not waver as each succumbed to the sound of her singing.

'More! More!' they cried eagerly at the end of the song, and Jamie and Anna gave them more.

Finally Anna decided they had performed enough. Elizabeth came quietly to her side. 'David is a lucky man. I hope we have more evenings like this. It's what the family needs. Thank you,' she whispered as she squeezed Anna's hands between her own.

'You have the most beautiful voice I've ever heard,' said Lord Strathwade breathlessly, dabbing his eyes with his handkerchief. 'You made me weep. It's the Burns, you know. Now where did Jamie find you?' he asked.

'Oh really, Bertie!' said Meg with more than a touch of annoyance. 'You don't find people like Anna as if they were a parcel or something. You obviously weren't listening when I told you she is a famous singer. People pay good money and lots of it to hear her sing.'

'Your father isn't Angus Frazer, the specialist from Glasgow, is he?' asked Lady Strathwade.

'Well, yes, unless there are two of them,' said Anna politely.

'Well, fancy that, Bertie. She's Angus Frazer's girl — you know, the Frazer who operated on your ears.'

'My word! Your father saved my hearing. Apparently there is no better surgeon in the country. A gifted family, aye what?' said Bertie.

'Please don't give us your operation story again, dear,' commanded Lady Strathwade. 'I want to hear more about Anna and her singing. Meg tells me your young brother plays the trumpet. How charming. We find it very difficult to get people to play the Last Post for us at the Remembrance parade. Do you think he would like to play for us?'

'Actually, he plays the flute not the trumpet, and he won't be in Scotland often anyway because he starts at music college in London in the autumn.'

'I must say, all this education seems quite unnecessary. We never did it in my day. Think of what it must be costing the taxpayer. I'm sure your brother is very good at his flute, but surely he can't expect to earn a useful living doing it, can he?' inquired Lady Strathwade, her ample bust expanding alarmingly as she spoke.

'You are wrong on all counts!' interceded Meg angrily. 'Firstly, students pay back their fees when they obtain employment and, secondly, someone with a music degree is unlikely to be unemployed, even if they don't end up playing music for a living.'

'My sister is a fountain of knowledge on all things, always was the brightest of the family,' said Jamie.

'Talking of the family, how is David?'

asked Lord Strathwade. 'Poor boy, he must be shattered . . . such a dreadful thing. Of course, we never met the wife, didn't come up here, did she? But we had good times with David when he was a lad. Brilliant shot . . . could never understand him becoming all lefty. I mean, he used to love shooting and all the country things. Damn shame. Traitor to his class, I would say . . . ' Bertie's voice trailed off as his wife gave him a very unsubtle dig in the ribs.

'We must be going,' she announced. 'Now, Miss Frazer, do let Jamie bring that brother of yours over and he can pop a few birds. I take it he can handle a gun?' asked Lady Strathwade bossily, as she got her glasses and car keys out of her snakeskin bag.

Anna thanked her for the invitation, saying she would talk about it with Jamie.

'You'll be able to drive over now you have your licence back, won't you, Jamie dear?' said Lady Strathwade.

'That was rather unnecessary,' ventured Anna to Jamie as the Strathwades disappeared down the drive.

'Do you know what that woman needs?' Jamie hissed under his breath.

'No. What?' asked Anna innocently.

'To be covered in mud and given a bloody

good fuck,' replied Jamie, bellowing with laughter.

'I heard that,' said Meg quietly, coming out of the drawing room and giving Jamie a playful slap. 'You're a disgrace, Jamie. I hope nobody else heard what you said. What can Anna think, hearing you talk like that?'

'Well, she's going to have to get used to it. From what I hear, she'll be seeing a lot of us. I suppose, as usual, I'll be told it's none of my business, but I never did think that French woman was right for David. Now this one,' Jamie said, putting his arm firmly round Anna's shoulders, 'this one is a very different matter. I reckon my little brother is on to a winner here all right.'

26

Charles lay on Veronica's snowy white sheets
with his eyes closed, enjoying the scent of
tuber rose wafting gently from the adjoining
bathroom. It was always a relief to come to
Veronica's immaculately run flat and escape
the pressures of life in Vincent Square. But
on this occasion the calm in Prince of Wales
Drive was more than usually necessary.

At least Meg had taken off for Scotland
with Polly, and Lavender was to follow
shortly when she returned from a magistrates'
seminar in Cheltenham. He had put her on
the train to Cheltenham this morning. Mrs
Duvver had left him his supper in the fridge.
He wouldn't eat it of course, and Mrs Duvver
would not comment. She understood that
Charles pushed off the moment Lavender
went away, but she never asked questions.
She knew only too well how he must need
to have what she would call 'a bit of a
change'.

Charles thought now about the last few
weeks and the unexpected turn of events
which had thrown the family into chaos.
He had never really had much time for

Joelle, although he had admired her sharp intelligence and her crystal good looks. One thing he couldn't understand, however, was a woman who neglected a child. Of course Lavender had been anything but a perfect mother, but she had taken a fervent interest in the children's education and, who knows, if Mrs Duvver had not come on the scene so early and taken up the role of mother hen, she might even have been domesticated. He had to admit she had an impeccable record on the Bench and was highly respected. And to be fair, she had always told him she didn't want to stay at home and look after children.

But Joelle was a different matter. She had been a bad wife and an indifferent mother. Charles was proud of the way David had coped with his situation, the loyalty and restraint he had shown with regard to his wayward wife. How bizarre that he should now be behaving like a man in total grief. Charles didn't talk a great deal to Veronica about his family, but tonight he was going to get it off his chest. She might have an objective view which could help him figure some of this out.

He heard the clink of ice and the scent of tuber rose intensified. He felt Veronica get on to the bed beside him as she handed him an ice-cold vodka and tonic. She lay opposite him, propped up against the brass end of the big bed, her head resting on one of the many outsize white Egyptian cotton pillows, stuffed with the best duck down and only available from a smart shop in Bond Street. She wore a pink and yellow silk kimono which fell open a little to reveal her still perfect breasts.

Charles caressed her manicured toes with their red-painted nails and admired a tiny glimpse of her rounded thighs and mons Veneris which he had just enjoyed with all their usual mutual satisfaction. A few years ago he would have started to make love to her all over again but now he needed more than sex, he wanted the benefit of her view on the situation.

He took a refreshing sip of his drink and was about to start to tell her what was on his mind when Veronica preempted him.

'How is everything? You must have had a terrible few days. Is your little granddaughter getting through it?'

'I need to talk to you, Veronica, see what you think.' Charles hesitated a moment, switching his attentions to her other foot. 'It's not Polly who is worrying me. She is an extraordinary child. She seems to be coping well. No, it's David. He is behaving very strangely. Admittedly he must have had a horrendous time and the press haven't helped. They have, as you know, had a field day with the story . . . Wasn't too bad at first but then they tried to read more into it all. Perhaps it's this that has sent David into such a weird state. What do you think?'

'Since you ask me, darling,' said Veronica gently, 'the press don't usually sniff around these stories unless there's some truth somewhere, and surely you must have realised that David's wife was not exactly faithful. She was obviously having an affair with Felix Khamul.'

The foot massage stopped abruptly. 'I suppose you must be right,' said Charles slowly. He hadn't wanted to believe it, though not because he couldn't believe that Joelle had been unfaithful to David. Of course she had, the marriage had been more or less over anyway and now David had just found himself someone else, someone very special in all the ways Joelle was not. No, the problem was the manner of Joelle's awful death, the idea that the bomb was meant for her lover and she had been killed by it; that this Khamul had not even come to the ceremony that David had arranged; that Khamul had just disappeared from the scene.

'Look, Charles, I expect David is scared

stiff with the press sniffing about. You have told me about his lovely new girlfriend. Suppose the press get on to the fact that he was having an affair with her when he wasn't divorced from his wife? It's all good stuff. David must be very careful. He probably shouldn't see Anna until the rat pack have run their course.'

Charles was deep in thought. He suddenly had a mad thought that Joelle might have been mixed up in something far worse than just the everyday story of adultery. 'Could the bomb have been meant for her?' he asked Veronica.

'Naturally that had crossed my mind, but I have a gut feeling it was as it seems. I have friends in the Foreign Office, as you know, and from what they tell me, Felix Khamul is a frightening man. Apart from anything else, he is probably the most powerful man in Cairo. He is an unofficial adviser to the president and also, and I know this to be true, he is CIA and consequently has a lot of enemies.'

'What can you mean, CIA? That, surely, is fantasy land; it's like a James Bond novel,' said Charles.

'Look, Charles. The man spends months at a time in the USA, he has houses in California and Washington and, wait for it, an American wife, number two to boot. He is a Muslim, you know, he can have more than one wife if he pleases. But I understand he has fallen foul of the fundamentalist groups, perhaps one of them had it in for him. Whichever way you look at it, he wasn't the kind of man to bring sweetness and light. He is dangerous, in every sense, as history has proved. Look at poor Joelle.'

Charles felt a headache coming on. He was suddenly angry with Joelle. How could she, the wife of his gentle son, become involved in anything so sordid? No wonder David had gone into a shell. It wasn't grief, it was more like disgust and horror. He must be shattered by all that had happened. According to Gloria, David's secretary, he had been working harder than ever, even doing a kind of sympathy kick in the constituency. Thank heavens they were coming up to the recess, although the House would be sitting into the first week of August because of the extra time required for the blood sports issue.

'The odd thing is, David is throwing himself into his work as he has never done before,' said Charles.

'That isn't odd at all, it's the only place where he feels normal. It's the best kind of therapy. You must just let it take its course; everything will be all right, you'll see. David

245

is not his father's son for nothing,' said Veronica reassuringly.

'I have to be frank. David hasn't been happy for years. He is completely unsuited to politics, he should have gone into the arts. It was his mother who pushed him, and something to do with his brother Jamie. Jamie is the apple of Lavender's eye, can do no wrong, even though he has virtually destroyed Lavender's family home,' said Charles pensively.

'I thought the estate in Scotland was a great success. Didn't you tell me about all the enterprises your son keeps getting into, including a wind farm?'

'He has many grandiose ideas but none of them is profitable. He has had quite a drink problem as well but I gather he now has that under control. But what I meant to say was that I think David went into politics as a sort of gesture. He felt our family were too spoilt, that Jamie had abused our privilege. He wanted to do something for society. He has a very sharply developed social conscience, but he is disillusioned by politics and I can't say I blame him.'

'Oh come on, Charles. Yes, your family is lucky, but for heaven's sake, you inherited a tumble-down white elephant in Sussex with no money to support it, and I've seen what a worry it has been to you. Thank goodness you've handed it on to Meg and David. I hope they will have the sense to get shot of it, something you should have done years ago. And as for the thing in Scotland, it's the same, unless your son is really prepared to get his hands dirty . . . it's also doomed. The odd thing is if it had gone to David, from what I hear of the man, he could perhaps have made a go of it. After all, letting grouse moors is big business. But you have to be a glorified hotelier and I suppose your son is too high and mighty for that.'

'You're very sharp, Veronica. I feel you know all my children, even though you've never met them. If only Lavender had your insight. I wish you could meet them. I . . .'
Charles looked searchingly at Veronica, his friend and lover, the person who had given his life stability and the woman who still made him feel like a young man embarking on a romantic affair. He wanted to tell David, to share his good fortune, see him getting some of the approbation he so richly deserved but never received from Lavender. He knew how well David and Veronica would get on. How nice it would be for his son to see him in such a different light, bathed in the glow of Veronica's all-embracing beneficence.

'I know, darling,' said Veronica understandingly when he put this to her. 'But, Charles, we have discussed this before and it just wouldn't do. Apart from anything else, I have always felt our relationship never threatened your wife in any way and I don't want to change that. It would be very damaging for me to meet your family. Imagine the disloyalty they would feel to their mother and, besides, the strength of our love affair is its separateness. It takes you away from all your family difficulties. I like to help by talking to you objectively; I don't want to become involved and lose that special private place we have together.' Deftly changing tack, Veronica turned to the subject of her Bill for Conjugal Rights for Prisoners.

Charles willingly switched into the correct mode, rather relieved to be drawn away from the saga at home.

'I think we must put an additional element into the Bill, Charles,' Veronica said firmly, getting up and refilling their drinks. Charles admired her fine legs as she returned to the bed. 'It's the matter of this resistance to compulsory AIDS testing in prisons,' she declared forcefully. 'It's ridiculous. Why, if you send a young man to prison where we know rape buggery is rife, surely prisoners

248

with AIDS should be segregated? I want to take this to the European Courts if necessary. Will you help me?' Veronica looked her most beguiling and Charles felt a definite stirring. It was only seven thirty, there was plenty of time before dinner.

'Of course, I think you're absolutely right,' he said approvingly, thinking that at least the dreadful spectre of AIDS was one thing he didn't have to worry about in his troubled family.

Veronica moved and lay beside Charles. Later they watched the sky over the trees in Battersea Park. When the light faded they lit candles and had dinner of lobster mayonnaise and raspberries and cream at a round table in the window of the white drawing room. Afterwards they went to bed and Charles held Veronica's magnificent and still desirable body in his arms. He slept well for the first time in weeks.

27

There was no question about it, David was ill. Whatever it was that had reduced him to such a state, it could no longer be put down to Joelle's death alone, of this Meg was certain as she prepared a late breakfast for him, although she knew it would probably be left uneaten.

She took the fresh croissants from the oven and put them on a tray with coffee and orange juice. It was ten o'clock. It was going to be yet another glorious day. She looked out of the open terrace door on to the cottage garden and saw the heat haze was beginning to lift from the Downs. She wondered what Polly and the rest of the family were doing up at Bonniemoor. Yesterday had been the glorious twelfth, and the grouse shooting would have begun. Anna's brother had been invited to remain at Bonniemoor by Jamie; the two of them had struck up quite a friendship. Meg hadn't heard from Anna in France and, truthfully, she was relieved. What could she tell her if she asked about David? Not the truth, surely. The awful truth was that David, her brother, the person she loved most in all the world, the person she had come to rely on, the one person who was always there for her, was a shadow of his former self.

She had known there was something terribly wrong by the tone of his voice on the phone, and so she had come back from Scotland to the cottage, where he was staying. Parliament was in recess and he claimed it was his wish to be left alone. He had told Anna the same thing, and she had departed for France without seeing him when she returned from Scotland. Meg didn't warn him she was coming, she just turned up, to find the cottage a tip and Ross sitting mournfully outside David's room, the door shut. The place was stifling. None of the windows could have been opened for days.

Slowly she opened the bedroom door. David lay on the bed, his face a strange grey colour, even allowing for the stubble. One arm dangled down the side of the bed on to the floor. Ross hurried in and tried to lick his master awake. Meg shook him but he didn't respond, and for a terrifying moment she thought he must be dead. But then she saw he was breathing. Eventually he opened his eyes. He took in her frightened face and reassured her that he was perfectly all right. He had taken two sleeping pills at seven o'clock that morning as he had been unable to sleep.

As the day wore on, Meg realised it was far more serious than insomnia. He wouldn't eat, he had lost a lot of weight and, worst of all, he seemed unable to make the simplest of decisions. She asked him if he would go to the village to get some provisions. She handed him a list and gave him a carrier bag, then left him and went upstairs to clean up and wash his sheets and piles of dirty clothes. Half an hour later when she came downstairs again, she found him still standing in the sitting room, saying he had forgotten what he was supposed to be doing.

While she had been clearing up his room, she had found some pills in a press-out blue foil sheet. They were not sleeping pills. They had the days marked and she saw he had pressed out seven of them.

She sat him down gently and asked him about the pills. He told her they were antidepressants prescribed by the doctor. He admitted they made him feel a good deal worse, but the doctor had assured him they would kick in after two weeks. He would begin to feel better and then he should continue to take them for three months. 'By that time I'll know the worst anyway,' he said absent-mindedly and then he had put his head in his hands and cried — big childlike sobs, the most shocking thing Meg had ever witnessed in her life. She tried to make him talk, but he refused. He told her not to worry, said he had it under control, whatever it was ... That had been two days ago and, if anything, he was worse. So today she was determined to make him talk to her.

When he came down with the tray and the uneaten croissants, she noticed at once he was wearing odd socks, one blue and one yellow, and had developed acne on his forehead. One of the spots had bled and he had cut himself shaving. He looked pallid and gaunt and his eyes didn't focus properly. He started to load his breakfast dishes in the dishwasher and dropped the milk jug on to the quarry-tiled floor. It smashed and lay in several pieces amidst a trickle of spilt milk. He stared at it as if not knowing what to do next.

'Leave it, David, it doesn't matter. Come and sit down. We need to talk.'

He sat down, his hands hanging vacantly between his knees.

'Wait there. I'm just going to get something,' Meg said firmly.

She went upstairs. The pills were on the bedside table; today's had not been taken.

She took them and joined David at the kitchen table.

'Shall we throw these away?' she asked bluntly. 'Let me be your cure, David, help you to help yourself. It's up to you.' She handed him the pills.

He seemed to collapse in on himself, as if he did not have the strength to argue. 'All right. Come with me.'

She followed him into the downstairs lavatory. He lifted the seat and one by one he popped the pills out of the foil and flushed them down the pan.

'Well done, that's the first step. Now let's talk.'

They went back into the kitchen.

David looked at Meg with haunted eyes. 'There is something, Meg . . . It's not just depression. I don't get things like that and it's not Joelle's death. I could have coped with that for Polly's sake, if nothing else. It's something almost worse. I've told no one. I couldn't . . .'

'You must tell me, David. Nothing could be worse than what you've been through, and it's over now. Tomorrow is another day. You have to get on with your life. You have so much going for you and you're letting it all slip away. I mean, what about Anna? You'll lose her if you're not careful. You must take a grip,' said Meg anxiously.

David's face suddenly became distraught. He stood up abruptly. 'That's just it, Meg, that's just it. Joelle was HIV positive and I'm convinced I've got it.'

Meg was too stunned to speak. The silence was oppressive; she started to sweat. She held on to her chair to stop herself falling. She hoped, for a brief moment, that she would awaken and find she was dreaming.

'Oh God, David, please tell me you don't mean it! You're stressed, you're imagining things. It's because you feel guilty and you're trying to punish yourself.' Meg began to sob uncontrollably. She stood up and went to David. She put her arms about his neck and buried her face in his hair. It smelt of the sea, of all the things she loved about her brother, and perhaps for the first time she faced the truth of her dependence on him. She simply couldn't imagine life without him.

'Her lover . . . the . . . he gave it to her . . . she didn't know . . . I mean, she wouldn't have . . . ' David stammered.

'But I thought . . . Surely you didn't sleep with Joelle, not . . . not since you started your affair with Anna?' The implications of what she was saying rose before Meg like the awful knowledge of pain after a drug-induced sleep.

'Oh God, Meg, that's what I can't live with. The thought of what I might have done to Anna.'

'Please, David, we must be practical. Have you told Anna?' Meg tried to keep her voice steady. She held on to the back of David's chair. She couldn't look at his face. She felt a frantic desire to raise her voice, scream, wake herself from this nightmare, and yet she knew she must remain calm. It was as if they were children again. How often it had been she who had been the calm one, the one who got them out of a childhood scrape with her quick thinking, her instinctive desire to protect her brother at all costs. This could not be true. She wouldn't let it happen.

She took a deep breath and regained her composure. She sat down opposite David and quietly asked him to tell her everything.

He told her the facts. How he had been to the doctor, how the first tests were negative . . . how the doctor had been cautiously optimistic. He had not slept with Joelle for over a year, but he still had this gut feeling he had it . . . He had not been blameless in his wife's infidelities. Perhaps he deserved it.

'Oh, for heaven's sake, David, spare me the guilt trip! Joelle had a choice.' Meg banged her open hand on the pine table. She felt hot and she began to perspire again.

'Have you told Anna?' she asked again, her face going white as she imagined gentle Anna being confronted with such an unspeakable thing.

'No,' David answered flatly.

'Why on earth not? You must tell her at once. What if — ' Meg broke off.

David's ashen face looked directly at her. 'You mean what if Anna has caught it from me and sleeps with someone else?'

'No, of course I didn't mean that,' said Meg hastily. 'I meant surely you're morally obliged to tell her.'

'Do you think I haven't gone over this again and again? For God's sake, Meg, I feel like a drowning man. My love for Anna is all I have to hang on to.'

'No it isn't, David. You have me, you will always have me. We will confront this thing together. I've always been there for you, just as you have been there for me,' said Meg angrily. For the first time she felt resentful of Anna. After all, it was she who had always been David's mainstay, his rock, even when he didn't know it. Her love for him was the centre of her life. This was part of her problem, no other man could be the friend he was to her. She had been happy to share him with Anna, but as an equal in his affections. Joelle had never been a serious rival, she had always been separate from them. David didn't deserve this, she would steer him through it. He would survive, she would find a way.

'David, I don't believe you've got AIDS. We must hold on to that. You mustn't let fear take over. Your best defence at this point is to stay fit and healthy. Anna's friend Jason has been HIV positive for years, and he leads a perfectly normal life. We live with it nowadays, it's reality, but you, well, you've never seemed part of all that. I've always thought of you as removed from that sort of thing.'

'You mean I've finally been woken from my ivory tower existence,' said David with more than a trace of bitterness.

'No, of course I didn't mean that . . . ' Meg hastily got up and blew her nose on some kitchen towel. 'Oh God, David! Have you told anyone? Does Dad know?'

'No, and I don't want anyone to know. I wasn't even going to tell you but, Meg, my dear Meg . . . ' He held out his hand and reached for hers. He took it and held it to his cheek. 'I've grappled with this and I've decided I must stall until I have the final test. It's not too long, only a couple of months. Why spoil everyone's summer? I mean, if the worst is true, they'll all have to know soon enough anyway. I couldn't have given it to Anna. We were always so careful, she didn't want to get pregnant . . . '

'Which doctor are you going to? If it's Desmond, he's bound to tell Dad.'

'Yes, it is Desmond. He is, after all, our family doctor. He knows all our secrets and, don't be ridiculous, it would be more than his life's worth to tell Dad. It would be wholly unprofessional. I trust him completely.'

Meg thought for a moment. 'I'm going to stay here with you, David. We can get on with Loverstone together. I'll look after you. You mustn't be alone, not now. I'm due some time off, I can take extra holiday. I love you so much, David. If the news is bad, we will beat it together. There are new drugs, you know. But you have to tell Anna.'

'Meg, you're a lovely woman. If I get through this, you, Anna and I will be a team and then I will have to find a big brother to join us and we can make a foursome,' he said with a laugh. 'And, Meg, I want Polly always to think well of her mother . . . '

They looked at each other in the silent room and things seemed suddenly simpler. The situation was in their control. They both knew, in the cerebral shorthand they had developed over the years, exactly what the other was thinking.

Meg nodded. 'Let's enjoy what's left of the summer. Come up to the house and let's see what they've done with the roof. Did I tell you I've got sponsorship for the project from a Japanese record company?' she said, flushing with excitement.

'Meg the miracle worker,' said David affectionately 'What would I do without you?'

28

Veronica was good at disguising her feelings. It was one of the many qualities that equipped her so well for public life. She had just received some bad news — her brother, to whom she had always been very close, had just been told he had cancer; he was having to give up work and start chemotherapy. She did not show her distress now as she sat waiting for Charles in the L-shaped dining room of the House of Lords. It was one-fifteen, and he was already fifteen minutes late. Veronica was apprehensive about the final stages of her Bill that afternoon. Charles had been preoccupied with the dramatic events in his family and had not kept abreast of things. The time had come when she needed him on-side. She felt somehow wrong-footed by being kept waiting. She had ordered iced Perrier water, for she would not drink wine today. She must keep a clear head.

Charles arrived, looking harassed. 'I'm so sorry, my dear. I never caught up today, after last night. As you know I was very late into the office,' he said, raising his eyebrows and sitting down in a flurry. He wore a faded light brown tweed suit and his customary bow tie. Today he had chosen red with white spots and he now dabbed his forehead with a matching handkerchief.

'Everything all right?' he asked.

'No. My brother Simon has just found out he has cancer. It's always such a shock. It reminds one of one's own mortality.'

'Oh dear, I am so sorry. I suppose that means Phillamores will be looking for a new chairman. What a shame for him when the firm is doing so well. I notice the shares have just been floated on the Stock Market. Quite brilliant when you think of all the competition from the other leading auction houses. I suppose your brother's expertise in the art world has been very much responsible for their success.'

'Will you keep it under your hat for the moment, Charles? Nobody knows yet. I . . . .' Veronica's lip began to tremble slightly but she pulled herself together almost at once.

Beryl, Veronica's special waitress, had been standing waiting to take the order. Hearing Charles's remarks to his luncheon companion of so many years, she gave a wry smile and informed them of the specialities on the trolley.

'You choose, my dear. I'll have whatever you have,' said Charles absentmindedly.

Veronica ordered the vegetarian main course for them both.

'After last night I could hardly eat a thing. Will you be having a starter?' she asked.

'No, we never need a starter, my dear,' he muttered under his breath, with a twinkle.

Beryl's eyes rolled to heaven as she heard these exchanges. She walked away with the menu cards.

'Everything all right?' the head waiter asked her.

'This lot in here are never too old for a bit of malarkey. One day I'm going to write my memoirs.'

'Will they include me?' he asked, slyly pinching her bottom behind the service console.

'That depends,' said Beryl. 'But I must say that Lord Lovegrove is still a very attractive gentleman and he has lovely manners, better than some others I could mention,' she said pointedly, inclining her head to a rowdy table in the other corner from which came frequent bursts of laughter.

'I always said the place would go to the dogs when they got rid of the belted Earls . . . A lot of riffraff now, not the same at all,' the head waiter remarked disapprovingly.

Charles also heard the ribald noises emanating from the corner and thought they struck an uncomfortable note against the traditional splendour of the opulent room, with its plum-coloured curtains and magnificent decor. Not for the first time he mentally conceded that the reforms had not brought the improvements that had been hoped for. In fact he had long ago decided the removal of the hereditary peerage and the substitution of working peers had turned the whole place into a kind of provincial town hall. The average age of peers, already verging on the senile, seemed to have risen by a decade and the level of debate was not any longer to his erudite taste. The Chamber, as he first knew it, was a catholic place and the eccentricities of the landed families, with their unpredictable and sometimes unconventional contributions, had been the perfect antidote to the vote-conscious and accountable decisions that came from the Commons.

'Now, let's get down to this afternoon,' said Veronica firmly.

'Not before I tell you how wonderful last night was,' said Charles quietly, his knee gently pressing hers under the table.

Veronica's ample bosom swelled visibly and she gave him one of her most brilliant smiles. She patted his hand briefly, then brought the conversation back to the Conjugal Rights for Prisoners Bill.

Charles listened attentively as she spoke fluently and then his mind wandered just a little until he saw her fuchsia pink lips enunciate the information that, during the Bill's passage through the Commons, an amendment to extend the rights to gay and lesbian partners had been added. He choked on a piece of bread roll, his face reddening. He grabbed a glass of water and tried to speak. Finally he managed to splutter out some words, far more loudly than he intended. They came with a surge of air on the wings of yet another violent coughing fit.

'Good God!' he boomed to a now attentive dining room. 'Do you mean to say we're going to have licensed buggery in prisons now? You'll be telling me they are getting sex aids next! They'll all be queuing to get behind bars at this rate.'

Beryl's hands shook a little as she placed the vegetarian curry in front of Veronica. 'Will you be wanting hot chilli chutney, my lady, or is it hot enough already?' she asked helpfully.

'No, I'm sure it's hot enough,' said Veronica politely, looking nervously at Charles, who was spooning chutney all over his soya beans. Beryl moved away disapprovingly to the service console and the dining room returned to normal.

'I didn't expect such a strong reaction from you,' said Veronica emotionally.

Charles thought she might be about to cry. He had never seen her lose her composure in all their twenty years together.

'Well, what am I supposed to do? I wish the whole thing hadn't come to light in the Commons. It was completely out of my control and unless someone filibusters the Bill, it will go through and if they do, it will only come back in the same form again. We're stuck with it, and I didn't get the amendment on compulsory AIDS testing.' Veronica reached down for her handbag and got out a lace handkerchief. As she daintily blew her nose, Charles could see she was very upset.

'You won't oppose it, will you?' she asked appealingly. 'Not after all the work we've done together? It's progress I suppose, we can't stop it.'

'It's not progress, Veronica, it's degeneration, but it's one way of controlling the prison population I suppose; they'll all get AIDS now.' Charles looked miserably at his cold soya bean curry and bit on a mouthful of chilli. The result was his immediate removal from the dining room.

★ ★ ★

At four-thirty that afternoon formal business and questions in the House of Lords came to an end. The bewigged clerk rose to his feet and called out, 'Conjugal Rights for Prisoners Bill, and House of Commons amendments.'

The late afternoon sun shafted through a window and framed Veronica, splendid in her cyclamen jacket. In spite of his reservations about the rest of the afternoon's business Charles felt a shiver of pride when he looked at her. She stood out in a sea of grey relieved only by the odd slash of floral easy-care. After an exodus of those disinterested peers and peeresses there were but two dozen remaining in the chamber, amongst them the ageing Lord Bancroft, a notoriously long-winded speaker. For a moment Charles's spirits rose as he saw the possible demise of the appalling legislation he had unwittingly brought to fruition.

'Would My Lords not agree that to be deprived of the normal physical relationships that keep families together is hardly in keeping with the reforming process we are implementing in our prisons? Keeping men and women in touch with their families is essential if we are to expect them to return to the outside world and resume normal lives,'

267

said Veronica fulsomely. She continued in similar mode until Lord Bancroft stood up and called for her to give way.

He was a ferocious opponent of gay rights. He launched forth in a stinging attack on public morals, broadening out into a more specific condemnation of what he called perverts and sexual deviants. As the minutes ticked by Charles saw the chamber gradually succumbing to the post-prandial nap. He caught sight of Veronica's face and was engulfed by a mixture of feelings. He respected the conviction behind her work, but the way things had gone had horrified him. Yet as he heard Lord Bancroft's voice rising in a crescendo of graphic indignation, he didn't like what he was hearing.

Charles had always prided himself on his ability to take a brief and fight it on its merit, regardless of his own prejudices. Several times Veronica called for 'the Noble Lord to give way' and Lord Bancroft ignored her.

Charles did not speak as frequently as some of his colleagues, but when he did the House would usually fall silent and attentive, for he rarely disappointed. His call for Lord Bancroft to be silent met with a rumble of approval. He spoke slowly and firmly, and the snores from various parts of the chamber ceased and a hush descended as he sombrely beatified Veronica's Bill. It was at moments like this that Veronica reminded herself of what a remarkable man Charles was.

29

'So you insist on being faithful to your dreary MP who is probably shafting a nubile researcher as we speak. Don't old lovers count? For God's sake, Anna! Here we are under the stars, full of red wine. You look more beautiful than I have ever seen you. Everyone else has gone to bed and I want to make love to you.' Justin put his arm round Anna's bare shoulders and pulled her close. She was wearing a white cotton dress with a full flowing skirt and a halter neck. Her skin had turned a soft gold in the last few days.

Anna felt much happier than when she had left England but her confidence in David had completely evaporated. She had had just one phone conversation with him before she departed for France. He sounded so odd, it was impossible to believe he was the same man. He said that for both their sakes he thought it best if they didn't meet before she left for France. He needed to be alone to sort himself out and he didn't want to do anything to bring the media sniffing round the cottage. While she had been in Scotland a story had appeared in the press about their relationship. It wasn't much of a story and the picture of her and David in the doorway of his house was quite harmless. There had also been some innuendo about David's marriage having been in difficulties for some time prior to her arrival on the scene, so she was happily spared the tag she had dreaded.

Anna had travelled in a minicab to the airport feeling depressed and full of doubts about her future with David. Of course Justin had been there to meet her off the plane at Lyon, looking wonderfully handsome and tanned. He had hired an open Mercedes and together they had driven into the valley of the Loire to Solmes and then on to the chateau.

They swept into a cobbled courtyard through ornate wrought-iron gates to the front of the chateau which backed steeply on to one of the tributaries of the Loire. The building was on the site of an old monastery, which accounted for the verdant fruit and vegetable gardens and a small vineyard which adorned the lower levels of the land between it and the river. The monks had provided produce for the entire neighbourhood and were famous for their honey and peaches. Espaliered fruit trees covered the old walls of the grounds as far as the eye could see. Justin explained that the labyrinth of buildings owed much to its ecclesiastical origins. There were more than forty bedrooms, all now with bathrooms, and a magnificent medieval hall, originally the monastery chapel, which had been turned into a concert and opera hall. It could seat two hundred people in comfort and each had a perfect view of the raised stage where concerts and semi-staged opera were performed in repertory each night, with master classes on Sundays, for an eight-week season. Visitors were put up in the village, in the converted stables, in small hotels or with enterprising locals who had taken to offering bed and breakfast. The price of a ticket included supper after the performance, prepared from local produce in the chateau's kitchens, and the chateau wine.

They were to have a week's rehearsals of the early French repertoire and *Lieder*. These would take place in the afternoon while the already prepared programme finished its three-week run in the evenings. Anna was in a pleasantly equable mood by the end of her first day. She loved the Rameau opera she was to perform in. As usual, Justin took her to the very limit of her potential. His grasp of the authentic instruments used by the small orchestra was impressive, and his body language with Anna implied a passionate physical relationship between them — a situation not lost on the rest of the performers who clearly assumed they were lovers. This heady atmosphere had blossomed over dinner at a long communal table on the flagged terrace. The scent of rosemary from the barbecued lamb mingled with the fragrance of the jasmine and sweet geraniums from the gardens below. Her unhappiness about David had been mellowed by the red wine and the perfection of the surroundings, and she had not needed much persuasion to follow Justin to this quiet corner by the swimming pool where they now sat on a swing seat, watching the bats darting for gnats in the reflection of the underwater lights of the pool.

'No, Justin, I can't. I told you that before I came out here. Please don't spoil everything.' Anna lay back on the soft cushions. It was dark, the sky peppered with stars. The sound of crickets and the distant tones of this evening's singers floated down the terraced vines. Anna could feel Justin's breath on her face as he moved closer. His long persuasive fingers remorselessly edged up her bare thighs. She half-heartedly pushed his hand away. Sensing the ambivalence in her reaction, his fingers merely began the well-travelled journey all over again.

'Why save yourself, Anna? Who is going

to be any the wiser? And besides, your voice is showing distinct signs of hormone deficiency.'

Justin's hands had reached the top of Anna's thighs and his lips sought her mouth. She tried to resist but the sweetness of the night filled her and she responded, driven not so much by her need for the familiar closeness of his body as anger at David's apparent rejection.

'For God's sake, let's go to bed,' whispered Justin. 'I want you so much, Anna. It's no good between Felicity and me. I've been going mad. I — '

'What do you mean?' said Anna, drawing away from him. 'Am I the bit on the side that keeps your marriage bearable? Well, I have news for you, Justin. I'm not in the business of providing that sort of marriage therapy. I'm not going to bed with you.'

'Oh, stop it, Anna! Don't be so pompous. Since when have you been so high and mighty about a little adultery? I can tell you want me. Don't forget, I know every bit of your body. I bet your stuffy MP doesn't know what a full-blooded woman you are. You need passion. You're half whore, half nun.'

'Well, you can have the nun half. I'll keep the whore for my stuffy MP,' laughed Anna.

Anna stretched her legs and threw off the light blanket. She got out of bed and padded across the tiled floor to the window. When she pulled the shutters aside, the morning sun hit her like a warm bath. She sat for a moment on the hot tiles of the deep window ledge, her knees bent up, and looked out at the perfect day. Below two gardeners were busy watering and tending the greenhouses.

A soft, dry breeze blew the bougainvillaea outside her window towards her cheek. The day was going to be scorching. She had on a white cotton nightdress and her unruly auburn hair tumbled about her shoulders, catching a fiery glow from the pellucid early-morning light.

'What a beautiful sight. Can I come up? I have something for you.' Justin stood in the courtyard below, his voice echoing on the cobbles. 'You look ravishing, Anna. I'm on my way.' With that, Justin's lean linen-clad figure disappeared inside.

Anna had only time to clean her teeth before he was outside her door. She could hear him humming some bars of *Der Rosenkavalier* as he tapped. Anna knew she should refuse to let him in but she didn't. She had been in France for a week now and she had not heard from David. She was slowly beginning to think she had better forget him. She had got hold of Meg at the cottage yesterday, but she had been uncommunicative. She said vaguely that David was back in London and was going down to Chequers for lunch with the Prime Minister. 'So he must be better then!' Anna said excitedly, and then, 'Why don't you suggest he comes out here? He would love it, it's the most beautiful place and the music is gorgeous. I am starting my stuff the day after tomorrow. It will be just what he needs. The place even has a pool. I'm sure I can fix a room for him. Will you ask him to ring me?'

Meg had sounded strange, evasive, not her usual self at all. David had not rung back.

Justin knocked again and she let him in. He did not waste any time enfolding Anna in his arms. The smell of her, the erotic mass of hair, the freshness of her face without makeup, and behind them the rumpled intimacy of the huge four-poster inviting him to make love to her were more than he could resist. She did not pull away from him as he tugged open her white nightdress and felt her brown nipples harden under his practised touch.

The phone rang. She pulled away from him roughly.

'Oh, it's you! Why haven't you rung before? Where are you?' he heard her say breathlessly. She seemed to have forgotten he was still in the room. She sat down on the bed, her nightdress hanging open and both her breasts visible. The sight of them aroused Justin almost as much as the feel of them had. He did not leave the room. He knew she was talking to David Lovegrove. She had told him she wanted him to come out and join her, but Justin somehow doubted he would.

Anna's dejected expression when she put the phone down told him he was right. He sat beside her on the bed and gently pushed her back on to the pillows. She lay quiescent on the tumbled bed, her body limp, unresisting. 'My darling Anna,' he whispered, his lips moving gently on her mouth, 'why do you go on doing this to yourself when I am here wanting you? I need you, Anna, I want to be inside you, feel your beautiful body respond to me the way it used to. He isn't coming, is he?'

She didn't reply.

He lay on top of her, his weight on his elbows. He pushed her hair away from her brow and saw she was crying silently. The obvious depth of her feeling for this David Lovegrove surprised him. He knew he must tread carefully. Lovegrove had had his chance and missed it. He would not make the same mistake. Tonight would be all the sweeter for his patience now. He would take her to the pool after dinner. It was the last night they would have together before the performances started.

Justin stood up slowly and looked gently down at Anna as she lay with her eyes closed, shuddering slightly. She would recover, he knew. She would forget David Lovegrove, she would forget because her voice, that beautiful instrument, meant more to her than any man could and he, Justin, was the only man who could take her to her full potential. He had been through some of *Der Rosenkavalier* with her the previous day. She would be a truly great Octavian. She had that rare quality, the power to move people. He hoped to prove to her that they needed each other. Together they would become great, one of the great duos. The chemistry between them was unique. When their eyes met across the footlights, she was transformed and she knew it, but she did not yet know that in many ways her future lay in the power of his musicality. She had the voice, the beauty, but he had the musicality, and the ambition, energy and inspirational genius that would make her his star, his own creation. What a life they could have together. That was what he wanted. He had missed her so much. As for his marriage to Felicity, that was over. She had told him she had found someone else and she wanted a divorce. He hadn't told Anna yet.

'Come, Anna,' he said, 'he's not worth it. Let's work. I will see you in the music room. Bring the score of *Kavalier*, I want to work on 'The Silver Rose' scene with you. It will be your greatest moment, what you have always dreamed of. Together we will make it perfection.'

He left the room quietly. He wasn't entirely sure she would come at once, but if she didn't he would send some flowers from the garden to tempt her down. She would come eventually. He wouldn't let her go again. When he thought of her in some other man's arms . . . no, Anna was his now and for ever. He felt triumphant, confident, as he walked down the long gallery humming Octavian's Silver Rose duet.

Anna lay for a moment, her mood veering from misery to anger and then to a feeling of betrayal. Was it possible that all men were the same or was she somehow the cause of this pattern of male behaviour? They were always a disappointment. First her father, perhaps the most disillusioning of all, and then the one or two relationships she had embarked on as a student, then Justin, and now David. She had never realistically expected to marry Justin, not even when she became pregnant, but just for a while, with David, she had allowed herself to dream.

If he really loved her he would surely have found a way to join her in France. He had said Joelle's mother was coming to England, but while she accepted that he obviously had an obligation to be with Regine, she couldn't help feeling he was using this as an excuse. If he hadn't been so strange since Joelle's death, she might not have attached so much importance to it. He had withdrawn from her both physically and mentally, and against such a wall of noncommunication she felt quite helpless.

Anna took a deep breath and decided she was lucky to have Justin here. He would not let her wallow in feelings of rejection and self-pity, he lived in the real world, not a comfortable daydream of fidelity and security. She felt she had grown one more skin. The next time, if there was a next time, she would not give so much, she would not expose herself to the slings and arrows of consuming love. Justin had once said that she would find her fulfilment through her music and the rest would be the subplot. He was right.

30

'Well, I'm entitled to at least one nervous breakdown in my life, and this was it,' was the last thing David said to Meg as he left for London.

Meg had been wonderful. It was odd, David had thought, how he spent so much time advising other people about their problems in such a clear-sighted and objective way, and yet when it came to his own life he fluffed about in a fog of indecision. But Meg was right, he must tell Anna. Meg had passed on her message suggesting he join her in France and he had decided he would go so that he could talk to Anna face to face — this was not something you could blurt out over the telephone. But now it would have to wait until after Regine's visit.

She had rung yesterday. Her voice, so like Joelle's, had given him a start.

'David, I'm flying in to London tomorrow,' she announced. 'I've booked into my club in Sloane Street for a week. I've a lot to do and would like to see something of Polly. Is that all right?'

David's mind had raced. He would have to put off the trip to France. There were things he must discuss with Regine. The Foreign Office were conducting their own inquiries but they seemed to be leading nowhere. David wanted to know more about Felix Khamul but there was still no information about where he was. One theory suggested he had gone back to the Lebanon. David assumed it was he who had given Joelle the AIDS virus, and if so he wanted to know how long she had been having an affair with him. The importance of this was obvious. Perhaps Regine would have some answers.

'Of course, Regine. Polly is back in London now, she's with my parents. But let's plan the details when you arrive. I'll meet you at the airport.'

As David put the phone down, he suddenly felt terribly sorry for Regine, a woman alone grieving for her only daughter. She sounded harassed and upset. She had seen so little of Polly over the years that naturally she would want to pick up the threads. Polly was all she had left.

David lifted the phone again and dialled France. He hoped to God Anna would understand why he couldn't join her just yet.

★ ★ ★

David dropped Regine at her club at teatime. She looked tired and drawn. She said she would have a rest and a bath and then have dinner with him in the quiet dining room where the food was excellent and they would be able to talk.

At eight o'clock they sat together in the window at a small round table. Regine looked much better. David had to admit she was still a very beautiful woman. She wore her regulation smart black dress and minimal gold jewellery. As he looked at her, he thought Joelle would have looked much the same at her age if she had lived. The same figure, the same short dark hair, the same lively face and hands. The difference was in Regine's eyes. There was a look of Polly in them, soft and tinged with an approachable kind of humour and sadness. They held the gaze, whereas Joelle's had always been on the move as if she didn't want to miss anything.

While they ordered their food they made polite conversation, but when the waiter had produced the bottle of wine and they each had had a drink, Regine unexpectedly put her hand on David's.

'I am so sorry, David dear,' she said

quietly. 'If only she had been honest with you and called it a day a year ago, before she went to Rome, you would have had nothing to worry about. As it is you must be going through hell.'

David pulled his hand away. 'What has Rome to do with any of this? Joelle's assignment there was nine months ago and as far as I'm aware it had no connection with what she later got involved with in Cairo.'

'You're right, there's no connection. But she slept with someone in Rome. It was a one-off, it meant nothing. She never saw him again, but after she got back from Cairo, she found out he was ill with AIDS. She only came out with all this when I went to Cairo, not long before she was killed. She summoned me. She was distraught, didn't know which way to turn. But she was very strong, you know. She pulled herself together remarkably quickly, and she didn't need me to tell her she had to return to London to sort things out with you.'

David took a gulp of wine, remembering how he had gone to pieces at just the possibility he might be HIV positive, even believing he was already showing signs of full-blown AIDS.

'I had no idea about any of this,' he said unhappily, twisting the stem of his wine glass

285

in his fingers. He looked up at Regine. 'Joelle and I didn't sleep together for more than a year before she died, you know,' he added quietly.

Regine's face lightened. 'So that means you're in the clear. Oh David, I'm so glad, not just for your sake but for Polly's as well. If anything happened to you, Polly would . . . ' Regine didn't complete the sentence. 'I want you to know, David, I didn't approve of Joelle's plan to remove Polly to Egypt. It wasn't safe, I told her so . . . Now I feel I'm all she has left of her mother. Perhaps one day you'll let me take her to Egypt, just for a visit. I'd like to show her some of Joelle's past, where she spent part of her childhood.'

David nodded. 'Yes, of course, one day.' He didn't want to discuss that now. 'Regine, when we were on the Red Sea with Joelle's ashes, what did you mean when you said Felix Khamul murdered your daughter?'

'I don't want to talk about that man. It's just that the bomb . . . it was meant for him. He was expecting it. He shouldn't have let Joelle go in his car.'

'They were lovers, weren't they?'

Regine nodded.

'Did Joelle tell him she was HIV positive?'

'I've no idea, but she did mention that he

286

had an obsession about safe sex. I suppose he had to have, he had so many mistresses. It doesn't matter now anyway.'

'Why not?' asked David.

'He's dead. The people who were after him in Cairo caught up with him in Lebanon — another bomb, but this time in the house where he was staying.'

David wondered briefly why the Foreign Office had not seen fit to tell him this bit of news. Surely they knew. He hadn't seen anything in the papers about it, but then he had not been following the news very closely lately. It didn't matter. Nothing mattered right now except that he was healthy and his life could once again move forward. The terrible limbo he had been living in was over. He would ring Meg with the good news as soon as he got home, however late it was. And tomorrow he would call Anna and arrange to fly out to France.

Regine watched him. She saw the glow of animation return to his face and was glad.

31

Anna tried to hang on to the conception that the things that had happened to her were her karma. Perhaps she never was meant to live an ordinary life, get married to a man she really loved, have a middling career and babies. Her voice, she knew, was going from strength to strength, thanks in large part to Justin. His concentration on her had been absolute and he had even paid for Jason to come out to France to work with her. Now that she had the programme for the festival safely under her belt, they began to work seriously on Octavian.

This morning she was working with Justin in one of the old chapels which had been converted into a music room. A concert grand piano stood next to a large window which looked out over the chateau's vineyard towards the tributary of the Loire. The river water was like a silver millpond and Anna had watched boats negotiating the lock. Bright geraniums decorated the window boxes of the lock-keeper's house. When they had finished their work, Anna planned to take a picnic to the cool of the low-hanging willows along the banks of the river, past the little house. Earlier she had been to the village and bought pâté, baguettes, cheese and enormous peaches. She had found a shop that sold baskets and had bought one lined with quilted red and white gingham. It stood ready packed with the food and a bottle of wine.

Justin closed the lid of the piano and stretched his arms. 'You're superb, my darling. I still believe Richard Strauss had the female orgasm in mind when he wrote that music,' he said softly, looking directly at her. He wore khaki shorts and a crisp white shirt with the sleeves rolled up. Anna had allowed herself to admire his smooth, tanned skin and his taut body. He was not as tall as David. His father was of Polish Jewish descent and it was from him he had inherited both his dark good looks and his musical talent. His father, Joseph Stein, though not a professional musician, was an accomplished violinist. He had chosen to study medicine and Justin and his two brothers had all been university educated. The brothers had both gone into law. Justin was the only one who had read music. He had pleased his father by getting a music scholarship to Cambridge and gaining a first-class honours degree. Justin had been a golden boy in every sense of the word. His marriage to Felicity, whose father owned a chain of garages, had put the icing on the cake; it was her father who had bought them the commodious house in Surrey. It would be Felicity's alone now. Justin had told Anna that Felicity wanted a divorce. She was welcome to it, he had said lightly. It would allow him to get on unencumbered with what he really wanted to do. He had promised to tell Anna exactly what that was on the picnic today.

Anna moved round the piano and spontaneously bent to kiss the top of Justin's head. He grabbed her and pulled her to him, pressing his face into her body and running his hands up the backs of her legs under her short cotton dress. Her buttocks tightened involuntarily as he found them but she did not pull away. His hands began to move between her legs. She stood enjoying the sensation, but she knew she should resist him.

'Let's go,' she said firmly, twirling away from him towards the door. 'I want to show you the lock-keeper's house before we eat.'

He remained seated. 'Darling Anna, you know I've fallen in love with you. I think I've always been in love with you. I know now I cannot live with a woman who does not share my passion for music.' He got up and crossed the room to where she stood and pulled her into his arms. Her head dropped back and her mane of hair fell over his hands as he kissed her longingly.

★ ★ ★

They chose a spot way past the lock-keeper's house under a large, old willow tree. Justin held back the ribbons of soft green for Anna to enter what appeared to be a cool shady room. When he let the long tendrils fall back into place, a slight breeze from the river moved them in ripples with a swishing sound. The ground underneath was mossy and soft. Justin spread the rug he had brought and set to work opening the bottle of wine. He handed Anna a glass and raised his own in a toast.

'To us, to you and me. Together we will do great things, Anna.' He put down his glass and took her in his arms, the rippling willow tendrils swaying sleepily about them. Anna lay back, submitting as Justin started to remove her scant clothing with practised expertise. He paid solemn attention to each part of her body. First he exposed her breasts, reverently tracing the white contours which the sun had not seen and following the tracery of faint blue veins to the velvety brown which surrounded her nipples.

Anna closed her eyes in a state of delicate, lazy arousal. Justin had never made love to her quite like this before. He usually seized his pleasure rather perfunctorily. Today was different.

'You're not allowed to move, this is for you. Stay still,' he said huskily. He removed her dress and underwear. She now lay naked in the mossy bower. He returned his attention to her breasts and then his lips slowly, tantalisingly, travelled down her firm belly to the musky hair he had thought of so often in the last few weeks. As Anna cried out they moved together into oblivion.

They stayed locked together in their green bower for some time until Justin saw the silhouettes of two white swans moving serenely over the water, past the green tendrils of their love nest.

'Sit up, darling. Look, it's you and me. You know they mate for life?' He pulled her up as the graceful birds majestically made their way down the river in tune with and in command of all they surveyed.

'I won't let you go, Anna. I love you and you need me if you're going to follow your star. And one thing you can be sure of, you'll never be bored with me.'

'You may be right,' said Anna sleepily.

'When we get back, can I move in with you?' asked Justin.

32

David woke slowly, and for a moment he couldn't quite think why he felt so content, and then the relief of his conversation with Regine came flooding in on him like a warm balm. Meg had been asleep when he rang her last night but she was overjoyed to hear his news. He looked at the clock. It was already nine thirty.

He dialled the chateau and asked to speak to Anna. 'Just hold on a minute, I will try Mademoiselle Frazer's room,' replied the voice in perfect English.

'Hello, darling, it's me,' he said as the receiver was lifted. For a moment he thought he must have been put through to the wrong room. There was muffled silence the other end and then Anna's voice.

'Who is it?' she asked.

'I hope I didn't wake you, darling,' he said. Anna often slept in after a performance.

'Oh, it's you,' she said flatly.

David felt confused. Her voice was cold, uninterested. 'I'm coming out to see you after all,' he blurted. 'I have things I must

294

explain. I love you, Anna. I've missed you so much. I — '

'David, I think it would be better if you didn't come at the moment,' Anna interrupted. 'I've a lot of work and I'm busy learning Octavian as well. I just wouldn't be able to spend time with you.' There was a pause. He was sure she had briefly put her hand over the receiver. 'Why don't we have dinner when I get back and everything is less fraught?'

He had no option but to agree.

'See you in about three weeks,' she said finally.

Disappointed and slightly puzzled, David went to make himself some coffee. He felt at rather a loose end. Polly would be with Regine today. Lavender had been less than enthusiastic about the emergence of the other grandmother. 'It's just another confusion for her,' she had said when David had told her Regine was coming to England. Polly, however, had been excited and said she wanted to go shopping with Regine and take a boat trip down the Thames.

The phone rang. David hurriedly picked it up, thinking it might be Anna. It was Gloria, his secretary.

'Can we do a diary plan, David?' she asked brightly. 'And do you have the directions and itinerary for the lunch at Chequers tomorrow with the PM?'

'Yes, to both questions,' said David, silently kicking himself. He had completely forgotten he was due at Chequers tomorrow. 'I'm coming into the office in a few minutes, Gloria. I need to get back into the swim, get back to normal.'

'It will be good to have you back,' said Gloria with barely disguised relief.

* * *

There was the usual gaggle of newsmen at the gates of Chequers as David arrived at twelve thirty on Sunday for lunch with the Prime Minister. As he slowed his car to show his pass to the security men at the gate, lights flashed for the usual silly season picture. He could imagine the caption: 'Bomb victim's husband, MP David Lovegrove, whose name has been linked with opera singer, rides into Chequers.'

The Prime Minister was standing on the steps to welcome his guests as David drew up. He greeted David with more than usual warmth and thanked him for coming.

Two smartly uniformed WAAFs stood in the hall and directed the guests into the long drawing room where drinks awaited them on silver trays. David had been to Chequers before but he had not really taken much note of the decor and the charm of the house, but recent events had somehow sharpened his appreciation of his surroundings. It was almost as if he was seeing things with a new pair of glasses. He thought of Anna somewhere in France and wondered if she would have enjoyed coming today, and just for a brief moment he allowed himself the luxury of thinking she might one day accompany him here. He would be so proud of her, beautiful, talented Anna. She would be like a bright star among the people he saw helping themselves to iced champagne in this beautiful room.

'Hello, David my boy. I want you to meet Peggy.' It was Jeff.

Peggy extended a firm handshake. Her picture on the Chief Whip's desk had not lied. Today she wore a red and white striped two-piece made of crisp seersucker cotton. She looked capable, efficient and comforting. Suddenly David envied Jeff his uncomplicated life. He almost wished he had his own Peggy to fall back on.

The guests helped themselves to the buffet lunch in an adjoining room and ate seated on gold chairs. David found, to his surprise, that he had quite an appetite. The food was excellent, far too much for the guests, and David remembered reading that the PM's wife took it back to Number 10 for the deep freeze. She was a doctor and had kept up her practice when her husband assumed office. They had four teenage children, all still living very much at home. The change of government had brought a welcome fresh breeze into the fusty corners of Downing Street. Despite the misgivings David had about the political life, he felt proud to be part of this vibrant new team.

He helped himself to salmon in a pastry case, new potatoes and salad, and made his way to his place at the Prime Minister's table. He sipped a little of the white wine grown in an English vineyard somewhere in Devon and again wished Anna could have been here with him. She would fit in beautifully with the new tolerance towards a wife who had her own career instead of the two-for-the-price-of-one attitude that had prevailed in the past.

He felt a hand on his shoulder. Turning, he saw it was the PM's wife, Margaret, who had been placed next to him. He got up at once and pulled out her chair for her. As they sat down, she leant confidentially towards him. 'I haven't been able to talk to you before, but I want you to know our thoughts have been with you.'

David thanked her for her concern, and was grateful when she tactfully changed the subject. She asked him what plans he had made for the rest of the holiday. When he told her he didn't really have any, her face clouded with concern.

'I have a brilliant idea,' she announced brightly. 'I know someone who has dropped out of the Commonwealth Parliamentary Conference in Barbados in September. Why don't you take her place? I'm sure it would be good for you to get right away.'

They talked for a little and David began to warm to the idea. Later, after lunch, Jeff came round with a hat and secured a cheque from each guest as a contribution towards the cost of the lunch. 'Have to do it,' he explained. 'Can't have the country thinking we're all freeloading on the state. It's as much as the PM can do to keep up appearances in this barn of a place. By the way, glad to have you on the team in Barbados. News travels fast in this place,' he added, slapping David on the back.

'So, David.' It was the Prime Minister. 'Care for a stroll in the Cromwell Gallery? There's something I want to talk to you about.'

'Yes, of course,' David conceded warily.

William Parry, the Prime Minister, was in every sense of the word a people's Prime Minister. Of medium height and build, he looked your average man, but his subtly handsome and urbane appearance disguised a wide intellect and ability. There was not much in life he had not done. He was an accomplished sportsman, and excelled at tennis and rugby. He had been a sports journalist before moving to local politics where his fresh English looks had made him popular. It had not been long before he stood for Parliament and came into Westminster on a by-election swing. He had a broad and ubiquitous smile and a tactile way of creating a bond. He did this now by taking David's arm.

'I love these paintings. I often come here to think,' he said. 'In fact,' he confided, 'I sometimes find it's the only place I can be alone. Now, David, I've been watching your work in the Whips' Office. I've been impressed, you've done well. How would you feel about a proper job in the autumn reshuffle? We thought Heritage. You seem to know so much about the arts, I think you would have a great deal to offer.' It was more a statement than a question and David recognised at once that a refusal would not be well received. The two of them stopped walking and David stared awkwardly at a spot somewhere on the thick carpet.

'Prime Minister, I would like time to think. I know it is a tremendous honour, but I have my daughter to consider. I never do anything without discussing it with her,' he joked.

'And how old is Miss Lovegrove?' asked the Prime Minister jocularly.

'Eight going on thirty,' answered David with a smile, glad the PM obviously wasn't going to press him. He was very tempted by the offer, and flattered, but he didn't want to rush into anything. He thought again of Anna. If, God willing, everything turned out all right between them, how would she feel about his becoming totally immersed in a government job?

The Prime Minister left the matter there and turned the conversation to the arts in general and opera in particular. David had the distinct impression he was fishing but he didn't rise to the bait. But he got the message: his affair with Anna was known and, furthermore, had been sanctioned.

'I hope things go well for you now, David. Chance comes but only to the prepared mind,' said the Prime Minister before he turned and walked swiftly back to the drawing room.

33

David didn't quite know why he stopped and looked in the jeweller's window. He hated shopping. He had been to the stationers to pick up the headed paper Meg had ordered for Loverstone. It showed a line drawing of the house above the words 'Loverstone Festival of Arts', followed by e-mail and postal addresses, and fax and telephone numbers. He really had to hand it to Meg. No sooner had the idea been born than it became fact. She was already planning events for the first season and had handed in her notice at work. 'You must be crazy!' he said when she told him. 'How are you going to survive?' She said she would live at the cottage and Lavender had agreed to chip in towards her living expenses until the project got off the ground and she could draw a salary. The sponsorship from the Japanese had come through, which would see the completion of the roof repairs, and she had got an overdraft from the bank for renovating the kitchen and rewiring. A local firm had agreed to install central heating and modernise the plumbing with a deferred payment.

The jeweller's was a small family shop between Pimlico and Westminster. Its window displayed a mixture of dependable antiques and safe reproductions, but what had caught his eye was a silver rose brooch, about three inches long, gracefully budding on to a double leaf. He stood and looked at it for some time and then went in and asked the assistant if he could have a look at it.

She took it from the window and laid it on a red velvet display tray.

'What a lovely thing. What is it made of?' asked David, holding it up to the light.

'It's platinum and diamonds. A wonderful buy, if you're interested. It's quite rare. Brooches like these usually get broken up for the stones.'

'Where does it come from?' asked David.

'It belonged to an opera singer. She passed away and her son asked us to sell her jewellery — he's a single gentleman and she had no daughters.'

David looked at the price ticket. It was a lot of money, more than he could really afford, but he wrote out a cheque, reminding himself to ring his bank manager before the cheque could be presented.

There was something about the brooch. He didn't really believe in omens, but the way it had spoken to him from the window — somehow he felt better with it in his pocket.

He showed the brooch to Meg on Friday evening at the cottage. She arrived after him and was pleased to see him looking so well. His few days in London had obviously done him good.

'You look very cheerful,' she said approvingly, flopping into a chair. 'I could kill for a G and T.'

'I'll get you one, but first I want to show you something,' said David excitedly. He went to his desk and opened the drawer, carefully taking out a dark blue leather box. He set it in front of Meg and opened it. 'What do you think?' he asked expectantly.

'It's beautiful,' said Meg, looking puzzled. 'But whose is it?'

'It's for Anna. It's Octavian's rose. I want her to have it when she first sings Octavian and if, well, if . . . ' A shadow crossed his face.

'Have you spoken to Anna recently?' Meg asked gently.

'Yes, I rang her again yesterday, but she sounded more distant than ever.'

Meg was silent. She had heard on the grapevine that Justin's wife had begun divorce proceedings. It probably had no bearing on Justin's relationship with Anna, but she couldn't help wondering at Anna's apparent coolness towards David.

'After Joelle's death,' David went on, 'when I thought I could be HIV positive, I must have seemed pretty distant myself. I was a fool. I owed it to both of us to talk to her, like you said, but I didn't and now I'm terrified I've lost her.'

'Why didn't you explain everything over the phone to her if she won't see you in France? The longer she feels you somehow rejected her, the more difficult it's going to be to get through to her.'

'That's just it. I can't get through to her now. She sounded so busy and distracted when I rang. It's going to have to wait until we're both back in England.'

Meg was puzzled. 'Both back in England? Are you going somewhere?'

'Yes. I've been invited to take part in the Commonwealth Parliamentary Conference in Barbados. I'll be leaving the week after next. I won't be here when Anna gets back.'

That won't help your cause at all, thought Meg, but she kept her misgivings to herself. Things would just have to take their course. The turmoil in David's life had, in a peculiar way, made her focus on her own life — Loverstone and the festival. She had a passion of her own now, and she felt sure it had a future, one which, moreover, could affect all their lives. In fact, it was already beginning to. Polly was coming down tomorrow with Lavender and Charles, both of whom wanted to see the work on the house. To her surprise, they were becoming quite excited by her plans for the festival.

She carefully put the brooch back in its box. 'Now, how about that gin and tonic?' she said brightly.

★ ★ ★

'Why don't we speak in French, Daddy?' asked Polly between mouthfuls of Rice Krispies. They sat at breakfast, just the two of them. Meg, Charles and Lavender had all gone off early to Loverstone.

'Why do you want to speak in French? I didn't think you liked it very much,' replied David.

'Well Regine says I have all these French cousins and things and I want to be able to talk to them.'

'Has your grandmother asked you to call her Regine instead of Granny?' asked David, while he digested this matter of the cousins.

'Yes, she has, actually, and I think it's a good idea because nobody could be like Granny Lavender. And I don't think of

Mummy's mother as a granny really. I mean she does look very young, doesn't she?'

'Yes, she does, darling. Now tell me about these cousins.'

'There isn't much to tell really because I haven't met any of them, but Regine says I will meet them one day soon and I can take Melissa to stay with her in France and we can all speak French together. I've already told Melissa about it and she thinks it's really cool.'

'Do you tell Melissa everything?' asked David, hoping to distract Polly from the cousins. He remembered Joelle had had very little time for them.

'Yes, I do, and she tells me everything . . . Her mother is having another baby . . . ' Polly thought for a moment. 'Do you know what I want, Daddy?' David was used to Polly's sudden changes of subject. It was her way of dealing with life. She threw all her problems in the air to be caught by the wind. Some of them landed in the right place and some were lost, and perhaps better so. He had been advised to let her talk about her mother's death when she felt like it, not to press her on her feelings. So far, she had not said a word on the subject. But it was good to hear her chatter about other things, although 'the French connection', as Lavender called it, was an unexpected development.

'No, darling, tell me what you want,' he said.

'I want a proper family like Melissa's, and then I won't need French cousins. When will we see Anna again? And I want to see Shamus, too. He was almost like a brother. It's not fair, grown-ups are so stupid. They never get it right . . . '

'I agree with you, Polly, grown-ups are stupid. So how about you trying to help me get things right?'

'You never have time to get things right, Daddy, because you work so hard and you don't like what you do anyway because you always look fed up and cross when you go to work and you don't have any fun. Perhaps that's why Anna went to France. She hasn't got any French cousins, has she?'

'No, she hasn't. She went to sing, you know that. And all fathers have to work, you know that too,' said David. He was rather shaken by Polly's words.

'Yes, but you should find something you like doing and get paid for it.'

34

Sunday lunch at Vincent Square had become something of an occasion lately. Lavender and Charles had taken to inviting friends, but today it was just family. The departure of Regine, and David's imminent trip to the Caribbean had left a natural slot for a get-together. There were so many things to be discussed, questions to be answered, quite apart from the healing process of all being together.

Before lunch Lavender took David into the garden ostensibly to look at the roses, but she led him straight to the garden bench.

'So what is happening with you and Anna?' she asked without preamble.

'Nothing at the moment,' David replied truthfully.

'Why not? I know I haven't said much about it, especially while Joelle was alive, but can I speak freely?'

'When have you ever not?' asked David with an affectionate smile.

'Yes, well,' said Lavender, fussily picking cats' hairs off her navy cardigan, 'she is clearly a very special girl, David. I feel I know her well because Polly never stops talking about her. She is another high-flier but not like poor Joelle. I know I shouldn't say it after all that has happened . . . ' She paused for a moment, trying to find the right words. 'There was something about Joelle right from the beginning. In a curious way it was as if she knew she had only a limited time . . . I hope she has found some sort of peace, David. I pray for her each night, you know.'

David patted her hand. 'Yes, Anna is a wonderful girl and if I could wave a magic wand I would marry her tomorrow. She adores Polly and I know we would be happy, but things are a bit difficult at the moment. I hope when I get back from Barbados we'll be able to straighten everything out.'

'So do I, David. I wasn't sure the girl was right for you at first, but after listening to Polly and Meg, and having seen the way you blossomed — before this terrible thing with Joelle, that is — I have revised my opinion. I think we all deserve a little happiness, don't you?' Lavender added wearily.

As they walked back into the house, Jamie arrived. He came bundling into the hall, leaving the door wide open. As Lavender went to shut it, Jamie restrained her. 'No, Mother, I'm not alone. There's someone I want you to meet. I hope it's all right if she stays for lunch.'

'Elizabeth! How wonderful to see you!' cried Meg down the stairs.

Charles was coming upstairs from the basement with a couple of bottles of wine when he first set eyes on his future daughter-in-law. He understood at once, as people sometimes do at moments like these.

★ ★ ★

'Maybe we're going to get some of that happiness you mentioned earlier, Mother,' David said later in the drawing room, after they had all enjoyed one of Mrs Duvver's special roasts of pork with crackling, red cabbage and golden roast potatoes followed by treacle pudding.

Elizabeth, Polly, Meg and Jamie all sat round a large jigsaw puzzle. The French windows were wide open and the smell of Lavender's climbing roses wafted into the room in the heat of the afternoon sun.

'If you will forgive me, I must have forty winks,' said Lavender, settling back into her armchair.

'Good idea, Mother. I can see Father had already fallen asleep in his favourite spot at the end of the garden,' David said, looking out of the window to where Charles lay in an old swing seat under the medlar tree.

'Uncle Jamie,' said Polly, 'can we go for a walk in the park? I want to show you my roller blades and Ross is simply dying for a run.'

Elizabeth, Jamie and Polly left the house with Meg who had to get back to her flat, and David found himself alone in the house with his sleeping parents.

Later, he walked down the long, narrow garden to where his father lay breathing gently under his old Panama hat. He felt a surge of contentment and gratitude towards his family, for all their odd, scratchy awkwardness. It was a long time since he had thought about them like this — too long.

'It's all right, my boy, I'm not asleep,' said Charles as David approached. 'I've been wanting to get you alone.' Charles sat up and shook out his old hat which he laid carefully on the seat beside him. He got out his big spotted handkerchief and wiped his forehead. 'Oh, damn, where have I put my glasses?' he muttered. David retrieved them from a pile of crumpled Sunday papers on the ground.

Charles patted the garden chair next to him and David sat down, leaning forward, elbows on knees and head bowed.

'Dad, I think I've come to a rather dramatic decision.'

Charles liked it when his son called him Dad. 'Tell me,' he said simply.

'I think I'm going to get out of politics. Joelle's death has made me look very closely at my life. Perhaps if I had not been so committed to something I've never really been terribly good at, I would have had the wisdom to ask what the hell it was all for. I don't think a man can embellish other people's lives if he isn't happy and fulfilled by what he does. At least if you do a boring job, it can give you time to compensate in other areas. I'm going to look for a job in London, something to do with the Arts. It's what I should have done years ago. And I'm going to help Meg with the Loverstone enterprise. Meg has a friend who has done a feasibility plan and it looks good. We can make it work. I might convert part of the house and give Polly a proper base at weekends. I need to wake up in the morning looking forward to what I have to do. It's so long since I've done that, I've almost lost the art of how to do it.' He looked apprehensively at his father.

'There's no need to try and convince me about this, my boy,' said Charles. 'It's music to my ears. But you had to come to it in

313

your own way. But you'd better get used to the idea that rich you never will be,' Charles added with a smile. 'Did you know the chairman of Phillamores is resigning on health grounds? It's not yet public but you are just the sort of chap they need, with your contacts in the arts and your degree in fine art. We must get on to it at once.'

David thought this typical of his father. Once a decision had been made, he never went back over dead ground. He bounded forward.

Charles felt in the breast pocket of his faded summer suit and got out his pocket diary. 'I'll ring my contact tomorrow first thing,' he said.

Before David could thank him he moved on to the next item on the agenda. 'Now, tell me, what about that beautiful Anna? Something has gone wrong, hasn't it?'

David admitted it had but, as with his mother, he didn't go into any details. He owed Anna a full explanation but he felt it would be unfair to Joelle's memory publicly to blame all his problems on her admission that she was HIV positive. He was only too aware that he had handled the situation badly, and he had himself to blame for that.

'There's something you're not telling me,

David, but I flatter myself that we have very few secrets between us but those we have are to protect someone. So all I will say is, sort out your life a piece at a time and the rest will fall into place.'

35

'So poor little Felicity has had the last laugh,' said Jason over a ham sandwich. He and Anna sat in a corner of the Lilian Baylis rehearsal room which had been converted from an old recording studio. They had arrived back from France a week ago.

'I suppose you could put it like that,' replied Anna thoughtfully.

'Don't let him fool you, Anna,' said Jason.

'What do you mean, fool me?'

'I can just hear it all, Justin telling you that you can only succeed under his gracious patronage, that you owe your success to him, that you can't do without him, that with you it will be different, he will be faithful, and all the rest of that crap.' Jason took a dainty bite of his sandwich and carefully wiped his mouth on a silk handkerchief.

'That is more or less verbatim,' said Anna with a laugh. 'You must be psychic or something. But he has been wonderful recently, quite different. So caring and thoughtful, I think perhaps he really has changed. At the same time, I can't help remembering the way he treated Felicity. Adultery was a way of life for him, and I want to be able to trust the man I live with. It has to be all about trust, doesn't it?'

'Of course it does, darling. If Guy and I couldn't trust each other, I would kill myself. I suppose his nibs is trying to move in with you. I expect he thinks he is on to a good thing. But take care, Anna. He's never going to change, and he'll never make any woman happy.'

'Well, he can't move in. The house I'm buying is too small and, anyway, it would be unfair on Shamus, just when I'm giving him some stability.'

'What I want to know is what has happened to your MP? He sounded special. He can't suddenly have become a villain, can he?'

'When his wife died he just went cold on me and then, after putting me through hell, he suddenly changed his mind and wanted to come out to France. And now, when I'm back in London, he's gone off to the Caribbean. He's just playing games with me, or that's what it feels like, and frankly I don't want to see him when he gets back.' Anna started to cry and Jason produced one of his immaculate handkerchiefs and put his arm round her shoulders. She rested her head on his shoulder and he continued to ask her about David. She told him all she could and the more she spoke of his behaviour, the more puzzled by it she became. It was as if talking about it created more questions.

When she had finished, Jason produced his thoughts on the matter. He felt very strongly about Anna. She was perhaps the only woman he had really cared about, and the best friend he had ever had. He could tell her anything and he knew he could ring her up in the middle of the night and she would come if he needed her. He felt protective of her in much the way he would have done if she had been his sister. He didn't care for Justin, although he recognised his genius; he thought the man was a control freak.

'Anna, I'm going to give you some hard advice, because I really care about you.'

'I'm listening, Jason,' said Anna quietly, fiddling with the handkerchief and looking at the floor.

'You don't need Justin. He's not a nice person, whatever you think, and I know you always try to think well of people. This is a tough old world, but you've got what it takes. Your singing ability owes something to him but that's as far as it goes. You don't need him now. Why don't you concentrate on your career? Forget about meeting Mr Right at the moment. You never know, your

MP might suddenly realise what he's missing and play straight with you. If so, well and good, but you don't need him either. Just give yourself some time. And I'm here if you need a friend.'

'I know you are, Jason. Thank you,' said Anna.

The rest of the singers drifted back into the room and the second act of *Der Rosenkavalier* started in earnest. Anna had her period and felt distinctly under par. It always affected her singing, and she often envied the Continental approach where opera houses had a clause in the contract for singers to withdraw at that time of the month. On her first top note her voice cracked and she felt like bursting into tears. Justin stood at the door; he had taken the opportunity to come and listen to the run-through with the *répétiteur*.

'It's all right, darling,' he called. 'We all know what you meant.'

Anna didn't know whether to laugh or cry. She decided to laugh.

36

For a minute or two Anna could not remember where she was. She had been dreaming about Polly and David. She could hear the cheep of sparrows and the distant noise of a train. She felt deep contentment as she gradually opened her eyes and remembered where she was. A shard of morning sun slid round the curtains, and the room felt light and clean. There was a smell of paint.

She sat up and looked happily round her bedroom. This had been her first night in her new house. She plopped her feet on to the wooden floor and searched for her slippers. She felt a sudden rush of happiness; here in her very own house, surrounded by her own things, the start of her independence, in a sense she felt protected from the slings and arrows of her relationships with men. Having Shamus here with her completed her feeling that she had finally arrived at a stage in her life where she could safely say she was confident about her future.

She had slept well for the first time in days in the new bed Justin had insisted on buying as a house-warming present. He had even bought linen and a duvet. Anna would never have spent so much money on a bed but Justin would not be deterred. Anna looked at the bed as she pulled back the makeshift curtains and the room became bathed in September light. She opened the window wide and felt the faint chill of autumn. The acacia tree outside the window was starting to shed its leaves. Anna looked down at her tiny garden and thought about the summer which had flown past so swiftly. She had ridden on the crest of a euphoric wave when she had met David, her life had appeared to fall into a pattern which nothing could break, but the wave had broken, leaving her in a state of confusion and hurt more painful than anything she could remember feeling with Justin. After all, she had always known Justin was a shit, albeit a very beguiling one. He hadn't swept her off her feet as David had done. She felt angry when she thought about David. She wondered what he was doing.

He would be returning from the Caribbean any day. Perhaps he had found someone else, perhaps he had simply been jogged out of love with her. Whatever his feelings, she knew she was still in love with him and this is what upset her the most. Resuming her relationship with Justin was a form of compromise, although a very different Justin had emerged in the last few weeks. A caring, helpful Justin who thought of everything. There really didn't seem to be any sense in rebuffing him; after all, it made an enormous difference having a supportive man about. But she wouldn't let him move in. If he wanted her, he would have to work very hard indeed to convince her he wouldn't slide back into his bad old ways.

He was living in his old London flat having moved his things out of the marital home in Surrey and put them in store. 'For when I can set up home with the woman I love,' he had said.

★ ★ ★

When David called, Anna was unprepared for the thrill she felt at hearing his voice again. He asked her to have dinner with him at their favourite Italian restaurant. The warmth and urgency in his voice was hard to resist, and Anna hesitated for only a moment before agreeing. Later she had second thoughts and chided herself for her weakness. Shamus disagreed.

'You must go, Anna. You owe it to yourself as well as to him to give him a chance to explain himself. After all, you refused to see him in France. And anyway, what harm can it do? Even if you never see him again, you will always regret it if you don't go.'

She dressed with care. She wanted to look her best, retain her dignity. She wore a long, crushed velvet skirt which clung to her slim hips, and a tight bodice of rough silk. She gathered her hair behind her ears with combs. It had grown longer during the summer and it now hung down her back in rich waves. She put on David's favourite pair of gold earrings and a thick gold choker necklace which snaked about her neck. As she looked in the mirror, she was pleased with the result; she looked every inch the diva.

As Anna swept into the restaurant at eight o'clock, several people turned to look at her. The head waiter took her hand with a bow and then gestured to her and David's usual table in an intimate corner half hidden by an elaborate plant stand. 'The gentleman has been here for some time,' he said.

When David saw her, he leapt to his feet and stood very still. The head waiter punctiliously pulled out the chair for Anna, shook out the thick linen napkin and placed it on her lap. He listed the specialities of the evening and then told her she was the most beautiful woman in the room. In the kitchen he informed the other waiters he would serve the couple in the corner himself. They were not to be interrupted with unnecessary offers of pepper and Parmesan.

'I'd forgotten just how beautiful you are, Anna. You take my breath away,' said David.

Anna's voice shook as she tried to respond. The last thing she had expected was such a direct declaration and she was surprised by the strength of her own feelings. She felt an irresistible desire to touch him, and then she realised they hadn't even given each other a cursory peck on the cheek.

When they had ordered their meal and were sitting with a bottle of red wine, David raised his glass to her. 'To the future, whatever it may hold,' he said, and leaned towards her. He took her hand and raised it to his lips. Her stomach constricted as she looked into his eyes. Nothing had changed about her feelings for him. She knew she must take control of the situation before her emotions made her blind to logic and reason.

'I must tell you, David, things have changed between us. I was terribly hurt by your rebuttals after your wife died. I know it was traumatic and horrifying, but you shut me out.'

324

'There were reasons, Anna. I — '

'If someone loves you, David, they are there to hold you, comfort you, take you away from the horror. If you reject what they have to offer, you reject their love. You reject them.'

'Will you give me a chance to explain, Anna? That is all I ask. You mean so much to me. The thought of the future without you is bleak. Joelle's death left a legacy I couldn't cope with. I didn't know what to do.'

The waiter came with Dublin Bay prawns and mayonnaise.

'What legacy? What are you talking about?' asked Anna as soon as he had gone.

'Before I tell you, I must ask that none of what I say ever goes any further. It was Joelle's last wish, to protect Polly. But you have the right to know.' He paused. 'Joelle was HIV positive.'

Anna stared at David. 'When will you know?' she asked.

'Know what?' He looked confused.

'If you have it,' she answered simply. Nothing in her face betrayed the terror she felt inside, terror that was changing slowly to anger.

'I know now,' he replied. 'I don't have it. I couldn't have. Joelle contracted it after we had stopped sleeping together.'

'Then I don't understand. How does it have any bearing on your extraordinary,' she chose the word carefully, 'behaviour?'

'I only found out she had it when I got back from Egypt after her death. She wrote me a letter which she must have posted the day before she died. She didn't say how long she had had it. I couldn't be sure of anything.'

'But you could have passed it on to me . . . I simply don't believe it! How could you have been so stupid, so . . . ' She searched for the right word. Not finding it, she ran her hands through her hair. One of her combs fell out on to the white cloth; she picked it up and stabbed it back in position. The vehemence of her anger took David aback.

'I went to a great many people for advice, Anna,' he said. 'They all told me something different but the one consistent thing was that you would have been unlikely to have caught it. We were always so careful. I didn't want to ruin your summer until I had found out more. I needed to find out how long Joelle had had it, where she got it from. I had decided to come out to France to tell you, I couldn't tell you over the phone, but then Joelle's mother announced she was arriving. She told me the whole story. Poor Joelle, it was a one-night thing in Rome about nine months ago.'

The waiter came with baby chicken wrapped in sage and garlic, and deep fried courgettes. Anna realised she had eaten the first course without noticing. David poured her some more wine.

Anna wanted the facts again and again. She wanted to be certain of each and every detail before she allowed her mind to deal with the emotional impact of David's story.

'It must have been a nightmare for you,' she said eventually. 'But the more you tell me the more angry I am. How could you exclude me the way you did? Do you think I'm the sort of person who would have done a runner? None of this makes things better between us. I can't just slot back into our hopes and plans together. A month is a long time in a new relationship, nothing stays the same. I'm not made of stone, I'm flesh and blood. There are plenty of chinks in my armour, and this summer . . . ' Her voice died. David gave her a quick darting look. She blushed a little and evaded his eyes.

'It's Justin, isn't it?' said David quietly.

'I can't tell you anything which will make you feel better at the moment,' she stammered. 'I don't think we should see each other for a while. It's not just all this, it's my work. I can't afford distractions. I don't need dramas of any sort. Frankly, I've had enough of those. David, I am seeing Justin again. I don't know what my future holds, but he has been a fantastic support.' She looked down.

'I assumed as much, Anna, but this doesn't alter my feelings,' said David.

He could see she had made up her mind. He hadn't really expected a miracle, a resumption of life as if nothing had happened — too much had happened. He felt in his pocket for the silver brooch. He opened the box and laid it on the table between them.

'Darling, I want you to have this. It is Octavian's silver rose. It belonged to a great singer. I don't know who she was but the rose found me and it is meant for you, I know that much. I'd like you to have it, even if we never do make a life together. I won't pressure you but, Anna, there is something I haven't told you. I've come to a big decision. I'm leaving politics. I've been offered a wonderful job, chairman of Phillamores. It's what I've always wanted to do. I'm starting afresh. Meg has got substantial backing for the festival at Loverstone and together we're going to make a real go of it. Don't you see, Anna, we would bring so much to each other and to everyone else — just think what you could bring to young musicians.'

Tears welled in Anna's eyes. She knew she could not refuse the brooch, it was magical. As she took it from the box, it caught the light.

David held her hand in his. 'Anna, when I see you wearing it, I will take it as a sign.'

She noticed he used the word when, not if.

The waiter brought coffee and the bill. Anna said she had to go, and David walked her to her car. As he held the door open for her, he did not try to kiss her.

'I will wait, Anna, for as long as it takes,' he said. He couldn't tell what she was thinking. She touched his hand fleetingly and drove away. She didn't look back as he stood on the pavement and watched her car turn the corner.

★ ★ ★

Meg gazed at David through the kitchen window in the cottage. He was sitting on a bench on the mosaic terrace, apparently deep in thought. He had looked fit and well when he came back from Barbados, and his tan was still evident, but she knew he wasn't happy. She had tried to draw him out about his relationship with Anna, but all he would say was that she 'needed space'. Meg knew that Anna wasn't being allowed much space by Justin.

Meg still counted Anna as one of her dearest friends, but there was no question that the rift between her and David formed something of a barrier to their former confiding friendship. Since Anna had moved into her house in Kennington, Meg saw much less of her anyway, but she fervently hoped she and David would get together again. She decided to join David on the terrace. She had some news of her own to tell him.

'I've got two bits of good news,' she announced as she sat beside him on the bench. 'The first is I've got tickets for all the family, including Polly, to go to the gala concert at the Coliseum. It's to help with fundraising for the new theatre. And guess what? Anna will be singing. It's one of the last things I'll be helping to organise there before I leave.'

'How marvellous,' David said with a smile. 'That really gives us something to look forward to. What was the other bit of good news?'

'I shall be bringing someone I want you all to meet.' Meg blushed as she spoke.

'Oh, and who is that?'

'Someone local, he lives down here. He's a solicitor and works in Lewes. I met him a month ago when I went to his firm to get some of the papers drawn up about the transfer of Loverstone into a charitable trust. You've been so preoccupied, David, I've rather got on with it all, as you know, and I couldn't have done it all without his advice. His wife died two years ago . . . I don't think it was romance at first but . . . '

Meg looked at David and saw she had his full attention.

'Yes, go on,' he said encouragingly.

'Well, it's hard to explain. I'm so used to other people's accounts of what it feels like to be in love and I never believed them, but it's as if the whole world has become a brighter place. I can't imagine life without him now. It's like coming out of the cold into a warm room. I suppose it's all the more wonderful for me as I'd more or less resigned myself to a lonely old age. I wasn't looking for love, it found me, David, just when I had given up on it. The nicest thing is that after having been the understudy, as it were, I now feel like the central character.'

David looked at his sister more closely than he had bothered to do for years. She did indeed have a radiance he had never seen before. It made her look years younger. He supposed they had all rather taken Meg for granted. She had always been there to listen and to advise, and no one had thought about her waiting in the wings for a Prince Charming who had lost his way.

'Darling Meg, I'm so happy for you. Do we have to wait until the gala? Couldn't I be allowed to meet him now?'

'Actually you did meet him once, although I don't suppose you'd remember. He remembers you, though. He liked you, said you were not at all what he expected, not like a politician at all. He couldn't understand how you could stand it.'

'Well, he was right, wasn't he?'

37

Anna laid out her clothes for the following day, something she always did, for waking up the morning after a performance her mind was never at its best. She checked the music for tomorrow's gala concert. She would run through it again before she went to sleep, a trick she had learned to help commit scores to her memory. Of course she had performed this music many times before, but lately her mind had been preoccupied with the dilemmas in her private life.

Justin was becoming more and more pressing, yet, try as she might, she couldn't stop thinking about David. It wasn't just him she missed, it was his whole family. But did she really want to be part of David's life, with all the complications he would bring with him? They were not part of her scheme as it had now panned out.

Justin had been instrumental in perfecting her gifts as a singer. Life with him would offer unimaginable excitements; he had already talked of contracts in America, of her accompanying him on a tour to Australia. Sydney Opera House was interested in her.

If Justin could nudge things in the right direction they could be the next Sutherland and Bonynge.

The silver rose brooch lay in its box on her dressing table. Anna took it out tenderly and laid it to her lips for a moment. It would look marvellous with the red velvet dress she planned to wear on stage the following night. She took the dress from its plastic cover on the wardrobe door and held it up against her in front of the long mirror.

Closing her eyes, she thought of tomorrow. David would be there with his entire family. They would all be watching her, and he would be radiating love. She could imagine it now. She had never felt so torn. She swiftly put the dress back in its cover, irritated by her own sentimentality. A warning voice told her to keep a cool head. Of course she was still in love with David, it would take a long time to get over the feelings she had for him. But Justin had opened up the possibility of something she had always dreamed of. She knew in her heart she was approaching a watershed and as she replaced the brooch in its box she felt utterly confused. She had not worn the brooch but she had looked at it often. She had made up her mind that if she wore the brooch it would only be when she had decided to follow her heart and not her head. If she decided to throw in her lot with Justin, or even go it alone, accept neither of them into her life, she would return the brooch. It would be a matter of honour.

At last everything was ready for tomorrow and she went to bed. As she closed her eyes, she could smell the freesias on the bedside table. Justin had sent them to wish her good luck. He was expected back from America the day after the gala.

Anna's mind would not rest as her body wished it to. She knew she must sleep if she were to be at her best the next day. She tried not to think of Justin or David or the choice she knew she must make, for it wasn't fair to leave either of them in limbo. She considered what Justin would do if she ended the relationship. She suspected he would quickly find a replacement, but David was different. She knew his love for her was deep and enduring, and that he would probably go on waiting and hoping, whatever she said. There was something comforting and safe in that certainty.

★ ★ ★

David arrived at the Coliseum in plenty of time. The foyer was filling up fast with smartly dressed guests, and there was a heady buzz of excitement in the air. The gala had been given a lot of advance publicity, as Meg had been working overtime. She wanted to leave her job in a blaze of glory. David had in his pocket a cutting from today's *Times* in which Anna had been interviewed on the arts page. Somewhere in the rave profile she had been asked about her personal life. 'I don't have one,' she had answered. 'I get all the emotion I need on stage.'

David took a deep breath as he walked into the foyer. It was going to take a lot of effort to disguise his feelings as he watched on the stage tonight the woman he had loved and lost.

But, looking on the bright side, this was to be a special evening for the family, with both his brother and sister happy and accompanied by their partners, though for David this only added piquancy to the occasion. He knew he should be happy for all of them and he was, but his heart ached when he thought of Anna and what might have been. He had allowed himself a moment's daydream when he had imagined how it would be if they could all go backstage to Anna's dressing room after the performance and he could gather her in his arms for all the world to see.

He looked around the foyer and spotted his mother. She was wearing the sludge-green cocktail dress she kept for special occasions. She was deep in conversation with Meg's new boyfriend, Peter Henley. He was tall and gangly and rather earnest. He was leaning towards Lavender, concentrating on what she was saying. Charles, Jamie and Elizabeth were looking at their commemorative programmes. As for Polly, she looked radiant in the party dress Lavender had bought her in the summer. She had never been to an opera and could hardly contain her excitement. David watched her for a moment, wondering where she had hidden the tragedy of her mother's sudden death. She must have compartmentalised it somewhere in her mind, but David had no doubt that the bonds that had been forged between her and her extended family had been vital to her overcoming her loss. He felt relieved and grateful as he watched her standing securely between her grandparents. Recently David had begun to value his family as never before, and he consoled himself with the thought that even if he had lost Anna, in some curious way he had gained a family, and his heart filled with happiness. Life had a way of putting things right; it had been a long journey for them all to reach this state of harmony.

'There's Daddy,' called Polly, diving from

the group and running to him, flinging her arms about his waist. 'Daddy, look! Anna is in the programme. Isn't she the most beautiful person in the world — except for Auntie Meg and Granny Lavender of course,' she cried excitedly.

'Oh, there you all are,' came Meg's voice from somewhere in the middle of the throng. She emerged in a black velvet trouser suit and high heels. David had never seen her looking so good. She went at once to Peter, and their gazes locked for a moment in mutual admiration. David felt a pang of envy and then chided himself. Meg had been an outsider in the game of love for too long.

Charles was wielding a bottle of champagne. 'To all of us,' he said, handing David a glass and lifting his own to Meg and Jamie. 'We seem to have a lot to celebrate.'

'Thanks, Dad,' said Meg, looking affectionately at Peter.

She broke away and came to David. 'I want to show you something,' she said quietly. 'Look, here in the programme. It's Dolores Man in her heyday.' She pointed to a black and white photo under the title of 'Golden Singers from the Past'. Under the picture was a tribute to Dolores, an ardent supporter of the company until her death the previous spring. It went on to describe the trust she had founded for the benefit of young singers connected with the company. 'She was one of the greatest Octavians, and do you see what she is wearing?' asked Meg.

Dolores Man was dressed in what looked like a black velvet gown, and on the shoulder was a diamond brooch.

'Meg, it's the brooch I gave to Anna!' exclaimed David. 'It has to be the same one, there can't be two of them.'

'It's a sign, David, I know it is. You wait and see,' said Meg.

'I wish I could believe you, Meg, but I've given up expecting things to turn out all right. If they do it's a bonus. But this is your evening. I like Peter very much. I'm so happy for you, little sister. And you've done a magnificent job tonight. A great start for your new challenge at Loverstone.'

'Our challenge, if you don't mind, David. I know when you start your job at Phillamores I'll be left doing most of it, but I wouldn't even attempt something like this if I didn't think you were right behind me.'

'Now then, talking shop as usual,' Charles broke in. 'What I want to ask David is, are we all going round to see Anna after the show?'

'I don't think so, Dad,' Meg replied, hastily giving her father a sharp nudge in the ribs.

'Well, Jamie has booked a table somewhere for dinner afterwards, and it doesn't matter if we are extra,' Lavender chipped in, just as the bell began to ring for the audience to take their seats.

David began to feel sick as the family took their places in the stage box left.

The Opera Company chairman came out in front of the thick velvet curtains to make an appeal for funds. He explained the importance of private funding if the People's Opera was to survive, and thanked the government for its latest grant. David felt proud to have played a part in that but glad he had decided to change his career. If his personal life was to remain unfulfilled, at least he would be enjoying his work. Tomorrow he would tell his constituency he was leaving parliament. He tried to stop his mind going over the speech he had prepared, but he knew he would be in no fit state to concentrate the day after seeing Anna on stage.

The performance started. Anna was to take part in the second item, a scene from the opera *Lakme* . . . Suddenly she was there, her voice soaring in the flower duet. He could hardly breathe as her beautiful voice rang in his ears. He had never experienced such desolation and such love in one moment. She wore a red dress, her hair piled up on top of her head, her creamy skin contrasting with the rich colour of the dress. He had a brief memory of the feel of her body when he had last made love to her.

'What's the matter, Daddy?' came Polly's whispered inquiry. She had seen him brush the corner of his eye.

He was almost relieved when Anna left the stage to rounds of enthusiastic applause. The programme continued, and he pretended to listen. At the interval he longed to excuse himself, run for cover, anything to get away from the exquisite pain he felt, and then he felt ashamed. He had no right to spoil Meg's evening. He put aside the emotions he felt and made polite conversation. He saw his father glancing nervously at him as he talked to Meg. Charles came to him and pressed his shoulder sympathetically.

For the second half David sat at the back of the box. As the curtain swept up for the final trio from *Der Rosenkavalier*, Anna stood centre stage, turned slightly away from them. She wore a black velvet dress. He had never seen anything so perfectly beautiful in his life. As the three women's voices surged, he lowered his eyes and buried his head in his hands. Then he looked up. Anna turned to face the box as if she sang for him alone, and something caught the light. It flashed for a moment, dazzling and bright like a star, and he saw Anna was wearing the silver rose brooch. He felt Meg's warm hand on his shoulder. She whispered in his ear, 'She had to tell you in her own way, David. We'll be nine for dinner.'

THE END

McLEAN AT THE GOLDEN OWL
George Goodchild

Inspector McLean has resigned from Scotland Yard's CID and has opened an office in Wimpole Street. With the help of his able assistant, Tiny, he solves many crimes, including those of kidnapping, murder and poisoning.

KATE WEATHERBY
Anne Goring

Derbyshire, 1849: The Hunter family are the arrogant, powerful masters of Clough Grange. Their feuds are sparked by a generation of guilt, despair and ill-fortune. But their passions are awakened by the arrival of nineteen-year-old Kate Weatherby.

A VENETIAN RECKONING
Donna Leon

When the body of a prominent international lawyer is found in the carriage of an intercity train, Commissario Guido Brunetti begins to dig deeper into the secret lives of the once great and good.

A TASTE FOR DEATH
Peter O'Donnell

Modesty Blaise and Willie Garvin take on impossible odds in the shape of Simon Delicata, the man with a taste for death, and Swordmaster, Wenczel, in a terrifying duel. Finally, in the Sahara desert, the intrepid pair must summon every killing skill to survive.

SEVEN DAYS FROM MIDNIGHT
Rona Randall

In the Comet Theatre, London, seven people have good reason for wanting beautiful Maxine Culver out of the way. Each one has reason to fear her blackmail. But whose shadow is it that lurks in the wings, waiting to silence her once and for all?

QUEEN OF THE ELEPHANTS
Mark Shand

Mark Shand knows about the ways of elephants, but he is no match for the tiny Parbati Barua, the daughter of India's greatest expert on the Asian elephant, the late Prince of Gauripur, who taught her everything. Shand sought out Parbati to take part in a film about the plight of the wild herds today in north-east India.

THE DARKENING LEAF
Caroline Stickland

On storm-tossed Chesil Bank in 1847, the young lovers, Philobeth and Frederick, prevent wreckers mutilating the apparent corpse of a young woman. Discovering she is still alive, Frederick takes her to his grandmother's home. But the rescue is to have violent and far-reaching effects . . .

A WOMAN'S TOUCH
Emma Stirling

When Fenn went to stay on her uncle's farm in Africa, the lovely Helena Starr seemed to resent her — especially when Dr Jason Kemp agreed to Fenn helping in his bush hospital. Though it seemed Jason saw Fenn as little more than a child, her feelings for him were those of a woman.

A DEAD GIVEAWAY
Various Authors

This book offers the perfect opportunity to sample the skills of five of the finest writers of crime fiction — Clare Curzon, Gillian Linscott, Peter Lovesey, Dorothy Simpson and Margaret Yorke.

DOUBLE INDEMNITY — MURDER FOR INSURANCE
Jad Adams

This is a collection of true cases of murderers who insured their victims then killed them — or attempted to. Each tense, compelling account tells a story of cold-blooded plotting and elaborate deception.

THE PEARLS OF COROMANDEL
By Keron Bhattacharya

John Sugden, an ambitious young Oxford graduate, joins the Indian Civil Service in the early 1920s and goes to uphold the British Raj. But he falls in love with a young Hindu girl and finds his loyalties tragically divided.

WHITE HARVEST
Louis Charbonneau

Kathy McNeely, a marine biologist, sets out for Alaska to carry out important research. But when she stumbles upon an illegal ivory poaching operation that is threatening the world's walrus population, she soon realises that she will have to survive more than the harsh elements . . .

TO THE GARDEN ALONE
Eve Ebbett

Widow Frances Morley's short, happy marriage was childless, and in a succession of borders she attempts to build a substitute relationship for the husband and family she does not have. Over all hovers the shadow of the man who terrorized her childhood.

CONTRASTS
Rowan Edwards

Julia had her life beautifully planned — she was building a thriving pottery business as well as sharing her home with her friend Pippa, and having fun owning a goat. But the goat's problems brought the new local vet, Sebastian Trent, into their lives.

MY OLD MAN AND THE SEA
David and Daniel Hays

Some fathers and sons go fishing together. David and Daniel Hays decided to sail a tiny boat seventeen thousand miles to the bottom of the world and back. Together, they weave a story of travel, adventure, and difficult, sometimes terrifying, sailing.